Halloween Haven

By
Michael Gore

www.DarkInkBooks.com

First Published by Dark Ink Books, Southwick, MA, 2024

Dark Ink and its logos are trademarked by *AM Ink Publishing*.

www.AMInkPublishing.com

To those who have been gutted like a jack-o'-lantern themselves.
May a light turn the emptiness into something magical.

TABLE OF CONTENTS

Cabbage Night

"Devil's Night, Gate Night, Goosey Night, Moving Night, Mat Night, Mischief Night. Each place has its own name, but around here, my friends, we call it Cabbage Night! The term was first recorded all the way back in 1861 when the *Daily State Gazette and Republican* in Trenton, New Jersey, mentioned that people noticed sundry boys armed with cabbages causing chaos the night before Halloween. Why the term Cabbage Night stuck here in New England and not one of the other countless names, no one seems to know. Though it is said that in the fall, farmers used to pile unused cabbage to be used for bonfires, making for easy ammo to steal and throw at houses."

Nick's palms were already sweaty when he looked up from his paper to see Mr. D raise a finger to stop him. Nick's heart froze, he was nervous enough about presenting this damn research paper, now he was getting stopped when all he wanted to do was get it over?

"Nick…" He watched as Mr. D moved his scrunched-up cheeks into his "I'm about to give you bad news" face. Mr. D, with his "hip" tweed jacket and thin glasses sitting on the top of his head, was perpetually trying to be some cool teacher in a '90s sitcom. Regardless of his occasionally funny dad jokes, the man had failed him two quarters in a row. Nick swallowed hard.

"Your report was supposed to be about what fall means to you. This is a research paper about a night of vandalism."

Nick's mouth opened and closed a few times as he tried to think of a way to express why it was important to him, but nerves were holding his tongue tight and drying his mouth out with the power of an industrial fan.

"In your research, did you learn about Detroit in the '90s, how many fires were caused and how traumatic it was?" Mr. D asked. "Millions in damage, thousands hurt, some even died. They now have…"

Nick jumped in to finish. ". . . almost fifty thousand people a night to protect the streets, and they call it Angel Night, because out there it was called Devil's Night. I was about to get to that in the report! With Cabbage Night just a few days away, I figured . . ."

Mr. D pulled the glasses off his head, raised his hand to stop Nick again, sighed heavily, and got up. With the arm of the glasses touching his lip, Mr. D nodded in deep thought as he slowly walked up to Nick. Using the glasses, he made a gesture, showing Nick it was time to sit down. Nick's face flushed with a tidal wave of blood. It was embarrassing enough getting up to read, let alone the fact that Maddie was in the room staring at him—he could tell she was trying not to laugh. The rush of embarrassment quickly turned to anger and then rage as he sat in the hard, small seat, fidgeting with nerves. He couldn't concentrate and didn't even hear the comment that Mr. D said about his report that made everyone laugh to the point where the class had to be calmed down before calling up the next student. Through the entire next essay about "The Significance and Joy of Spiced Lattes in the Fall," Nick pictured smashing Mr. D's head in with rock-hard cabbages.

Not even ten minutes into the next class, as he absentmindedly watched Ms. Alden demonstrate how to make a "pumpkin candy" dish in pottery, Nick's phone buzzed. The school's grading system was letting him know that Mr. D had put in a grade for his project. It was a *zero*. In the comments section, there was a note attached: *Nick, next time read the requirements so you don't waste everyone's time like you did today.* Without knowing, Nick blurted out a loud and angry "fuck!" that took Ms. Alden, who should have retired ten years before Nick was even born, by such surprise she crumbled the bowl on the pottery wheel. A minute later, he was on his way to the principal's office to have his phone taken as he spent the rest of the day in-house. For the next two hours and twenty-four minutes, Nick did nothing but seethe and plan as the coach tasked with babysitting the "delinquents" giggled to the Netflix show he was watching on his phone.

Almost three hours without a phone at sixteen years old is like not seeing the sun for over a year to an adult. It causes depression, anxiety, and a sense of being disconnected from the world, and Nick considered it cruel and unusual punishment. Part of him wanted to write a paper to

2

start a movement in the government to ban taking away a cellphone from anyone in any situation. When Nick got his phone back after the last bell, a rush of relief came over him, making him forget about the patriotic stance he was about to take. But his relief was quickly crushed by seeing he had 38 alerts; the flush and rage came back as he knew what they would be. Sure enough, four different memes were made by the multiple kids who took pictures and videos of his face turning red as he walked back to his chair in Mr. D's class. One short meme played the *Curb Your Enthusiasm* music as he took his seat, another one with his cheeks bright red said, "When you shit your pants in front of the class," and the one that made him the maddest had a caption that read, "Nick the Prick after the teacher wouldn't suck His Dick." The irregular capitalization made him even angrier, although none of his spite was funneled at the students who made the memes, it was all aimed at Mr. D.

Normally, he would meet a few friends in the parking lot, and they'd go off and mess around for a few hours or play Xbox at one of their houses before he had to be home for dinner at 5:00 p.m., but today he chose to run home and sulk. Some days they'd go and play video games at Luis' house, the richest of his friends who had a dedicated "game room." Other days they'd hang out at Wendy's and try to score as much free food as they could from their friends working there, and sometimes they'd go out to the quarry to smash the discarded beer bottles and jump in the reservoir if it was hot enough. Of course, no matter what they did, the consistent thing was their phones, almost constantly they would all be on them, no matter how much they talked or bullshitted, it was like a third hand. Knowing this, Nick could not stomach going to any of those places today, as his friends would do nothing but howl at how hysterical the memes about him were, and then they would all try to make new ones and make sure to share them to the entire school. Nick himself had been guilty of this many times.

When Luis spilt milk on his lap at lunch, he made the "when you haven't jerked off in a week and Ms. Blaire walks by" meme that got the most laughing emojis of any post in his life. There was also the time when Kim, one of the girls who hung out with his normal group, got her shirt wet in a water balloon fight. Nick took a picture and captioned it, "Finally, evidence that Kim is a man!" Kim didn't come around for two weeks and didn't talk to Nick for a month after he showed the entire school the revealing photo of her flat chest. That one he felt a bit bad about, but he told himself it was worth all the likes it got from the non-loser kids. Luis still called it an "epic burn" to this day. While Nick was now on the other side of the "teasing," not a single one of them would ever consider it bullying. Boiling with anger, he knew the second he could make another meme of someone else, he would, because it would take the attention off him. The greatest revenge would be memes made about Mr. D, or better yet, a prank video.

Even though he was an only child and his mom was at work for another few hours, Nick still felt the need to shut and lock the door of his bedroom when he got home. At sixteen, no one, *no one*, could see him cry. The tears that came out were angry and wet. Burying his face into his powder blue pillowcase, Nick felt like a teen girl, but then he told himself the tears were not from being embarrassed, but from anger at how stupid Mr. D was. *The damn paper was good!*

Stifling his tears, he sat up, pulled his Chromebook out of his laptop bag, opened up his report, and looked at it. It made no sense to him why Mr. D would give him a zero. He had all the requirements, just because Mr. D didn't like the topic, *fuck him*. Staring at the screen, he saw the words "Cabbage Night" in all caps at the top of the document—he had even made the color of the font green. It was then, staring at the word "Cabbage," that the idea started to set in. Cabbage Night was tomorrow, so maybe he would have to give Mr. D a real reason to hate the night.

The light blonde hair tickled Tim's nose. He comically blew it away and yelled out, "Crash-landing," as he shook his tiny daughter's body up and down on his feet before quickly pulling them away and catching her on his stomach. Sydney laughed and laughed before saying "again!" over and over. Tim loved playing airplane with her, even though after hitting forty, half the time his back would hurt for a few days afterwards, but it was always worth it. The poor girl missed most of the years she should have been playing. He didn't care if she was eight and getting a bit too heavy, as long as she was willing to be thrown up in the air, he would throw her.

"No more right now, Sweet Sydney, Daddy needs to grade some papers, okay?" Tim set her down, mimicked the sad look she was giving him, and then rapidly kissed her four times on the cheek.

"You're always correcting papers, Dad." Sydney said with a pout. That comment stuck in Tim's gut. She was learning how to manipulate him with just the right words, but he refused to break down this time.

"I know, my little butter bean, but you know my response, right?" The girl rolled her eyes then said with him in unison, "If Dad doesn't correct papers, he doesn't have a job. If he doesn't have a job, I don't have toys." Tim winked at her and then handed her the TV remote, telling her to watch Disney Junior *only* before heading down the hallway, although he knew she would switch to the regular Disney Channel as soon as he was out of hearing range.

Flicking on the office light, Tim sighed heavily, sat down at his desk, and fired up his computer. Within seconds he was reading essay after essay. It was not the reading nor the work of correcting that bothered him, it was the lack of effort and brains that drained the life out of him on a regular basis. When he first started teaching almost twenty years ago, when he himself was a mere kid of *twenty-two*, he was optimistic and students shockingly *tried*. The amount of kids who failed his class was less than his daughter's age now. As each year went by and the addiction to phones and tablets and social media grew and grew, he saw the quality of writing decline rapidly. Some students even wrote like they were texting, using words that only exist between teenagers: *gr8t*, *2day*, *irl*, *ppl*, and dozens of others were mixed into normal writing. One writing assignment that was turned in last year didn't even have a single period or capitol letter in it, and when he asked the student why, the confused kid said, "Why would I use those? It was just homework." This infuriated Tim, who had a master's degree in English and had spent years teaching students the mechanics of written communication, yet he still tried nonetheless, even if the passion was gone.

Tonight was no different. About forty percent of the written assignments were mediocre: *students trying to get an okay grade and nothing more.* Fifteen percent were good: *the high achievers striving for perfect transcripts.* Thirty percent were poor to crappy: *students who didn't give a crap or actually could not construct a sentence.* The last fifteen percent fell into the category of: *dear lord the world has no future.* One particular gem finished with the line he detested and told his students to never write, yet they still did countless times: *Thank you for reading, I hope you liked this essay.*

The damn line made him think of Nick Cotter's paper from the other day. He had not read it, but just given him a zero for the fact that he didn't follow the directions. According to his course expectations, the grade was justified. If he gave them a grade for not following the topic, what was he teaching them? If you got the wrong meal at a restaurant, you don't eat it just because it was presented to you, you want what you paid for. It was a lesson students had to learn, coddling them like most teachers was what was going to ruin this world. However, Tim knew he had a penchant for grading certain kids harder than others. If the kid was a dick or didn't listen, he was going to follow the rules to the T, but if the kid was normally good and messed up, he'd let it slide. Nick wasn't a dick, he was a good kid. He was just, non-existent, and his love of horror and scary things bothered Tim immensely, just like anything graphic did, ever since, it happened.

Squeezing his eyes shut, he brushed away the images of his wife covered in blood and went back to the thoughts of Nick. While it was subconsciously, any kid that was into the macabre, he found himself failing more than he hadn't since it happened. Sitting back in his faux leather chair, he took a deep breath and realized he was a bit harsh and quick to make the assumption that Nick's topic of Cabbage Night fell outside the scope of the project. With a heavy sigh, Tim went into the grading system, found Nick's essay, and opened it.

Shit. The essay *was* good, the best work Nick had done all year and better than most of the essays the other students did. Yes, he took the topic out of context, but the kid had done actual research, putting citations in *correctly*—which Tim almost never saw anymore—and his paper went four times over the required length and even made a convincing argument as to why Cabbage Night is a safe way for teens to get out their angst through menial pranks. Running his fingers through his hair, Tim sat back and felt like an asshole. Right before class that day Tim had found out that he had to teach tenth grade reading and writing the next year, the class everyone dreaded as it was full of kids who couldn't pass ninth grade English. On top of that, he got an email from the hospital saying his payment for Sydney's medical bills had bounced and he would be getting a late fee on top of the mountain of bills he already couldn't afford. After seeing the bill, he had opened up a job search site and started looking aimlessly for higher paying work while eating a dry sandwich as fast as he could during his twenty-minute lunch break so he could squeeze in a bathroom visit before his next class started. When the students came in, he was ready for a fight and Nick was the unlucky recipient, he realized that now.

With guilt weighing him down but also feeling the need to save face, Tim wrote a message to Nick in the school's online program that reiterated the class rules and stated that while he shouldn't get a grade, he had decided to read it anyway. Then, Tim praised Nick's work. Lastly, he left off by saying that he would change the grade in the system on Monday when they were back in school and that he hoped Nick didn't get into any trouble tonight, being that it was Cabbage Night, after all. After sending the message and leaning back in his chair, Tim felt better about the situation, but he had no clue those were the last words he would ever type with his fingers.

There were no elaborate blueprints or written-out plans, Nick's ideas were simple and juvenile. There was not going to be any TP-ing of someone's trees or throwing eggs at a house, nothing like that, but there was going to be some scares, property damage, and one hell of a pissed-off teacher. Talking Luis and Meg into the plan took some convincing, but like always they went along with Nick's scheme. The key was to tell them how epic it was going to be and that they would become legendary, just like the class of 1986 still was for their senior prank where they herded over seventy milk cows into the school.

"Can you imagine, kids talking about this shit almost forty years later!?" Nick asked his friends. "Hell, if we film it, it could go viral and we could make money on the video, we'd just have to post it anonymously so we don't get caught, not that we're breaking any laws."

In hindsight, the video would turn out to be the thing that destroyed them. Not only would it prove their involvement in that night's events, but it would also be used in court to show that they didn't just break the law—they broke over a dozen.

The irony was that Nick's plan for not getting caught would go on to cause all the uproar in the end. After the embarrassment he suffered in class, if he just hit Mr. D's house, he would be the obvious suspect. Therefore, the plan was to attack *every* house on the street. The classic "kill a bunch of people to hide the fact that only one was the target" strategy that good old Agatha Christie came up with. At least he thought it was Christie who came up with that gem. Getting all the supplies cost almost two hundred dollars, but like always, Luis sprung for all of it; Nick loved having a rich friend. The hard part was waiting. Nick "went to bed" at ten, said goodnight to his mother and locked himself in his room. The plan was to meet at 1:00 a.m. Three hours was a long time to kill when you were hyped up on adrenaline and pumpkin spice energy drinks. Nick tried playing games on his phone, then watching Netflix, then porn, then cleaning his room… but after all of that, only an hour had passed. The next two were torturously slow. When it was finally time, Nick launched out of his window like a rocket.

Luis was parked right around the corner liked planned and within four minutes, they had picked up Meg. On the way over, just like Nick expected, Meg started her speech to try and talk them out of their plan, suggesting they just park and get high and then go home. Nick brushed it off by simply saying, "And what would we do with all the stuff Luis graciously bought us? We can't return it!" Meg sighed in the back seat. Nick could tell she was nervous, he was too, but he didn't have the words to comfort her. After a short, silent ride, they pulled into the parking lot of a closed Arby's and parked on the side, quickly shutting off the lights in case the cops drove by. The ticking of the cooling engine was the only noise in the silence as they all took a moment to get some courage.

Nick started to laugh a little. He looked at Luis, slapped him on the shoulder, and then glanced behind him at Meg, giving her a wink. It made no sense, but Nick was desperate to try and lighten the mood, and the other two forced a laugh. The three had been friends for only a year, but in that time they had become so close that everyone teased them about having a ménage à trois, and that term even became their nickname, being said in conjunction to all three on a regular basis: "Oh, the ménage à trois left a few hours ago." They brushed off the nickname and forced down the anger they felt at all the jokes. They would have fought back, but they didn't to protect Luis. They all decided it was better for the school to think he was banging Meg than to know he was gay. The worry wasn't over bullies, it was instead the fear of his father sending him to conversion camp again. Luis still had scars from it that would never heal and we was not going back there anytime soon. As much as the anger boiled in Nick for his best friend to have to hide and suffer, he would do anything to protect the two of them, so he kept Louis' secret safe. Nick saw them as his only family, being that his only real one was his mother, who was hardly there. So it was just the three of them through triumph and mischief.

"Come on, let's have fun with this!" Nick got out of the car, knowing as the leader of the night, they would follow. Popping open the trunk, the three stared into it like some heroes about to grab their weapons before heading off to a fight. The truck was stocked with bags and bags of stuff and two dozen perfectly cut pieces of thin plastic that were three feet by three feet. After a few seconds of hesitation, Meg and Luis each took a small stack of the plastic bags and one of the prepackaged bags, leaving one big black duffel bag in the middle. Nick grabbed that bag, closed the trunk, and set it on top.

Unzipping the duffel, he reached in and pulled out the three black jack-o'-lantern masks. While each one was different, all three had vines wrapping around the sides of the evil facial features. Party City had over a dozen of the masks ranging from menacing to friendly. They also had matching hats, gloves, and other items to make them into full scarecrows, but Nick liked the masks by themselves. Putting the masks on, they looked at each other and this time laughed genuinely. Wearing black hoodies, they pulled the hoods up over their heads, making them look spooky and suspicious.

"Okay, you each have your cameras?" Nick looked around and made sure Luis and Meg both nodded, though it was hard to see in the dark.

"Good, remember, go as fast as we can. Almost every house is going to have a motion-sensor light, and from what I can count, about six have doorbell or security cameras. Don't freak at the lights, animals set them off all the time, so it won't wake anyone. Only abort the mission if someone opens a door or yells. If they do, head back to the car and we'll leave. But don't worry about that. If we're fast, we can all be done in under five minutes."

Luis and Meg glanced at each other uneasily before looking back at Nick and nodding. His heart was slamming, and he could tell by his friends' heavy breathing that they were nervous too, although their masks didn't make that task easy.

"Let's do this." With that, Nick ran off, struggling to hold all of his stuff.

There were twelve identical houses on the street, all old "L" ranches from the 1950s, each of them with three cement steps leading into the main door of the house. Having a childhood friend who lived in an identical house, Nick knew the front door led into the living room and that virtually no one used that door as an entrance, which meant approaching that way made it a bit easier to not get seen, as the side door was the one everyone used. With only twelve houses, they were each tasked with attacking four. Meg took the first four on the left-hand side, Luis took the right side, and Nick took the last four in the cul-de-sac, meaning he had to lug the stuff the farthest.

Racing down the road, Nick felt a surge of excitement like he'd never had before. It was a mix of adrenaline, fear, and anticipation; he loved how it felt. At his first house, when no lights snapped on, he dropped all the stuff in the front yard. Grabbing the first sheet of plastic, he raced over and set it on top of the cement steps. Then he ran to the next three houses and repeated the same thing. At two of the houses, the lights snapped on, making Nick's heart jump each time, but he told himself that no one would wake up and kept moving. With everything in place, he ran back to the first house, opened the bag, and grabbed two bottles of baby oil, popping open the lids and squirting oil all over the sheet of plastic. Two minutes later, all four houses' steps were lubed up.

Back at the bag a third time, Nick's hands were shaking so hard, he didn't know if he could pull the tabs on the color smoke bombs. Looking down the street, he could see that Luis and Meg were about done as well. So far neither of them had taken off, and it was all going as planned. Nick took a deep breath, took out the four canisters, pulled the bag over his shoulder, then ripped off the tab of a red smoke bomb. Nick had only seen them in photographs and on TV in races and stuff, but they looked so cool, a giant plume of colored smoke continuously spraying for up to five minutes. The idea was to freak people out without causing any interior property damage while all hell would be breaking loose on the exterior. The firecrackers they would light off last would wake everyone up. They would look outside, see the smoke, and rush out to see what was going on, and that's when they would slip on the baby oil. *America's Funniest Home Videos*, *Ridiculousness*, and a thousand other shows like those replayed people falling all the time. If they filmed half a dozen people falling, one after another, it would be insane. If one video of a fall got millions of views, Nick couldn't imagine what his video of multiple people slipping and falling on their asses would get.

Putting his finger through the loop of the smoke bomb cannister, he pulled back, and instantly a giant spray of red smoke came gushing out. The site of it made his heart slam. With all his might, he threw it at the house's picture window. The window *shattered*, shocking Nick. He had no clue the tiny can would break the glass! As the smoke bomb hit the curtain and fell into the house, a big smile crossed Nick's face so much, it matched the grin of the grotesque grin on his pumpkin mask.

Forget the original plan, he was going to break *all* the windows.

At the next two houses, Nick did the same thing with the smoke bombs, only one of the windows must have been newer, as it required three throws to break it. When he got to Mr. D's house, he looked around the yard, picked up a rock, and threw it into one of the smaller windows before hurling a purple smoke bomb through the picture window. He wasn't sure why he broke a second window—maybe because he desired doing just a bit more damage to Mr. D's house. He desperately wanted to stand there and wait for Mr. D to rush out in a panic and then flip him off, but he was smarter than that. Instead, Nick ran. Running down the street was the most surreal experience of his life. Lights were snapping on everywhere, smoke was filling every single yard with red, yellow, purple, green, and blue clouds—it was stunning, and it made him feel like he was in a powerful cinematic moment. He imagined himself running in slow motion while some indy rock band played a powerful ballad.

When he got back to his co-conspirators, even though they had their masks on, he could tell they were pissed.

"You broke windows? What the fuck, Nick! The plan was to put them outside of the houses! Let's just get out of here," Luis said, turning to go.

Nick grabbed the large black bag from him, violently pulling it off his shoulder before turning it upside down and pouring out its contents. Reaching into his pocket, he pulled out the lighter, bent over, and lit the pile of Black Cat fireworks. This was what was supposed to get everyone out of their houses, not the smashed windows. Just as the first wick started to sizzle, Luis ran.

"I'm fucking out of here, you can come or not," Luis said over his shoulder as he bolted. Meg followed close behind Luis without a word. Suddenly filled with anger, Nick stood up and watched his friends leave him. They were supposed to film with him so they had multiple angles to catch everything. He was torn between making sure he had a getaway ride and filming. Revenge won out.

Just as the first incredibly loud snap of the firecrackers destroyed the night's silence, Nick pulled out a GoPro and clicked it on. Feeling the need to be creative, he started the shot on the firecrackers, then titled up to reveal the smoke before spinning the camera around to get a shot of the whole street. It looked amazing, but he had to get to Mr. D's house for the money shot. As he ran down the road, away from his friends, away from the plan, he kept the camera as steady as possible to get a good shot as the doors on the houses started opening, just as expected. One after another he saw people slip, slide, and fall. Nick couldn't help but laugh.

Running up to Mr. D's house just in time to see the door open, Nick slowed his pace and steadied his shot. The door swung open, but something he didn't expect happened, Mr. D was holding a young girl in his arms, and his teacher was rushing so fast, Nick didn't even have time to yell at him to stop. Mr. D's foot hit the plastic, slid straight forward, and sent his legs in opposite directions. As he fell forward, grasping his daughter tighter, his other leg stumbled forward, trying to grasp for purchase but hitting the oil instead. This time he spun around and fell backwards onto the iron railing, cracking his back and instantly letting go of his daughter, who dropped headfirst towards the steps. Mr. D rolled forward and slammed his forehead onto the opposite post. When Nick saw how violently his head snapped back and how hard the girl's face hit the cement, his heart dropped, as well as his camera, which settled on the ground with a sideways, albeit perfect shot of the scene unfolding.

Nick ran faster than he ever had, but this time it was not an enjoyable jaunt. Instead of picturing it in slow motion and hearing powerful music, he saw people lying on the ground, some sitting up, others crying, and a few screaming, and through it all in the background, he could hear sirens.

At the end of the street, Nick was met with a cop who was pulling in. He comically froze in the headlights for a moment before cutting to his right and running as the cop car followed. Nick was not an athlete by any means, and being scared and having a hard time breathing behind the mask didn't help either. He didn't make it far before needing to stop and catch his breath.

Two streets over, he raced behind the garage of a house, pulled out his phone, and tried to call Luis, but of course there was no answer. Going into his text message thread, he saw a little red one on his school folder. He had felt it vibrate earlier, but he ignored it. On the run from the cops and needing an escape plan, his schoolwork wasn't exactly a top priority right now, but something made him click on the notice. When he saw it was from Mr. D, he almost fainted. Reading the first few lines, he started to cry, then dropped the phone just a millisecond before the police light shined on his mask.

The cuffs dug into his skin so hard, Nick thought his skin was going to peel off. The cop was more than rough with him as he brought Nick back to the street. The smoke was gone now, but the night sky was still lit up with colors, only this time with the lights from three cop cars, two fire trucks, and four ambulances. The scene looked like the end of a movie when they put the bad guy in a body bag and the hero sits on the back of an ambulance taking oxygen while talking to someone about how it was all over. Nick never thought he'd be in a situation like this, let alone be the bad guy.

What he was most shocked to see was Luis and Meg, also in cuffs, only their hands were comfortably in front of them. Seeing them made him feel more relaxed—they had each other and they had a lie in place to make a cover story. As he started to go over the alibi in his head, his heart dropped for the final time that night when both Luis and Meg pointed right at him. They were a good forty yards away, but he could clearly read their lips: "It was his idea." Nick closed his eyes and gladly went into the back of the police car, away from the nightmarish scene that was unfolding.

"Could you loosen the cuffs? They're…" The first hit came so fast he felt the impact before he saw anything coming. With the cop standing above him while he sat in the car, the gloved fist scraped down from his left eye to his chin, scratching him deeply while at the same time knocking him out. He could not recall the next seven blows, but every time he saw them on the body cam footage, it made him feel sick. But those punches also saved his life.

"One fatal heart attack, nine broken bones, two concussions, and six lacerations were shared by residents in eleven of the twelve houses. The twelfth house, however, had the worst trauma. A single father taking care of his daughter who had battled cancer her whole life, suffered brain damage, and became paralyzed from the neck down. His poor daughter, who was finally getting a new lease on life after years of suffering, surgeries, and chemo, got her face slammed on the corner of a concrete step. She got a twelve-inch gash across her entire face, crushing her nose and cheek bones and dislocating her jaw. The damage required over one hundred stitches and six plastic surgeries to date, but sadly, the doctors are not confident they can reconstruct her face to ever look normal again. All this damage because of a *bad grade*. This was not a harmless prank, it was cold, calculated revenge. The state would like you to consider trying this juvenile as an adult."

The prosecutor would have gotten her way too, and at fifteen, Nick would have been brought to adult court, but the state also did not want a multimillion-dollar lawsuit against them for the police brutality. Even though it was the cop's father who had the heart attack, hitting a cuffed kid in the back of a cruiser until he was unconscious and bloody was not a good image for the small town, and it was an open-and-shut lawsuit.

With a scared mother, a town fearful of national headlines, and two slick lawyers, an agreement was made behind closed doors. In exchange for not suing, Nick would be charged as a minor and just have to pay a fine and do community service. He also had to write apology letters to each family and lastly, while not on paper or legal, it was strongly suggested by the judge that they move far away from the town so everyone could all "move on." Nick's mother could not sign the papers and pay the fine quick enough. Nick didn't want to leave his town or Luis and Meg, but he clearly understood there was no choice. He shut his mouth, wrote his letters, and packed his stuff. Within forty-eight hours of being released from the detention center, he was in a U-Haul heading to New England to start a new life. On the bumpy road, he used his mom's laptop to type up the first of many letters.

Dear. Mr. D,

I guess this is my last essay for you. In a way, it started and ended with one. There is some irony in that, (see, I was paying attention to our vocab!). I could write a thousand essays about how sorry I am, but none of them would ever be enough. I know I came off as stupid, but I'm not dumb enough to think an apology, especially one as informal as a letter, will do anything to correct the pain and suffering I have caused you and your daughter. Nothing could ever fix that. But I do need you to know, it was supposed to be a harmless joke.

All I wanted was for everyone to laugh at you like they laughed at me. It was supposed to be a harmless prank to show you that Cabbage Night could be fun. Just like something on Jack Ass *or* Ridiculousness, *I thought you'd walk out, slip a few times, and maybe fall. I would capture it on camera and the school would all laugh and you'd find it funny in time, just like that time Jacob slipped on the juice Cory spilt in class. Remember how he did a cartoon-style run on the slick spot for like ten seconds before falling and knocking over three desks? You got scared, ran over and helped him, but then you laughed your ass off (sorry for the language) for like five minutes. It was the only time we all saw you truly let go and laugh. I honestly believed my prank would do that: shock, anger, and then laughter.*

I never meant for anyone to get hurt, I meant for it to be the most epic prank ever done in our town. I thought it would be legendary and funny and that people would talk about how cool it was forever. I thought the video would be on TV shows and get millions of views and that it would make Cabbage Night legendary again. I could not have been more wrong.

With you, I did let my anger get a bit out of hand. I can't stop wondering about the window. If I hadn't broken it, would you be fine? Would you have just gotten up to see what was happening and just slipped and fell like normal? Or if I got your note about the grade earlier in the day, would I still have gone through with it? But like my therapist keeps telling me, replaying and wondering doesn't change what is done.

Please pass on apologies to Sydney as well. Out of everything that happened, I feel the worst about her. I know what it is like to be picked on, so I do hope the surgeries go well and she can have a normal life.

I read a self-help book recently (part of my therapy) and it goes on about how the trauma in our lives makes us who we are. Part of me likes to imagine that with the time you have, you will become the first bestselling quadriplegic author and that your daughter will become a model because of her uniqueness, and it will all be because of this tragedy. Who knows.

Again, I can't express how sorry I am. You were a great teacher and didn't deserve any of this. I'm sorry.
Nick Cotter

The mild brain damage made it hard to focus on things, but it didn't bother Tim as much as not being able to move anything but his head. Being in a wheelchair the rest of his life was something he could not understand nor fathom, but what mattered the most was his daughter, Sydney. *His Sweet, Sweet Sydney.* Seeing her in the hospital, with broken bones and a laceration to her face that was so deep it would leave her permanently scarred, was the worst of all the tortures he was going to have to endure. They kept him calm with sedatives, which made it even harder to think. But when he heard that a total of six of his neighbors ended up in the hospital with broken bones, cuts, and more, he cried again. When he found out that Old Man Samson died of a heart attack because of the scare, rage started to settle in. Though when he was told it was Nick who did this to him, he cried softly and blamed himself...

until he got that fucking letter apologizing. Then it was just pure rage.

When he learned months later that Nick and his mother moved and pretty much disappeared after his pitiful punishment of community service, Tim's rage turned into fury and then depression, because a man who wants revenge but can't move anything but his nose is forced to just live with his anger. Part of him fantasized about training Sydney to become an assassin like in some great revenge movie—hell, she already had the scars across her face to show the audience the trauma she endured, but the thoughts were stupid fantasies and just something to pass his damn time. His depression, anger, rage, and thoughts of suicide, revenge, and countless other painful and harmful things bounced around in his head for months as he and Sydney practically lived in the hospital enduring surgery after surgery. It was like they took turns: this week it's your nose reconstruction, next week it's Daddy's tendon transplant surgery! *What will be next?* It was pure and utter torture. He wanted nothing more than to die, but then he would leave Sweet Sydney an orphan to be raised in a foster home looking like a monster. What sort of life would that be?

A year later, back in their now handicap-accessible home, living with two aides who took turns doing twelve-hour shifts to take care of Tim and help Sydney, the anniversary approached. The date nearing was like an evil little parasite teasing him, poking at his brain until it was all mushy and eaten by the disease. Sydney was the only one who could calm him down, but to truly be calm, he had to not look at her and just talk to her with his eyes closed. Seeing her horrific face broke his heart. Her voice through the crushed septum and split lip wasn't much better: a gurgling sound that while unsettling was still not as grotesque as her warped facial features.

He couldn't get used to blowing in the straw to move the chair, so whenever he wanted Sydney to come to him, he would sing out to her, "Sweet Sydney, Sweet, Sweet Sydney." He did it to be cute and loving, but he could tell it was wearing on him. Calling her to him on the anniversary, he saw her face and broke down crying. He was going to ask if she wanted to play a guessing game, but for some reason he snapped. The crying was so hard, his monitors sounded an alarm for a high heart rate and blood pressure spike. Looking up, he saw Sydney and her split face standing in front of him, her expression cold and dead. She did not have tears like his. She took a deep breath and spoke.

"I will take the pain away one day, Daddy, I promise." This odd but sweet statement caused Tim to hyperventilate. His aide raced in, and an hour later he was under observation in the hospital, Sweet Sydney by his side. They were once again going to spend Halloween in the hospital.

Looking at his daughter sleep in the chair next to his bed, a small bag of candy on the table next to her, the nurses gathered together as Tim thought of ways to die, but first he was going to have to teach Sydney how to get revenge when she was ready. Falling asleep, he looked out the window and saw a small green vine clutching onto the glass, as if watching him.

Seeds

It was probably the size of a dime, maybe a millimeter smaller, but it hurt like hell. *When* exactly it started, Sandy couldn't recall, though she definitely felt it in November last year and she could hardly remember what it was like to not be obsessed by agony. The pain was on the back of her head, behind her right ear. Some days it was like a red-hot ice pick slowly being forced in, then pulled out, only to be slid back in, somehow smoking hot once again. Other days it was like someone planted something inside of her and it was growing, pushing outwards on the nerves. It made living a normal life almost unbearable. There were days when Sandy stayed home, days she fought through the pain and went out and acted like nothing was wrong, and then there were days she thought of nothing but ending the torture for good. Those days got more and more frequent as time went on.

Brain tumor, cancer, aneurism, or a parasite was her first self-diagnosis as of course the internet chose to show her the most gruesome of possibilities for this malady before any other milder options. At twenty-seven, she had just been kicked off her parent's insurance the year before, making her constantly fear lifelong debt out of no fault of her own. Bartending at night and working temp jobs in offices during the day, she was not provided with insurance, nor could she afford it. After seeing a news article about how an infected cat scratch cost someone forty-five thousand dollars in the news, she was determined to refuse all medical care. She couldn't imagine the cost of the numerous doctor visits she would need to figure out what her pain was; it would be astronomical and certainly more than her savings balance of forty-seven dollars. God forbid it was a tumor and she needed constant care. In one of her searches, she found out chemo was over thirty grand for an eight-week round, while surgery cost more than forty grand and that was not including the twenty-six hundred for *each* MRI, let alone the countless office visits. In total, she was looking at over a hundred grand, to start. She already owed that much on her student loans, and they were stopping deferment in a week. So Sandy did nothing but take handfuls of every type of over-the-counter pain meds as possible. *Death was better than debt.*

When she wasn't looking up causes for what she started to call her "spot," she was looking for a job obsessively online. Her college boasted a ninety-eight percent placement rate for graduates. Somehow, even though she was in the top of her business management program, she fell into that fabled two percent who couldn't get a job. It was all about "experience." Every job posting wanted someone with a long list of "experience." *Must have four years or more of experience.* How could she have experience when she just graduated? She applied anyway and hardly got calls back. Three times she got interviews, but they all smiled at her like she was a sick animal who they weren't sure would get better one day and told her when she had *experience* to come back.

It was her frustration at everything that started to make her think the spot was some sort of anxiety-induced pressure headache isolated to one random pinpoint. What could she do, though? Worrying about it did nothing but make it ache more. So, just like the rest of the misery in her life, she ignored it and focused her anger at the rich, happy twenty-somethings on her favorite reality television shows, wishing she had their issues instead of her boring real-world ones. Really, how much drama could you have when you are worth millions before your twenty-fifth birthday and spend your summers in beach houses paid for by your rich daddies? They never once had to worry about being able to afford a doctor's visit, yet the shows found enough drama to fill dozens of seasons. *Simply obnoxious.*

It was a Tuesday in September when things started to go from painful and annoying to weird and scary. Leaving her tiny basement apartment, which was really just her parents' house with a private walkout entrance that she made a point to call an "apartment" since they made her pay rent now to make her feel more "adult," she took a walk. She had gotten up early, showered, and got ready to take a job, but there was no call from the temp agency that day. Being cool and crisp outside, she decided a walk would clear her head and the constant depression for a bit, and she could use some exercise after all. While blood pressure, anger, and the like seemed to make the spot worse, exercise seemed to do the opposite, as the pain faded during any brisk activity, meaning she had been walking almost daily. At least there was one positive effect of the spot: a smaller waistline.

Walking down the street with the crunchy leaves making a ruckus under her feet, she took deep breaths and smiled at the trees as if thanking them for the crackling cacophony. On the side of the road there was a smashed pumpkin. She wondered if it had fallen out of a truck bed. Being only late September, Sandy found this odd and paused and looked at the mess of orange goo. It reminded her of the last time she could recall doing something without pain, it was… when she went pumpkin picking with her mother almost an entire year ago. They did it every year, just the two of them, a hayride, hot cider, and pumpkins. Sandy looked forward to it every season and the pumpkins they got were always beautiful, as they handpicked them from the patch. Last year it was colder than normal and windy, but they still laughed and went on and on about their daily lives, little did she know she wouldn't be able to have another conversation without being distracted with pain in her head for the next year. They each tromped through the patch with other families with little children running around them. Thankfully, her mother only made a handful of comments about finding a man so she could have "grandbabies." Then, Sandy found it: a perfectly round pumpkin with a giant green stem staring right at her. She picked it up but quickly yelped as the sharp and unforgiving vine dug into her skin. Dropping it to the dirt, Sandy looked at her hand and pouted—there was a small slice on her index finger. Kicking into mother mode, her mom rushed over, took a look, splashed some water on it, and cleaned it with tissues before wrapping it with a Band-Aid she pulled out of her purse. The woman had not had a toddler in over twenty-five years, yet she was still prepared for anything.

A few minutes later, Sandy went back to the same pumpkin, but this time she picked it up from the sides. The memory was vague, but Sandy had a hazy glimpse of the pain tickling her scalp the moment she picked it up. That pumpkin sat on their porch for the next six weeks until they cut it up, baked the seeds for a snack, and then set them on the porch for trick-or-treaters to enjoy. Her parents were one of the few houses in Haven—also known as "Halloween Haven" in October—who went for "classic country fall" over spooky themes. The quaint and simple display always made her mom proud. This memory flooding back caught her off guard, she couldn't fathom that the pain had been there for a full year. With a sigh, she kept trudging on—no destination in mind, no speed necessary, just lazy, casual wandering. About four blocks away from her apartment, it happened.

It was almost like an old movie skipping in the theater, when the film got stuck in the projector and it shook violently, causing the image to jump around the screen. One single frame, flashing and jittering all over while sending shocks of bright white light around the edges—the old anomaly that every movie attendee in the '80s saw at least once, right in mid-step. Sandy froze, confused at what her eyes were doing and what she was seeing—her mouth dropped open, and her tongue involuntarily went back and forth as if it were doing an imitation of a windshield wiper. Her left arm rose and stopped halfway. If anyone passed at that moment, they would think she was doing some sort of lazy zombie impression. Suddenly, flashes of a kid wearing an orange pumpkin T-shirt, a child she had never seen before, slammed through her brain. She saw him smush a pumpkin like the one she saw earlier with the toe of his shoes, saw him in line at a haunted house, saw his guts falling out of him, and finally she saw his funeral with only a lone woman attending, the last image she saw was the woman shooting herself in the mouth, a tiny bullet coming out the back of her head, in the exact spot where Sandy's own pain was.

When the vision snapped off, just like when the film strip would get too hot and tear apart, her arm dropped, her mouth closed, and she took a step as if someone had un-paused her, letting her continue her walk. Sandy took another ten steps as if on autopilot before slowing down and realizing what just happened. This time when she stopped she was in control of her body, but she was terrified at what had just happened. Desperately, she looked around for a place to sit, but unless she walked onto someone's property, there was nothing but the curb. Having no choice, she settled down on the hard, slightly damp square edge and took three deep breaths. The images haunted her head, though now they were memories. She tried to make sense of what she saw, but more so, she tried to figure out what happened. *Was it a stroke? A mental breakdown?*

After wiping the few tears that fell and steadying her breath, Sandy came to the decision that she had a brain tumor and it had finally grown to the point where it was pushing on her nerves, causing her brain to short-circuit. It scared the shit out of her. A few thoughts of rushing to the hospital came into her mind, but then with clarity she found peace. If it was already that far along, what was the point? Dying was a much better option. Her life sucked anyway, no one would miss her besides her parents, so why not? The thought of ending it all had always been lurking in the back of her mind ever since she was twelve, so why not now, when she had a valid reason? If she went through all the medial procedures for a brain tumor, she'd either die anyway or be a vegetable, so why risk that and the chance of leaving her parents with hundreds of thousands in debt, why not just leave on her terms? Standing up, she suddenly had a newfound excitement in her life, because now she had something to look forward to. Well, maybe not *look forward to*, but a goal nonetheless. As she started her walk home, she thought of the things she would do before leaving the Earth, sort of a farewell tour of enjoyable things. How she would kill herself was something she would think of later.

With a smile on her face, she walked briskly for another ten minutes, passing houses that were just starting to put up their Halloween decorations. Her mind was racing with various thoughts of what to do before she died. It was a bit overwhelming, to the point where she had to force the thoughts out of her head and relax, otherwise a panic attack was inevitable. Just as she was about to stop and sit again to focus, she saw a house so covered in Halloween decorations, it made her stop in her tracks to take it all in. It had enough decorations for ten houses and an odd, long black tube that ran around the house like some sort of man-made tunnel. Smack in the middle was a printed sign complete with grommets stating, "Haunted House Open Halloween Night! Make Sure to Vote for Scariest House!" Reading the sign, she smiled to herself, it was the first year she hadn't been looking forward to the season, the damn spot distracted her too much. She used to love all the events as a kid, she even came in third place in the "Children Under Ten Costume Contest" when she was eight for her homemade *Bride of Frankenstein* costume. She missed those days, when things were simpler and she didn't have to worry about anything other than getting more candy.

Standing there, taking in all the decorations while going down memory lane, Sandy was at peace. For once, she wasn't thinking about the spot or death. As the warm memories wrapped around her—watching scary movies for days before Halloween, getting bags full of candy, the costume contests, the school dance party, and the local haunted houses—she knew that was going to be the day: Halloween. She'd die on a day she loved so much growing up. With the decision made, she had just one worry: there wasn't much time, just over a month to be exact.

Just as she was about to turn and walk away, a plump man came out of the house carrying an armful of plastic skeletons. He looked flustered but happy. Sandy waved at him, and yelled, "Looks great, can't wait to see the haunted house!"

Smiling, the man put the bones down on the yard and trotted over to her. "It's going to be amazing this year, I promise! You have to come and you have to tell all your friends and vote for me! I'm trying to beat my brother. He wins every year."

The man was so excited, it made Sandy jealous that she did not have any of that excitement in her life and never would again. They talked for a few moments about the decorations, what sort of surprises he had in store at the house, and then she promised to be one of the first people to tour it on Halloween. As she turned and started her walk, a small smile resting on her lips, a sensation washed over her body, like a sudden chill shooting through her, only it was hot and prickly. She almost stopped, but she forced herself to keep going. When she dared a look back at the house, Spot thudded three times fast, like someone tapping her brain to get her attention. It made her stomach drop.

A few hours and eight aspirin later, Sandy poured herself a large glass of wine for lunch. Sitting at her small, cluttered desk in her dark basement apartment, she pulled out a notepad and pen and looked at it seriously. After a few seconds of contemplation, she wrote "Things to Do Before I Die" at the top in big block letters. It made her giggle a little. Then she jotted down several things: say goodbye to certain people, make a will, and a write a letter about how she wanted her remains handled—cremated and buried in the woods in a biodegradable box under a large fern.

After the list, which she was surprised was so short, she started on the first task: writing letters to her family. Again, she was surprised at how easy the letters were, they only took her bout twenty minutes each—one to her father and her mother and an aunt she was close to, and then she wrote a generic one that was to be shared with any friends who asked about her. Looking at the four letters, she felt a slight pang of loneliness over having so few people in her life, but then she shrugged it off as a good thing since she wasn't going to be around long anyway.

Setting down the pen, she shook out her hand and it began again. The room started to flicker, her mouth dropped open, and while she still had control of her mind, she briefly thought about how she was happy that this time, she was sitting down in her own home. The image of her room shook and then stretched and snapped, filling with brilliant white light before it was replaced with a different room altogether: a kitchen with a man wearing an apron. He was humming to himself and cutting something, but she couldn't see what just yet. Then, as if she were watching a horror movie, the image flicked quickly and she saw it was not a nice dinner, but the body of a small boy. It was followed by several horrific and fast shots that she desperately tried to close her eyes and not see, but it was no use—the images were embedded in her head, and there was no way to obstruct them.

When she snapped out of the trance or whatever it was, she flipped the pages of the notepad and found a new one. She did not want to see the images again, not at all, but she forced herself to think about them and write down what she saw. On a separate page, she also wrote the first vision—if that was what it was—down. She knew it was just her mind misfiring from the tumor, it had to be. She didn't believe in mediums and psychics and the sort, and she was not going to now. She knew it was the growth causing havoc in her brain, but why they had to be horrible and terrifying images was beyond her, especially since they had no context to her life and she had never seen the people involved. *Why couldn't they be of happy things?*

The next hour involved searches online about tumor-induced visions. She found a ton of stupid theories that were just that, theories made up by people with no medical training at all. Some even called it the *Phenomenon*, based on the movie with John Travolta, where he had similar visions caused by a tumor. There were a few scholarly articles about tumors causing odd images, but nothing that directly had to do with killings, murder, or death. Frustrated, tired, and wanting nothing to do with what was going on anymore, she laid in bed, snapped on Netflix, took out a whole bottle of wine, and started to drink. The alcohol did nothing to settle her or stop the visions that were suddenly coming one after another. Several hours straight they came in rapid succession as if someone was changing a channel; each time she wrote them down. Every single one involved death, murder, torture or something just damn awful. It was around 5:00 in the afternoon, after the bottle of wine was drained and she was exhausted, when the visions finally stopped.

Sandy laid in the bed, staring at the ceiling and breathing heavily. She was exhausted and simply scared—scared that the last days of her life would be filled with a nonstop horror show in her mind. After an hour of not moving and no flashes, she risked sitting up, and then she carefully moved around the room, stretching and loosening her body that had been so tense. Part of her knew if this continued, she'd have to move up her plan and kill herself much sooner to end the pure torture. She looked at her notebook and slammed it shut in anger. She didn't want to see the horrific details. Needing a break, she left her room and ventured upstairs, something she didn't do much anymore, as she tried to act like she was a true tenant and that it wasn't her parents upstairs but a landlord.

Her parents were surprised to see her, but more so, they both looked concerned at her appearance. She brushed it off as a headache and asked if she could have dinner with them and watch a movie that night. They giddily agreed and her mother started rushing around the kitchen as her father asked what sort of movie she wanted to watch, and she suggested something funny. Her parents loved her and would spend every day with her if they could. They only made her pay rent so she felt like she was an adult, and even then, Sandy knew they were actually putting it away in a savings account for her to use for a house one day. Sandy didn't want to be an adult anymore, she wanted to sit in the kitchen and read a gossip magazine while mom cooked, she wanted to laugh at her dad's stupid jokes at dinner and to cuddle up between them while watching a lame movie they only watched for her sake. And that night she got that along with two long and wonderful hugs. When she went back downstairs, she knew they were the last hugs she would ever have.

Back in her room, Sandy was thankful for one last night with her parents. She was especially grateful that the flashes did not come back, but just as she felt that relief, the visions took over, as if they purposely gave her a break. This time, they came back with a force so hard, it made her entire body ache with fear. Over the next six hours, Sandy found herself in various positions of pain: on the floor in a ball, pushing herself against the wall gasping for air, and throwing up in the bathroom as images of guts being bagged up raced through her head. It was the worst experience of her life and she needed it to end. The odd part was the visions—they were the same things in the same order, over and over. But as they played in her mind, vines came into her brain as well, almost as if they were making a picture frame around the visions. The vines stayed there on the edges of what she saw, slowly creeping inwards. There was a man with a scarred face who was hellbent on slicing people, a killer with a sick bloodlust, dark monsters, broken windows, pumpkin pie with blood as a topping—it was endless death and pain. This time, though, she saw more and more details of the horrors involved. When the last one in the series played in her head for the tenth time, she hoped she'd be given a break, but this time, a new one flashed, one of herself.

In this "vision," she saw herself sitting on a massive pumpkin, one of those blue ribbon winners that weigh over a thousand pounds. Only it wasn't in a parade or a fair, it was in the middle of a field, and all of these ancient warriors surrounded her as if protecting the pumpkin and herself was the most important thing in the world. Then suddenly she fell through the orange flesh of the pumpkin as if a trap door opened. Only instead of goo inside, there were long, jagged tan spikes that looked like they were made out of the shell of the seeds. Dozens of them pierced through her body, one right through her neck and two into her skull, which kept her from looking down at her body to see how many others cut through her. While it was all in her head, she still felt the pain of every single spike decimating her body. The pain was horrendous and so real she thought blood was pouring down her. She writhed in agony on her floor, but she couldn't scream—the imaginary spike through her throat had taken away her vocal cords. As the vision started to get blurred by the encroaching vines taking over her mind's eye, she realized that one spike had gone right through the spot in her head. As the last vine took over her vision, she passed out.

Waking, she didn't know if it was seconds or hours later. She gasped for air and tried to make sense of what just happened. She did her best to tell herself it was just her brain misfiring, but something told her it wasn't. Out of nowhere, a voice—soft, sweet, and raspy—started talking inside her head. *They must die, all of them, but you . . . you can save the world.* Sandy had never experienced anything like this voice before, it was so real and clear, right inside her head as if it were her own inner monologue, but she could not control it and it was so predominated, it was hard to hear her own thoughts over the voice. She was losing it, she was losing her sanity at a pace that was so rapid she couldn't understand it. She'd be completely mad by morning. If she didn't do something her family would find her, bring her to a hospital, and she'd end up in a psych ward forever... well, until the tumor killed her.

You are the chosen, the mother of the pumpkin queen. You choose if the world lives or dies, lives or dies, lives or dies . . . it's you or the world. The voice didn't stop, it kept talking to her as if it were a whole different person inside her head, telling her some sort of fairy tale. As it kept talking, it turned from a whisper into a full voice, the raspiness went away as if it hadn't spoken in centuries and just needed to clear its voice. Then it got a bit louder and louder until it was almost screaming inside of her skull. *You choose, you are the mother of the pumpkin queen! It is an honor, only once a century does someone get chosen to decide the fate of many. Watch them die or let them live, sacrifice one or many.*

No more. Sandy could not take it for another second. She was ready to go and run in front of a car to stop the voice—it was worse than the images she saw. The idea of not controlling her brain anymore was horrific. A quick end was needed. The voice started to laugh as she went into the unfurnished part of the basement, which doubled as her dad's workshop and grabbed a box cutter.

NO! You cannot die that way, they will never get what they need from you if you do. You don't want me living inside, then cut me out, but not that way! Sandy shook her head hard, ignoring the voice, she looked at the box cutter and took a deep breath.

STOP. You must cut it out, cut it out, cut out the pain, that little knife won't do. She again ignored the voice and said out loud that it wasn't real over and over to try and reassure herself. It didn't work.

I will prove to you we are real, that you must do this to save everyone. Look up a name and then we will help you end this all. Nick Cotter, Cabbage Night, look now, look, look, you will see. The voice stopped. The silence was confusing but more than welcomed. Looking at the box cutter, she repeated the name to herself, wondering if her mind was trying to help her or if it was just fried. What did a few extra minutes matter anyway? Sandy set the blade down and went to her computer.

With a mere few keystrokes, Sandy's heart sank. The image that came up with the name was the boy she saw in her vision, the one who squished the pumpkin then got stabbed on the table. Though this article wasn't about him getting stabbed, it was about some fiasco he caused a few states away last year on the night before Halloween.

"He is alive, you're lying to me." Sandy said out loud.

The voice came back, laughing. *We don't lie, what we showed you are things that are going to happen, not things that have already occurred.* It spoke another name, then another and another. Each one Sandy found on Facebook or another social media site. She had never met a single one of them, but they were all the people from her visions. *Real, real, real . . . not crazy.* Sandy took a deep breath, knowing she was not crazy but not understanding what was happening.

Staring at the computer, another vision came to her, though this one came softly and gently, as if it were protecting her, and this time it was a memory. Sandy saw herself, about six months before when she was on a date with a guy she met online. The date was good, he was nice and cute, they had dinner at Olive Garden, then went for drinks at a local bar. A recap of the date played in her mind without sound and on fast-forward, but then it slowed as they ordered shots. She remembered she only agreed to the shots because she figured she was going to sleep with him and wanted a bit of courage beforehand. The guy, Jack, she thought was his name, ordered some odd shot, it came in a bottle wrapped in orange foil and had a jack-o'-lantern on it. The name had something to do with a famous composer, but Sandy couldn't recall, she just remembered it was odd ordering a pumpkin chocolate cream shot in May, but she did it regardless.

What the vision showed her now was that when he was looking

into her eyes, he dropped something into her drink. Part of her started to get pissed thinking she was given a roofie, but the other part of her recalled she got home safe and never even got a kiss. The vision was persistent, it replayed the scene four times, each time showing his hand closer and closer—a seed, it was a *seed* that he put in her drink. Then the pumpkin patch from last year flashed into her head. Then the shots of her eating the seeds and laughing with her mother. One after another, there were tiny split-second moments over the past year of seeds being slipped into her food and drinks, sometimes by strangers and waitstaff, other times by people she knew—they were all making her eat pumpkin seeds. After she saw her consume each one, her spot throbbed as if it grew just a bit each time. The vision stopped.

Get the seeds out and get your life back.

You were chosen, you are the mother of the pumpkin queen now!

Get the seeds OUT.

GET THE SEEDS OUT.

The sentence started to grow to a chant. The voice splintered into two, then four, then a dozen and more. Flashes of the warriors standing around her on the pumpkin jolted her brain. It was them, they were all chanting to her.

Understanding what she *had* to do, she stood up, walked back into her father's workshop, and on autopilot got an electric drill. As a teen, she helped her father make all sorts of things, so she knew how to change the bits and what to use for various things. What she needed was a wood drill bit, one of the big corkscrew-looking ones. With ease, she found it in a drawer alongside many others. She chose the half-inch one, thinking it would be the right size. Slipping the bit into the chuck and tightening it, the chant stopped as the warriors noticed what she was doing. It took a bit of adjusting and then a lot of duct tape, but she was able to secure the drill on the vice with the bit facing out. A length of tight duct tape on the trigger kept the drill going at full speed. Looking at the spinning bit, she had no expressions, no emotions, she was just happy that she already wrote her letters. She had already experienced unimaginable pain, so she was not worried about what she was about to feel. Facing away from the bench, she knelt down and positioned herself so the rapidly rotating corkscrew was right behind her head. Adjusting herself a bit, she found the right spot, took a breath, and ignored the chant that was starting again in her mind.

Just as she was about to slam her head backwards, she recalled a viral video she saw about hair getting stuck in a drill and it stopping cold, all tangled in the locks. The last thing she wanted was her parents to find her scalped but alive. With a sigh, she got back up, got scissors, and cut off all the hair she could on the back of her head. This made her sad. She liked her hair, but it was better than it being ripped out. Kneeling back down, she was ready.

Get the SEEDS OUT.

She didn't understand what was happening or what was going to happen because of her death, but it didn't matter. With a sigh, Sandy slammed her head back.

The thin bit of flesh on her scalp was peeled off instantly. Her skull took a bit longer to crack through, actually smoking a bit as the metal corkscrew worked. Sandy could smell the pungent scent of smoldering bone, but then the drill bit popped through it like a piece of cheap plywood. Her brain, on the other hand, the bit went through like a watermelon. As one eye started to twitch, the voices in her mind stopped. She forced her head back harder, fighting the pain to get the bit deeper inside. Hot gobs of goo fell on to her neck and shoulders, but it didn't feel right. Curious, her head vibrating back and forth as the bit swirled inside her, she reached back and scooped up a bit of the goo off her shoulder and pulled it forward to look at it. Sandy was not surprised to see it was not red and mushy at all, it was orange with white seeds. It was as if she were carving a pumpkin. Sandy smiled as she let the seeds fall to the floor.

I'm the pumpkin queen's mother, Sandy thought as she started to pass out. As she fell forward to the floor, she heard the door open and footsteps approach. Through a blurred haze, she saw a man in overalls and a plaid shirt, a... farmer. He knelt down and rubbed her head, lovingly and gently. Then she saw a glass mason jar being set down in front of her. Like he was handling a baby animal, he scooped up seed after seed and placed it in the jar with such gentle care, it made Sandy jealous.

"I'm sorry they chose you, but someone had to do it. You are free now, darling. I'll find just the right queen to take care of your babies. You can rest knowing you may have just saved the town of Haven and hell, the rest of the world."

Sandy stared at the jar filling up with seeds, *her* seeds. She smiled and thought about how wonderful those pumpkins were going to look this Halloween season.

Alone on Halloween

The jack-o'-lantern had started to rot prematurely. Nick rolled it onto its side with the edge of his dirty sneaker; a slow-motion squishing sound softly emanated from the jagged mouth of the sad pumpkin. He shook his head with slight shame, but also as if inspecting it in the same way a detective in of those cop shows did when they hunched over a dead body.

"People always carve them too early," Nick said out loud to no one but himself, again taking up the role of a detective, his hands in his hoodie pockets.

"Day before Halloween, you want them fresh." This line was mumbled more than spoken out loud. With more slight movement of his shoe, he applied pressure to the triangle-shaped eye and mashed the face into a pile of orange mush. The fact that he did it gently somehow made it all right that he had just ruined some child's pumpkin. It was on the curb of the street, though, so he rationalized with himself that it was probably being thrown out anyway.

Shaking the pulpy mess off his shoe, Nick kept going on his walk. It was warm—warmer than most Cabbage Nights. Nick thought of the name "Cabbage Night" and the essay on it that ruined his life. Back in his hometown, that is what they called the night before Halloween. His new town didn't have a name for it; no one even seemed to know the traditions that took place on what Nick used to think was the most fun night of the year. What he did last year on Cabbage Night, well, that was why he was in a new town—one that didn't have such traditions. Under the strict urging of the judge, they fled, but his mom tried to play off by saying that maybe it would be "good for him" to get away and have a fresh start anyway, as if it were their choice. After all, everything that happened last year—the devastation, the uproar in the town, and the eventual ban of trick-or-treating that next night—was one hundred percent his fault. He would have never been treated fairly there again. He would always be the "kid who ruined Halloween" to the other kids and that "piece of shit" to the adults.

Leaves crunching under his feet, some of them sticking to the drying orange muck, he thought about how long ago that year felt. It felt like another lifetime. Hell, the six months he had been living in the middle of nowhere already felt like six years. And it wasn't just time and distance. He felt like a different person now. Looking back over the past year, thinking of that awful night that was supposed to be "fun as hell," he couldn't believe how stupid he'd been. Thankfully, no one in *this* town knew him as "oh, that kid" when people mentioned his name. Now he was just the "new kid who didn't talk much." While he usually had no problems meeting new people and making friends, in this new town, he didn't see the point. Nick was seventeen and a senior; making friends for half a year before they all went off to college seemed pointless, and most of them had already been together since preschool and had bonds he couldn't even imagine. Besides, the idea of losing friends again, like he did last year, was too painful of a notion. Keeping his head down and grades up was the motto: get through the year, graduate, and start a new life in college.

That's why the walk tonight seemed so . . . lonely. Last year, while traumatic, he was surrounded by his friends, his *best friends*. Friends he could trust with his life, or so he thought, until the night they pointed their fingers right at him when the handcuffs came out. Part of him realized that is why he didn't even want friends this year: if old ones would turn on him in a second, what would new ones do?

The walk, which he had already taken about a hundred times since moving into the new house, was simple and peaceful, but it had a singular purpose: snacks. While the ultimate goal was to get to the 7-Eleven for an energy drink and a few Slim Jims, Nick found himself using it as an excuse to get out of the house and enjoy the season. He already had his license, but his mother said he could not have a car until he turned eighteen and showed enough responsibility. Thankfully that was only a few months away. Regardless, Nick thought he would still take the walk. While he didn't believe in hippie crap, there was some sort of zen to the fourteen minutes to the 7-Eleven and fourteen minutes back that put him at ease, especially in the fall weather with the crunchy leaves making satisfying sounds under his feet—though he would never admit that to anyone and defend to his death that the walk was solely for the Slim Jims.

After two lefts, a right, and then a long straight stretch, Nick arrived at the dingy old convenience store and walked through the automatic doors. A cold burst of air hit him; they still had the air conditioning on for some reason, causing the store to be ten degrees colder than outside. The sudden cold made him hesitate with confusion for a second, but he quickly righted himself and headed for the cooler where they kept the thirty-two-ounce, overly caffeinated drink he had become so addicted to. Opening the cooler, he paid no attention to the pumpkin decals that adorned the glass; they had already been there for a month. What he did notice was that the inside of the cooler was warmer than the store. He shook his head in frustration, but grabbed two bright green cans anyway.

Three steps before the cash register, he grabbed two Slim Jims—the "Monster Size" ones—and a Twix. Throwing all his stuff on the counter, he pulled the crumpled money out of his pocket. He had the exact change ready, tax included, and put it on the counter to await his cheap plastic bag. The indistinguishably foreign man behind the counter just nodded and accepted the money without looking. He knew Nick and knew his routine and the fact that he always gave the exact amount, yet they never became friendly. As he cracked open a can and walked towards the door, he looked up and saw a bright orange flyer with little ghosts making up a border. Nick stopped, took a sip of the acidic sludge, and read it:

Alone on Halloween?
Don't be a Ghoul
Come Out, You Fool.
Get the Scare of Your Life
Even If You're Old Enough to Have a Wife
Treats for All
Even If You Don't Survive the Fall

34 Oak Terrace Ave – Starts at Dusk

Make Sure to Vote for Ruben's Home for "Scariest House" This Year!

It was a cheesy poster, but something about it intrigued Nick. He pulled out his phone and took a photo of the flyer and then started his walk home. The entire way he tried not to think about last year's events. Seeing the Halloween decorations, the flyer, and the countless pumpkins lining the way made him go over what happened again and again—not like he hadn't already a million times over the past year. He knew the anniversary would be hard, but he hoped that being two states away would help ease the memories.

So far it hadn't.

When Nick got home, he knew he had just missed his mother because there were pumpkins on the steps that weren't there before and her car was not in the driveway. He looked at the three round, squat, but almost perfect pumpkins with no emotion, then went inside to read her note. She *always* left a note rather than just texting; she said it was *more personal*. Inside, on the fridge like always, was the large, hot-pink sticky note. He read it quickly; it was the same old story: she had to rush off to her second job, there were frozen dinners in the freezer or pizza money in the drawer, don't go to bed to late, clean up, blah, blah, blah. The only difference in this note was that she asked him to carve the pumpkins for her. *All three, please, different faces on each.* It was the last thing he wanted to do, but since last year, there wasn't a single thing he didn't do that she asked. He'd been the perfect son, since November 1st of last year. He was also extremely thankful for his mother completely and utterly ignoring the Cabbage Night anniversary. His therapist would say it was unhealthy, but he sure would disagree—sometimes not talking about something is just a lot easier.

One by one he brought in the pumpkins, cleaned them off with wet paper towels, then set them down on spread-out newspaper. On the television in the kitchen, he popped on AMC to watch their horror movie lineup. Thankfully, Kane Hodder was on the screen wearing the classic hockey mask and gutting people left and right. Those movies always made him happy. Nick *loved* Halloween—actually, "love" was probably an understatement. And yet, last year, he didn't even see a minute of his favorite holiday: he was in jail, then the courthouse, while the little kids in his town cried about not being allowed to go trick-or-treating. That day, Nick knew what it felt like to be a monster—not one with latex rubber and a mask, but a real, live monster.

Pulling out the flimsy orange saw-like device that came with the pumpkin carving kit, Nick looked at it with curiosity. The thing was three inches long and could be bent by a strong wind, yet it did a hell of a job carving through the orange flesh. Holding the tiny blade to the pumpkin to start carving an eye, Nick suddenly stopped, pulled away the saw, and slid the miniature teeth across his left wrist. It stung and left a red line, but only one tiny droplet of blood, not even enough for a sugar test, oozed out of his skin. He stared at it, then dropped the saw on the counter. He had never done anything like that in his life and it scared him. His doctors asked him countless times if he was depressed, if he ever harmed himself, if he had suicidal thoughts, and he honestly told them "no" every time.

So, what the hell was that, Nick?

Staring blankly at the screen, seeing the giant machete in the killer's hand, Nick was suddenly happy that he did not attempt to cut the pumpkin with a real knife. With a big breath, he gently cleaned his wrist, decided it did not need a bandage, and then started to carve the pumpkins again. Watching the killer hack away on the television, he thought of his friends back home and wondered what they were doing tonight. Were they ignoring the day, refusing to relive what happened, or were they all together watching the exact same movie right now? They always got together after school and raced back to one of their houses to watch the horror movie marathons and eat junk food. *Man, he missed them . . . God, he hated them.*

By the time the last pumpkin was done, he pushed the thoughts of his friends out of his head and the incident with the flimsy blade seemed to be a fluke that was already in the past. Looking at the orange gourds, he was proud of himself; they were not bad at all. They were not going to win any contests, but they were classic-looking. After putting them outside and hoping there would be no Cabbage Night vandals like himself, he went back in and rinsed all the pumpkin seeds he had set aside. His mother didn't ask him to, but he knew she loved roasted seeds, so he washed them all off, spread them on a sheet pan, covered them in oil and sea salt, and set them in the oven to cook. *Nick, making homemade snacks for his hardworking mother—son of the year!*

Twenty minutes later, after one flip of the seeds, they were done. Using oven mitts, he grabbed the big cookie sheet with both hands and turned towards the counter where he had a trivet waiting, but just before he could set it down, both of his arms involuntarily pulled the tray against his chest. The red-hot lip of the pan hit his shirt with a searing popping sound, followed by the smell of burning. The heat almost instantly burned its way through the shirt and charred his flesh. This was no quick "tap the skin, scream, and throw the pan" like a normal person would. The lip of the pan stuck deep and hard into his ribs for a solid ten seconds, until the pan itself started to adhere to Nick's melting flesh. Even after he realized what he was doing, Nick never dropped the pan, nor did he scream. He simply set it on the counter, took off his gloves, and shut the oven door.

Once the off button was pushed on the oven, his screams began. Peeling off his shirt, he raced into the bathroom to see a long, fifteen-inch red, black, and brown thick line across his chest. It bubbled in parts while other parts oozed, and a few tufts of burnt gray T-shirt material stuck to his skin. Turning on the water, he quickly tried to splash his chest, but it was too late to do anything. Jumping in the shower, he turned the water to ice cold, stood under the spray, and screamed and screamed until he cried, partially from the pain, but also from not understanding what the hell just happened.

An hour later, with taped-together ice packs laid across his chest, Nick knew the burns needed medical attention, but he could not and would not put his mother through any sort of traumatic incident—not again, especially on the anniversary—so he was going to have to live with it for a while. Antibacterial ointment and bandages were going to have to do. If he went to the hospital, they would call her out of work. For a second year in a row, she would get a call from an official asking if Nick was her son and then telling her some horrible news. There was no way in hell he was going to do that to her again. He could live with this; it would heal eventually… he hoped.

With bandages and a new T-shirt uncomfortably on, Nick went to the kitchen to bag up the seeds. The pan itself was going to have to be thrown away. Nick just couldn't stomach trying to scrape off his own flesh to salvage the ten-dollar cookie sheet. With some painful effort, he concealed it at the bottom of the recycling bin along with the burnt T-shirt. With everything done, he skipped dinner and went to bed just as the sun started to dip down behind the horizon.

Lying in bed, Nick felt uneasy in a way he never had before. Part of him felt like he was losing his mind while part of him just didn't know what the hell was happening. The rational part was trying to tell himself that his mind was just processing last year's events in some messed up way, subconsciously punishing himself since he got off so easy. Maybe the guilt he thought he handled was really suppressed like his countless court-ordered therapists suggested. After endlessly talking to himself in his head, that was his best hypothesis: the date was bringing up suppressed guilt and he was subconsciously punishing himself. All he had to do was go to sleep. Tomorrow, the date will have passed, and he could start over. Nick also tried to trick his brain by telling it that he would now have a permanent, massive scar on his chest forever, which would recognize and pay tribute to his sins. He didn't think it would work, but he'd try anything to get to sleep. Which only came after four Tylenol PM.

This is a dream. Nick absolutely knew he was in a dream, it had to be.

Pumpkins could not talk, they could not get up and walk, they did not have legs, and they could not chase you—which meant he was dreaming. Knowing you are in a dream and waking up are two different things. When you are deep in the dream and it is still happening, when you are still running from the giant jack-o'-lantern monsters chasing you, your heart slamming, it didn't matter if you knew it was still a dream. Because it was *still* scary; it *still* felt real. As he ran for his life, he saw all the houses from the street last year, the street he had picked because it was Mr. D's, the street that everything happened on. Of course, the dream would be there; of course, the nightmare would take place on that street. If this were real life, he could run through any backyard, hop a fence, and be out of that awful street. But this was a dream; there was no way out. There were walls between each house a mile high with spikes on them; he could only run from locked door to locked door while screaming for help from those that he hurt . . . and killed. Of course, no one came to his rescue.

At the end of the cul-de-sac, at *his* house, Nick was out of running room; he was out of doors to try and open and windows to bang on. No one was coming to help him. *Why would they?* Turning around, he saw there were more pumpkin monsters than he thought—there were six of them. Each with horrific grinning jack-o'-lantern faces that looked to have been carved by a madman. Inside of each raged not just a candle but a burning-hot fire; flames and sparks flitted and popped out of the pumpkin creatures' mouths as they looked at him with hunger. While the faces would probably haunt his nightmares forever, it was the twisted vine bodies and legs that truly horrified him. Spiky, slithering veins of vines made up every inch of their bodies. Only when Nick looked closer, he saw they were not vines at all, but thousands of snakes writhing together.

Nick tried to speak, to plead with the monsters who were about to devour him, but his voice was gone. No words, not even a vowel, came out of his mouth. It was then that he realized his shirt was gone and the giant scar he had gotten earlier that day on his chest was glowing bright orange, as if the line of burnt flesh were made out of molten lava.

Seeing this, Nick started to cry. He wanted to fall to the ground, to run, to just give up, but he couldn't move, he was... paralyzed. He tried to scream, but he couldn't do that either. A giant scar was across his face, his mouth was sewn shut to help it heal. Helpless, the head pumpkin monster, the tallest one, took two steps forward, fire sparking out of his eyes, and pointed one writhing snake finger at Nick. Then all the other monsters followed suit and pointed their reptilian fingers at Nick. Seconds later, the lava on his chest burned so intensely, he thought he was going to explode, and, in a way he did: the burn on his skin split wide open, revealing an orange light shooting out of his chest, blinding him. The last thing he saw was all the pumpkin monsters rushing towards him.

Nick woke up screaming, the wound on his chest throbbing, sweat pouring down his face. As he went to wipe his forehead, he screamed again, as his fingers were slimy. His left hand was covered in orange pumpkin guts. Frantically, he shook it, flinging the stringy intestines throughout his room. Jumping up, he looked around to see if one of the monsters was actually there. Nothing. No pumpkins either. Cleaning his hand off on his comforter, Nick paced the room, wondering if he was still dreaming, but there was no doubt, he was awake.

It took a full ten minutes of slow box breathing to regain his composure and to think rationally. Even though he knew it was a dream and exactly what his mind was punishing him for, the pumpkin sludge was *real. Sleepwalking.* That was it—he had to have walked in his sleep and stuck his hands in one of the jack-o'-lanterns. *Right?* Regardless of what happened, he was scared and he felt awful; his body was sore from tensing, the burn was unbearable, and he was miserable. After gaining some of his composure, he dared to look at the result of last night's self-mutilation. Puss had oozed through the bandages and dried, sealing his shirt to his skin with a layer of crunchy browns, blacks, and reds. It took almost half an hour to pull the shirt and bandages off, and when he did, it just reopened the wound. The sight of the injury made him nauseous and also reconfirmed that he should have gone to the hospital and probably still should. Hell, if his mind continued the way it was, he would end up in the hospital for sure.

After an excruciatingly painful shower, more ointment, bandages, and a fresh shirt, Nick went into the kitchen to find a bowl next to a box of cereal and another pink sticky note. He wasn't surprised to read that his mom had to leave early, again, to go to her first job of the day. It also went on with almost the exact same wording as the day before and the day before that: *Sorry I missed you. Have a great day at school, honey. Let's catch up this weekend.* The only thing that differed this time was one line asking him to hand out candy tonight, and when he ran out, to shut the lights off. Nick hated that buying more than two small bags of candy was now a luxury his mother couldn't afford. Yet again, he was ruining some kid's Halloween, even if it was by just getting one less piece of candy.

Snapping on the television, he poured himself some berry-flavored, Frankenstein-themed cereal and enjoyed the irony of eating it on the one day of the year the cereal was relevant. On the screen before him, he watched as morning show hosts jumped around in asinine costumes that weren't meant to scare but instead get an "aww" from the crowd. Nick shook his hand with slight anger, but he pushed it away. It was that anger and thoughts about how a day should be spent that started the whole situation last year. A simple conversation about the origins of Halloween and why it was *supposed* to be scary. *Not cute, not silly, not sexy, scary.* Dressing up as cute princesses and superheroes made no sense at all. Demons were supposed to come to Earth on All Hallows' Eve; if they saw terrible monsters and fellow demons, they would be satisfied that Earth was in shambles, or better yet, they would get scared and retreat back to where they came from. A sexy nurse and a superhero would not scare a demon. That rabbit hole of a conversation brought up another conversation about Cabbage Night and what its true meaning was, which led to the paper, which led to the embarrassment, which....

Nick suddenly found himself standing. He didn't remember even getting up nor understood why he did. Then, with the speed of a falling cinderblock, Nick slammed his head into his cereal bowl. Thankfully, with a split-second thought, he turned his head slightly so the left side of his face took the brunt force instead of the bridge of his nose. The rim of the red ceramic bowl dug into his flesh and then exploded, sending tiny marshmallow bats, pink milk, and shards of sharp red chunks flying in every direction. Lifting his head back up, Nick knew without a doubt that there were going to be pieces of the bowl stuck in his scalp and cheek. As calmly as he could, he went to the bathroom and looked in the mirror. Sure enough, there were several marshmallows, a few cute pink pieces of cereal, a whole lot of milk, and half a dozen chunks of the bowl protruding from the side of his face. He removed the cereal first and pulled out the shards one by one, the entire time acting like he was doing nothing but gently pulling lint off his face.

Twenty minutes later, after washing his face and treating the wounds, which thankfully were not deep, he realized he had missed the bus, but he didn't care. There was no way he could go to school and risk doing something like that in front of a teacher. He'd end up in the looney bin before lunch. He had to stay home and make sure he didn't harm himself again. Things were getting way too concerning.

Nick desperately wanted his mom, but he just couldn't do that to her. He couldn't make her leave work, and worse, he couldn't make her worry about him . . . not again. The trial last year had almost killed her. She was so devastated that her hair went half-gray, she started taking anxiety medication, and she saw a therapist twice a week. While she claimed she was "fine" on a consistent basis, he could tell she was holding everything together by a thread. Nick did not want to be the one to cut that last string, especially since he was already the one who unraveled the others.

An hour later, Nick had devised a contraption to keep himself safe. It wasn't anything complicated or foolproof, but it should protect him enough from any other major impulses, at least he hoped. It involved several pillows, two oven mitts, and two old blue jump ropes he found in a storage box. With his hands in the gloves, the pillows all around him, his legs tied shut, and one hand tied to his bedpost, he figured one padded hand couldn't do much damage. Beforehand, he was smart enough to put some food and drinks next to the bed as well as the ever-important pee bottle. And that is how Nick sat for the next six hours, doing nothing but snacking and watching *Halloween, Halloween II,* and *Halloween 4: The Return of Michael Myers* all in a row. Having seen the movies ten times each, if not more, it was insanely boring to not be able to play on his phone at the same time, but at least the movies made it feel like it was officially Halloween.

When 3:00 p.m. came around, the time he would normally be home from school after the bus dropped him off and he got his normal snack at the store, he dared untying himself, as there hadn't been a single incident. Besides, he needed to stretch. To be safe, he kept the oven mitts on for the next hour as he cautiously moved around the house, as if waiting for someone to attack him. At 4:00 p.m., when still nothing had happened and he saw the first of the very little children start to go door to door, he slipped off the oven mitts, put on his orange pumpkin T-shirt, and got the bowl of candy ready.

Over the next two hours, he dutifully answered the door, put on a happy smile, and gave out candy while complimenting the costumes. Princess after princess, superhero after superhero, the occasional fireman or cop, and a few cartoon characters he didn't recognize came one after another—not a single monster, goblin, troll, or serial killer in the bunch. Of course, every single mother had cat ears, drawn-on whiskers, and a cheap tail, as if it were a law that once you became a mom, you had to wear the cat paraphernalia. It depressed Nick, but he was happy not to have harmed himself, especially in front of a child. Mostly, he was just happy he was getting to have somewhat of a Halloween this year.

As the last of the candy was handed out, well before 7:00 p.m. when the older, more demanding kids would start coming, Nick sighed and shut off all the outdoor lights and most of the indoor ones. Sitting in his room with just the television on, hearing the laughter from the hordes of gleeful children outside, Nick felt a deep depression wash over him. Guilt, self-loathing, anger, and the events of last year started to bounce around his head like sharp daggers, each one sticking in and causing a ripple of pain that wouldn't leave. Thankfully it was only mental pain, as he truly didn't think he could handle any more physical pain. Even the horror marathon on the television couldn't stop his mind; it was so fast and brutal, he wasn't even sure what movie was playing. As he tried to focus to see what masked killer was on the television, the desire to hurt himself crept into his brain. This scared him, as during the other times he'd felt nothing before they happened. This time, he knew something *was* going to happen. Jumping out of bed, he took deep breaths and paced back and forth. Air was not getting into his lungs enough; he simply couldn't get a solid breath. It was as if the air in the house was not clean enough. *He needed air. Fresh air.*

Less than twenty seconds later, Nick was outside sucking in glorious, clean autumn air. On the street there was dozens of kids. They all looked so damn happy, their parents laughing and smiling as they held their bags and went door to door. Nick missed his mom and he missed being a kid. It was so much easier then. The thought of going back in the house made him sick. Being outside with the fresh air and the happiness of the children made him feel . . . sane. So, he decided to take his normal walk towards the store. He didn't even know if he wanted to go to the store or where he was going, but it seemed to be the most natural path to follow. Normally the street was so lonely and peaceful he could walk it blindfolded and not bump into a thing or another person. Tonight, there were so many children and adults walking in every direction he had to zig and zag constantly — and it made him happy.

Here in this town, Halloween was still a happy event, and he was nearly invisible. No one was looking at him with disgust and anger; everyone he brushed past smiled or nodded, and some even told him, "Happy Halloween." The rejuvenating air and looking at costumes were helping him stay calm and keep his mind off everything. Slowing his pace, he started to relax and take in the beauty of the holiday. It was magical. It truly was the only day of the year you would see so many people out on the streets after dark. And while Nick still thought it was a night that was meant to scare away the demons trying to creep into our Earth, he couldn't help but love what it had become after hearing the laughter and excitement of all the children.

Leisurely strolling, watching the kids and teens run from house to house, he simply people-watched and enjoyed the seasonally warm air. Slowly but surely, his mind settled and he was enjoying the night. As a few teens walked by, he heard them talk about the "the kick-ass haunted house." It was then that he recalled the flyer he saw in the store the other day. Pulling out his phone, he opened his photos and found the shot he took, noted the street, and pulled up his map; it was only a seven-minute walk. As he headed directly there, he realized this town *was* pretty cool. His old town didn't have all sorts of contests for "Best Halloween Decorations" and "Scariest House." Hell, his old town was so stuffy, the city board once made a family remove a cheap plastic hanging skeleton from their yard, stating that it was "too disturbing" for locals. This town was *supporting* Halloween.

If I'd lived here my whole life, I wouldn't have pushed back so hard, Mr. D and Sydney would be fine, and I wouldn't have . . . whatever the hell I have right now, Nick thought to himself with a pang of sorrow.

As he walked, each street got more and more festive. Almost every house was fully decorated, there were entire displays in front yards, people hanging out and partying, music playing, and laughter everywhere. It was Halloween heaven. Turning down Oak Terrace, Nick was shocked to see it was even crazier than the last few streets he walked down. Instead of almost all the homes, *every* single house on the street was lit up with purple and orange lights, some lawns had bubbling cauldrons, others had intricate setups with flying bats and spiders on strings that would swoop down and scare trick-or-treaters. Not a single home had the lights off. Almost every resident was sitting outside in lawn chairs, some by fires, having a hell of a time handing out candy to every person. Nick even noticed that most of the houses had *cases* of candy to ensure they did not run out, not two bags. And it wasn't the cheap stuff either; they weren't handing out dollar store candy because of the volume. These people were handing out the real stuff. Some houses even gave out full-size candy bars. As he walked, looking at the house numbers, Nick realized he was smiling; it was probably the most real smile he'd had in a year.

As he came up to one particular house, he noticed a cave-like entrance with smoke coming out of it and a line of teenagers and adults waiting to get in, moving around with giddy anticipation. Nick was always more on the shy side and didn't really like to do things alone, which is why the last year had been so hard not having friends anymore, but without thinking, he joined the line. It was the house on the flyer, he wanted to judge if it truly was the best. Seconds later, there were a dozen more people behind him. Everyone was talking, laughing, and acting nervous, especially the girls holding onto the guys. Seeing that gave him a pang in his heart so strong it made him touch his chest, which reminded him of his burn. His pointer finger lightly touching his shirt felt like a bullet hitting his chest. He let out an audible gasp and hunched over, sucked air, and tried not to cry. As he whimpered, he could hear whispers behind him, so he pretended to pick a piece of something up off the ground and put the imaginary thing in his pocket, his chest still stinging.

Entering the mouth of the cave, his visibility was cut down to almost nothing. The dense fog and strobing lights made it hard to see, but he edged his way forward, trying to keep an eye on the shoulder of the teen boy wearing the Jason mask in front of him. It was a bit disorienting, but that was good: you shouldn't feel safe in a haunted house. A few seconds later, he was suddenly in what was clearly a garage, though there were black tarps up and giant pots with bubbling green liquid and two poorly dressed witches laughing ridiculously and cackling at the passersby. It was pretty cheesy, but Nick gave them a nod and a smile to show he approved of the effort these homeowners put in. Just as he did, the witch pointed at Nick and screamed his name.

"Nick, Nick, that boy was sure sick, sick." *No one* knew his name in this town. Hearing it caused him to stop in his tracks and the line of people behind him bumped into him. He stared at the witch, who didn't look away from him, even though her fake nose was held on with string, he was getting scared of her. As the group started to push him along, he saw the woman reach into the pot and pull out a human head. The second he saw the gray hair, he knew who it would be: Old Man Sampson . . . who he killed last year. Nick screamed and ran like he was in a bad horror movie, pushing patrons out of the way, getting dirty looks and called names, but he didn't care. He had to get out of the house. The line was clogged at the entrance to the basement—*damn, these people used their entire house*—so he pushed his way through a black tarp, ripping it off the wall and bursting out of the front door of the house. Someone ran out after him screaming, but they gave up when he reached the street.

Running was making his heart feel like Freddy Krueger was giving him a chest massage, so he slowed his pace and once again did some box breathing. *It was your imagination, nothing more. The woman didn't call your name and the head she pulled out was fake. Calm the hell down.* Sitting on the curb, he leaned against the tree and watched the wonderful world of Halloween walk by, slowly decompressing with each breath. Part of him wanted to go home, but the other part of his brain gave him a pep talk, telling him it was safer to be out with people. At least if he had a breakdown here, someone would call for help, and if he tried to hurt himself, some heroic soccer mom or dad would jump in and save him. Besides, even with his brain falling apart, he was still having the best night he'd had all year, and he hadn't even seen the "best" haunted house yet. With that in mind, Nick decided to stay out and keep walking around until the pumpkins started to get blown out.

After walking a bit more and taking in some displays that would rival real haunted houses and theme parks, Nick finally came upon house number 345 on Oak Terrace Avenue. Just like the other homes, there was a line of teens and adults alike waiting to go through the homemade haunted house. Nick was hesitant after the last one, but he joined the back of the line, ready for whatever lay ahead. This time, if something bizarre happened, he was going to ignore it and fight back against his brain—freaking out and running was worse than any delusion could do to him. He wouldn't let his mind win. This was his Halloween and he was going to enjoy it, even if it killed him.

Looking ahead to the front of the line, he noticed a little green light flicker on that told the next group when to walk through the black tarp tunnel that went along the side of the house to the backyard. All the houses seemed to have a tunnel like this, but it made sense. They all needed an entrance, after all. Thinking about just building one of these tunnels and setting up a light-based entrance system, Nick couldn't believe the amount of work put into something that was free and just for locals. It made him happy that there were others out there like him who truly loved and believed in the holiday. And while he wouldn't admit it out loud, he hoped one day he could turn his own house into a haunted one every year.

In front of him, he noticed a group of three teens. He recognized them from school, but he didn't know their names. Seeing them made him feel a bit nervous that they would think he was a loser for being alone. One girl was clearly with her boyfriend, as they couldn't keep their hands off each other, but the other girl seemed awkward as the third wheel. Nick tried not to pay attention to her, but she kept looking back and smiling at him. After three groups walked through the tunnel, she turned and talked to him.

"You're that new kid, right?"

Nick smiled and nodded, then quickly stuck his hands in his pockets. When he heard her name was Laurie, Nick laughed out loud, which got a strange reaction from her.

"Your name is the same as the main character in the *Halloween* movies," Nick explained. "I can't believe I'm meeting a Laurie *on* Halloween."

The girl laughed shyly and said her mom actually named her after the character because she wanted her child to be a "survivor." Nick's heart skipped a beat hearing this. As the line inched forward, Nick was introduced to the other two kids who didn't seem to care much about meeting him, but that was fine—he didn't care about them either.

As the line continued to move, he talked and talked to Laurie. She told him about a house where the homeowner wore insane makeup that made his whole face look like it was sliced up and stitched back together. Nick made a note to go back and check it out after. Eventually she asked if he would go through the house *with* her. He agreed without hesitation, thrilled he hadn't given up and gone home. The smile she gave back to him melted everything away and made him realize things would be all right in life.

A few moments later, it was their turn to walk inside. Laurie got close to Nick and he felt his heart race. For the first time that night, the pain of the burn was tolerable. The tunnel was darker than he thought it would be, and he actually got a bit creeped out. Unlike the other house, this one had a spooky ambient noise and a laser that made a vortex-looking image at the end of the tunnel. The first few jump scares were mostly animatronic spiders and monsters bought at the seasonal Halloween shop. They were effective but not terrifying by any means. The best part about them: they made Laurie jump and grab Nick's arm. The light touch of her hands on him radiated through his entire body. The touch was so subtle, but to Nick and his deflated heart, it felt like a giant fireworks display was being set off inside of him.

The tunnel curved around the back of the house; the other couple was a good ten feet in front of them. Nick could see there was a big scare at the turn that made the couple jump, scream, and scurry away. Knowing something big coming up made Laurie grab tight to Nick's arm, preparing for the jolt. A giant scarecrow jumped out from behind a black tarp, almost making contact with Nick's face. The noise and movement were so sudden, Laurie jumped away, losing her grip on Nick and running towards her friends, who were laughing and standing at the end of the tunnel. Nick, on the other hand, didn't move, for the face he saw staring back from the scarecrow was his own—not *really* his own, but he saw himself behind the rubbery, toothy grin of the macabre scarecrow. It was the exact same mask *he* had worn last Cabbage Night.

Suddenly, all the warm, fuzzy fun he was having drained from his body. There were all sorts of noises around him—yelling, screaming, laughing, haunted music, and canned cackles—but all Nick could hear was the sickening wet crack of Sydney's face hitting the step last year. Even if he wasn't there to witness the noise up close, the amount of times the police and lawyers showed him the picture of the damage, his mind manufactured the sound. *Shclack. Shclack.* As the scarecrow slowly moved away from his face and reset, Nick shook his head and tried to tell himself it was just a coincidence this time and not his mind slipping yet again. Nick wanted the warm firework feeling of Laurie's hands on him back; he could fight the past and have a new life in this town, maybe with Laurie. Turning to find her, he saw the door at the end of the long black hall shut; her friends must have pulled her in without him.

Racing to the door, he saw a red light on telling him to *Wait . . . or Else!* He ignored it and tried the door, but it didn't budge. Hearing the piston hiss behind him, sending the scarecrow launching at the next group, he couldn't stop himself; he shouldered the door and burst into the room. It was obviously another garage, but the owner had done a hell of a job setting it up to look like some sort of Satanic ritual. There was a man dressed as a cult leader in a red robe standing in front of a rubbery dead body laying across an altar, a giant red Devil-like hand was retracting into the ceiling, low-lying fog covered the floor, but Laurie was already gone. Nick let out a small laugh—not because he thought it was stupid, but because he was happy and excited about how cool the room looked. This was not some cheesy witch—this was *dark stuff, Satanic stuff.* If he had more time, he would have loved to take in the room, but he couldn't lose Laurie, so he started to jog across the room towards the exit. Something caught his foot, which he only saw a glimpse of, but it looked to be a giant hand made of . . . *pumpkin vines.* Being that he was jogging, the sudden stopping of his foot sent him flying face-first into the hard concrete. *Shclack.*

As his nose shattered, Nick saw a brilliant flash of light. When his two front teeth tore through his upper lip, he saw darkness. In the darkness, he saw the faces of Mr. D and Sydney. They were playing together, happy and content in the fall leaves. The image made Nick happy. He tried to smile, but his teeth protruding through his lip would not allow any sort of facial expressions to be made. In a hazy state, he felt hands on his body rolling him over. He tried to open his eyes, but the pain and blood pooling around them did not allow that either. All he could do was gurgle.

A bright light shone in his eyes; he could see the brightness through his bruising lids and he heard an adult talking to him, but he could still see Mr. D and Sydney playing, and he didn't want to let go of that image. Then the hands were off him and he was alone again. In his vision he saw Sydney jump into the leaves and disappear, but when she jumped out of them, she was bloody and her face was torn, just like his was now. The image shocked him back into consciousness. Opening his eyes just a tiny sliver, he saw a man—the same man he saw when he entered the room—fixing the door he had just broke. Two seconds later, the man was picking him up. Nick thought of Laurie and wondered if she was waiting outside and if she would ever talk to him again with a broken nose and split lip.

The sensation of being carried was unearthly, he couldn't help but wonder if the hands on him were made of pumpkin vines as well. Then, the man placed him, or more so, dropped him, onto the altar. This confused Nick, as he didn't know why the man wouldn't have just let him lay on the garage floor until the ambulance came. The table was uncomfortable and his head dangled backwards, sending blood dripping down his throat, choking him as if he were being waterboarded with his own blood. He tried to speak again, but he was choking on his own coagulating vital fluid.

"The judges are coming through next! Sorry, kid, but I'm not losing to my brother again this year."

Through blurry eyes, Nick could see a hidden monitor on the floor by the man's feet: three people with clipboards were coming down the tunnel. Nick then watched the man pick up a very realistic-looking knife as he heard the buzz of the door. The man started to speak loudly, some Latin-sounding chant, and raised the knife high above Nick. He raised his hand up for help, but the man ignored his tiny plea.

In the moment before the blade came down, Nick realized that everything in the past year had been leading up to this. That no matter how good he was, no matter what he did, it was his destiny to die. They were never going to let him live; he needed to be punished for what he had done. They just wanted him to suffer for a year before finally taking his life from him. Now, just like his horrible tricks turned wrong, he was about to meet his demise at the hands of another person taking Halloween just a bit *too* far. His vision getting cloudier, he looked to the man; the pumpkin monsters were standing over his shoulder, looking down at him with large laughing grins.

As the knife plunged into his chest, right into the burn line—as if it were a mark showing the man where to stab—he heard the gasps from the judges and one person say, "That is so realistic!"

With his last breath, Nick whispered, "I'm sorry," but then he tried to smile, because he knew that his death would become the stuff of legends and a tale that kids would tell to each other forever as they avoided this house every Halloween.

The Winning Prop

It was going to be a glorious day for Ruben. The day he yearned for forever. A day he had plotted, planned, and prepped for since last Halloween. This year, he was sure to win the "Scariest House" contest. It wasn't the prize he cared about (oh boy, two tickets to see the local production of *The Rocky Horror Picture Show*), what he really wanted was the satisfaction of finally beating his brother at something. For forty-six years, Lars has been the better one. Better grades, better job, better girlfriends, first to get married, and the best-looking. Ruben was constantly in his shadow. This was the year he was going to walk out from under it by taking the title of Scariest House away from his brother, who had won it the last six years in a row, beating Ruben every time.

Halloween was always a favorite holiday of his, but for years he just put out a pathetic pumpkin on his tiny little house's steps. Then ten years ago, the town started the "Haunted Haven" initiative to boost tourism as they went for the title of the "New England town with the most Halloween Spirit(s)." The town started holding an annual festival with pumpkin carving and costume contests, food trucks lining the main roads, autumnal parties that celebrated the season, and of course, the decoration and Scariest House contests. Within two years, they were second in line to Salem as the place to visit during the spooky season. Everyone started to jump on the bandwagon and do their houses up, and before he knew it, Lars won the house contest, motivating Ruben to join the competition. Finally, there was something he could have a chance to beat his brother at. The day after his brother won, Ruben went out and bought half-price decorations and stored them till the next year. Neither of them won that following year, resulting in both of them spending three grand each buying up decorations and lights for future use. Due to a faulty wire that made his electric chair prop not work, Ruben lost the next year as well. In fact, each year he lost, he could blame one prop over the other, as he always thought his haunted house decorations were still better, just if they all worked right. Then last year, just when he thought he had it in the bag, he lost because his brother hired an animal handler to bring in real flying fox bats that were on display, and people could take photos with them for a "donation" to the local food pantry. There was nothing scary about a dog-looking bird eating fruit and yawning for pictures, but it was those bats that won it. Ruben fumed and argued with the board about the criteria of what was "deemed scary," but he was brushed off.

That is why this year, instead of just the garage being haunted, Ruben added a tunnel and went all out. With over ten grand invested, his house matched the likes of professional haunted houses. At least he liked to think so. This year, Ruben was taking it further than anyone in town ever had. He bought over sixty tarps and dozens of pipes to make his haunted tunnel. It started in the front yard, wrapped around to the back of the house, and led into the garage's back door. Through the tunnel he rigged dozens of strobe lights, smoke machines, and various creepy decorations, even motion-triggered zombies that popped out and made noise when you walked by them. He even set up a camera system so he could monitor when people were coming in, especially the judges.

Of course, when they entered the garage, that was the best part: the finale! It took him days to cover the walls with black tarps, rig the strobes, set up the sacrificial altar, and make it look creepy. Ruben was to play the role of a Satanic priest. When people entered the room, they would see him standing behind the altar in a costume he had sewn himself made of red silk. Smoke would cover the ground and a giant fake body would lay on the altar. He would mumble some gibberish and swing down a giant knife into the chest of the dummy, sending blood spraying in the air (he rigged a pump that he controlled with his foot to shoot the blood out). At that exact second, he would trigger the speakers, loud booming screams and the Devil's voice would ring out over the scared visitors, telling them all that Satan had risen and would take their souls. Three seconds later, the attic door would pop open, spilling red light on the crowd as a giant hand reached out to bring them into Hell (this prop cost him a fortune and almost two months to get just right). At that point, Ruben would laugh and yell that all who wanted to be saved must leave now through the side door that he would open with a remote. Once outside, there would be a giant bowl of candy for them. It was brilliant, complicated, and needed hours of practice and tweaking of the machines, but it was all worth it, if he won.

As the sun started to set on Halloween night, Ruben cracked open the bags of candy, poured them into the massive bowl, and hummed to himself. His nerves were high, but he also was full of excitement. In a mere hour, the fun would begin and he would be on his way to winning first place. That and for the first time in decades, he had met someone; someone he might be able to share his winning with, Martha. After fixing her door and spending the last seven days having coffee with her, he was in love, and tomorrow they were going to have their first official date. If he could tell her he won on that date, it would be the greatest day ever. Life was good for once. In a matter of minutes, he had on his red robes and Satanic medallion necklace he bought on eBay. With a pat of powder and a bit of black makeup under his eyes, he was ready. Strobe lights of adrenaline flowed through him. The last time he was this excited, he was ten and it was Christmas morning. Of course, Santa had given the best presents to Lars.

With minutes left, Ruben did his last walkthrough. He checked every prop, light, machine, and inch of the wall to make sure no outside light came in. It was all beyond perfect. Satisfied, he ran to the front, put up the "Not Welcome" sign, and ran to his position to await the first visitors. It was not a long wait at that. Within five minutes he could hear screams and giggles as people entered into his award-winning (hopefully) display. Peeking at the monitors, he saw that it was time. Over the next two hours, everything went perfectly, though the judges had yet to come through. As the hours ticked by, the crowd turned to mostly teens. He *hated* teens—they were always tough to scare and broke shit just for laughs. But as they started to flood in, he realized it would be good practice—if he could scare them, he could scare the judges.

After going through four groups of teens who actually screamed and freaked out, he was picturing the award hanging up in his living room. As the next group of teens wandered in, he began his routine once more.

"Ahhhhhhh! More souls to send to Hell! Is that what you wish for?" Ruben screamed in his best theatrical scary voice. It was a small group of three, one teen boy acted tough with a girl holding him so tight he was having a hard time walking. The last girl stayed close to them, but she looked back nervously at the door as it shut.

"Musta, krakum, upulah, TEGUM!" He shouted, raising the knife high and swinging it down. Having found that the plastic knives bent too easily and didn't shine well enough, he was using a real eight-inch chef's knife. He was only plunging it into latex anyway, so it was safe. *Splurk!* The knife sank into the dummy. Blood spurted and the sound effects started to boom—it was beautiful, he had to do his best to not smile.

"Ewwww! Gross!" One of the girls cried out.

"What is taking Nick so long? He should have caught up to us by now!" The other girl cried out, grabbing onto her friends, obviously wanting her own companion to keep her protected. The attic door opened up, the hand started to reach out, and they all scooted back a bit.

"All of you who want to be saved, leave now . . . leave . . . or be forever in HELL!" The trio raced for the door, the boy laughing, saying something about how the "new kid" was on his own. With the door shut, Ruben let out a hoot of success, then quickly ducked under the table to check the monitors for more people. A slim teen wearing an orange pumpkin shirt was frantically hitting the door—their friend, Ruben assumed. Though the sign to wait was lit, the kid tried the door handle, shouldered it, and got it to swing open before Ruben was ready. There was a tearing, snapping, popping sound. Ruben was furious. The kid had just broken the remote-controlled mechanism on the door that opened it, and he was in before the hand could reset. The kid was ruining everything.

"You broke my damn door, kid, just get the hell out of here." He pointed to the exit door. The kid laughed and started a light jog towards the door. Then suddenly, he tripped. Ruben made sure the house was safe, it was part of the rules, after all, so there were no tripping hazards, but out of the corner of his eye, he could have sworn he saw a vine grabbing the kid's leg. But before he could process what he saw, his concentration was smashed, as the kid slammed into the concrete floor face-first. *Shclack.*

With the darkness and fog, Ruben couldn't see how bad the kid hit, but the wet smacking noise sickened his stomach, it couldn't be good, but he was more perturbed at the kid than anything. Annoyed, he waited a few seconds for the kid to get up, but he didn't. Grabbing the emergency flashlight from under the counter, he begrudgingly went to the kid. Rolling him over, he gasped at the sight. The kid's nose was flat to his face, two teeth protruded out of his upper lip, and blood was dripping everywhere.

"Wake up, kid, wake up!" Ruben yelled before lowering his head to hear if the kid could speak. There was a low gurgling sound that told Ruben the kid was choking on blood.

With panic setting in, he got up and shot to the door to get the kid's friends and call the police. As his hand hit the handle, the electric ding alerted to tell him the next group was about to enter. *What if it was the judges?* Racing to the monitor, he almost fainted as he saw a small group holding clipboards at the door. He had such little time. If he left the garage and called the police now, it would be all over with—he'd lose, probably even get a lawsuit. All this money and time would be for nothing. Back at the monitor, he switched the camera to the front of the house. The three teens were still there—the boy looked to be arguing about leaving.

"Go! That's right, just go. Your friend never came in here," Ruben muttered to himself as he watched the screen. Seeing the boy walk away and the two girls reluctantly follow, he realized that maybe this accident was a gift—a gift that could help him win.

Racing to the back door, he was thankful that the wire had merely popped off its wheel and not broken like he thought—an easy fix. With the help of a screwdriver, he had the wire back on in a second. Then it was off to his altar. Lifting up the fake body, he sat it against the altar, tipped its head forward and laughed at how good it looked. He should have thought about having more bodies around before. The hard part of lifting the kid up and placing him on the altar came next. It took several heaves and a few pulled muscles in his back, but he got the kid, who was thankfully skinny, on the altar. *Seconds left.* He raced to the door, looked at the body lying there, and made sure it didn't look *too* real. Thankfully with the lights and smoke it could pass as realistic but not *real*, besides, who would think a real body was lying on a thing like this? To be safe, he made sure the kid's head hung off the edge and tilted back, so if he opened his eyes, his face would be hidden by the fog a bit. *It was time.*

Trembling but ready, the door swung open, and Ruben said his lines, doing his best to not look at the judges' faces as he raised his knife high in the air. He could hear a few gasps and murmurs of, "How realistic!" Then, to his surprise, the kid raised his arm out for help. Ruben had planned to bring the knife down next to the body, but now that the kid was moving, he panicked as he swung the knife down. The blade plunged in the dead center of the kid's chest, plunging right into the nose of the jack-o'-lantern print. The boy lurched forward. Blood shot out of his chest and sprayed out of his mouth before he fell back and convulsed on the table. Ruben couldn't help but look at the judges, whose faces had gone slack with shock. Hitting the button for the floor, he prayed they thought it was just an amazing animatronics doll.

"Leave . . . LEAVE NOW!" The giant robotic hand came down, and they ran out with terror in their eyes. Ruben fell to his knees, gasped for air, and then laughed as he saw the blood and a chunk of flesh on his knife. As long as they didn't think it was real, he knew he'd win the contest. This kid was the greatest accident of his life!

Over and over again that night, Ruben brought the knife down on the boy until the hole in the chest was so large, he had to stab the kid in the stomach. Intestines and other chunks of innards started to spill out and pour down the altar, making it all the more gruesome. Every person who came through looked scared, but no one thought it was a real body. A bit before 11:00 p.m., one last group of teens went through, laughed at how "fake" the blood looked, and disappeared out the door. With the night over, Ruben shut off the power to the animatronics, switched off the fog machines, and flipped on the garage light. Brilliant, painful fluorescent light filled the room, taking away every ounce of creepiness there was. Looking over at the altar and seeing the mutilated body on top, the realization that he had killed a kid and was going to have to get rid of the evidence washed over him. He would have to delete the camera footage, figure out how to get blood out of concrete, and so much more. But first, he had to hide the body. As he started to wrap the legs in trash bags, the house phone rang, and the caller ID said it was his brother.

"Happy Halloween, bro," Ruben said, tension building in his stomach.

"Congratulations, you won. Don't know how you beat me, especially with my setup this year, but you did it. Mind if I stop by and check it out in a few minutes?"

Ruben could feel the tears streak down his face, smudging his makeup. *He won . . . he WON.*

"Sure. Sure, come by!" Hanging up the phone, he screamed, jumped up and down and cheered before kissing the dead boy's forehead. As his lips left the cold skin, he realized his brother would take more time in there than everyone else and would see the body was real. Grabbing the kid's legs, he pulled the body off the table and it smacked the ground, the head crunching against the concrete with a splatting noise that made his stomach drop. Part of the kid's shirt fell off him, having been torn open in so many places. It took a lot of effort and sweat, but he was able to pull the body out of the garage and behind the shed in the backyard just as he saw his brother pull up. Racing like a maniac, he put the fake body back in place on the altar, touched up his makeup, and shouted out the door for his brother to go in the main entrance.

Five minutes later, the two were chatting and Ruben was gloating.

"I thought the body on the altar would look more realistic, that's all people talked about," Ruben's brother said, shaking his head in disbelief. "Judges were amazed by it. Hmmm. I'm proud of you though, bro."

Proud? Proud. PROUD. It was the word he always wanted to hear from his brother. It was worth more than hearing he won the lottery. Ruben was so elated that he didn't realize two police officers had entered the tunnel until they were banging on the door.

"Oh, can I help you two or were you just going through for fun? Because if you were, I'll have to reset everything."

"Actually, we're looking for a kid," one of the officers said. "He disappeared somewhere around your house about five hours ago. Here's his picture, recognize him?"

With a huge gulp, Ruben mustered a laugh. "I saw hundreds of kids come through here tonight. I couldn't be sure."

"Well, if you think of . . ." The officer was cut off as the other one nudged him, walked over in front of the altar, and picked up a piece of cloth.

"Didn't they say he was wearing an orange pumpkin shirt?" The officer held up the orange cloth with a black half-triangle on it that was soaked with blood. Ruben rubbed his face, smudging the makeup more as his brother gave him a horrified look.

"That's, I mean, it could be . . ." he couldn't even get the sentence out. Within ten minutes, they found the body and put cuffs on him. As he was being walked to the squad car, he cried out to his brother.

"They won't take away the Scariest House title, will they? There's no rule saying we couldn't use real props, right? I still won, I beat you, damn it! I won! I won. I have to tell Martha! Please, call her and tell her for me!"

Slice

The blade went through the flesh without a second's hesitation. It simply slid right in. Jalen watched in awe at how easy it penetrated; it was almost like the skin wasn't there. As he sawed, he leaned forward and looked closer, wanting to see the blade go in and out. His rhythm sped up, making the blade suddenly get stuck. Frustrated, he pulled the knife out of the pumpkin, wiped it off, and started again on the eye. It was the last detail he had to carve, yet the cutting and slicing did not get tiring to him, the wet sawing sound was beautiful and soothing.

Jalen had always loved sharp blades, ever since his grandfather gave him a Swiss army knife when he was ten. His mother freaked out about it and took it away, but his grandfather—God, he loved that man—bought a new one and gave it to him in secret. It was in his nightstand drawer now, and his mother still didn't know he had it even seven years later. Though when he turned fifteen, she did let him get a small folding knife to use when fishing to cut wire and whatnot, what she didn't know was that while she let him buy *one* knife, he already had over a dozen of various sizes hidden in an old Lego box in his closet. She'd beat him relentlessly if she ever found out, but it was worth the risk. Why he needed them or had them, he didn't really know. He never used them for much. A few times he cut some branches, and he tried whittling once but couldn't make crap, so mostly he just looked at them and occasionally threw them at trees. It didn't matter that he didn't use them much, though, just having them and admiring their sleek designs and intensely sharp blades gave him pleasure, lots of pleasure.

When he was fourteen, he got a six-inch blade with a metallic green handle in the shape of a dragon. It was the first time that Jalen felt real love. Looking at the beautiful lines and sharp edge, his heart raced, his body felt warm and tingly, and he couldn't stop smiling. He bought the blade on the internet and had it shipped to his neighbor's house, (who never came home until seven at night), patiently waiting every day for the package to arrive. The day it did, he raced across the yard and grabbed the box before the mailman even pulled away. Back in his room, the second he saw the blade, it was like in an old '80s movie when the boy saw his first Red Ryder BB gun. Light shown on the knife, wind blew in his hair, and a metal band played a ballad in the background.

The first night he had the blade, he had an intense experience that was followed by such guilt that he prayed the next day, which he had not done since he was seven when his mother forbade him from doing so. The experience had to do with a bottle of lotion, one sock, and a four-inch gash on his left thigh. It was the greatest pleasure he ever felt, but it was followed by immense regret as the guilt weighed heavily and the cut, which probably needed stiches, hurt constantly for almost three weeks before it healed. Three years later, the scar was a reminder that the blades he loved so much could bring as much pain as they did pleasure. He had many scars on his body since that day, but that one, that was special. It was the one he found his fingers caressing every now and then. Every once in a while, he still used a blade when he touched himself, but now it was typically a razor, and he knew how small and how deep to go to where it would not hurt, get infected, or cause him to go to the hospital. The large blades were too unpredictable. Afterwards, he always sanitized the wounds and bandaged himself. The one thing Jalen did have was restraint, so while he pleased himself daily, he held off using the blade until the last cut healed, no matter how much he wanted to do it again. In a way it was like a reward for having patience.

As he finished carving the pumpkin into the classic face of a jack-o'-lantern, Jalen felt himself get hard; watching the blade do its magic on the flesh and meat was . . . seductive. Sticking his hands into the warm goo and pulling out the last of the seedy insides, he caught himself imagining horrible things—things he tried not to think of, but they would always find their way into his head. He pictured Tiffany at school, and imagined it was her body he was carving, *her* insides he was scooping out. His hard-on became painful as it ached inside of his pants. Without planning or thinking, he grabbed the knife, his hands still slippery with the orange slime, spun the pumpkin around, and eagerly cut a hole in the back of the gourd. Realizing he had emptied too much, he picked up the pile of guts and threw them back inside, right before unbuttoning his pants and sticking himself into the hole.

Jalen had never been with a girl before, but he could not imagine it would feel *this* good. Sticking both hands inside of the pumpkin, he cupped them around the slop and slid his hardness in and out. The edge of the rind was chaffing him a bit, but he couldn't stop and he knew it wouldn't take long, so he kept thrusting. Closing his eyes, he pictured pushing himself deep and hard inside of Tiffany's sliced-open stomach, and he came with a pleasure he had never felt before. His scream was so loud and guttural, his mother, who was only fifteen years older than him, ran into the room just in time to see his penis, dripping with gak and seeds, slide out of the gourd.

They both stood, not moving, staring at each other for a long second. Jalen had a quick memory about the movie where the guy fucked the pie, but that quickly evaporated out of his head as his mother picked up the knife and held it like she was a serial killer. There would be no comedic conversation about natural urges. Jalen had been hit and burned countless times over the years. One time he ended up on life support. When he woke up after a few days, the police questioned him about the kids who "jumped him," all while his mother gave him a death stare, making sure he kept her out of jail. As close to death as he brought her, seeing the knife made him wonder if she really thought this was finally going to be the time that she killed him. While she was half his size, he did nothing to protect himself. When the knife came down with a guttural yell from his mother, he was *not* relieved to see it went into the side of the pumpkin; he truly wanted it to have disappeared inside him. When she pulled it back out, he hoped the next stab would go into his chest, but instead the woman who gave birth to him, whom he already towered over by a foot and a half, grabbed his penis that was just starting to soften with her left hand. Jalen couldn't move. Looking down, he saw her tiny fingers and perfectly pink nails wrapped tightly around his shaft, strands of orange flesh and a few white seeds oozing between her fingers. Jalen felt blood rushing hard down there. Then, she started to stroke him.

Jalen could feel himself starting to lose his breath. No one had never touched him before. The sheer feeling of fingers around his dick was exhilarating, but knowing they were his mother's and she was holding a knife a foot from his face short-circuited his brain and aroused him even more. While it was probably only three slow strokes, it felt like an eternity of the most confusing pleasure that made the pumpkin he so enjoyed a moment before feel like it was, just a pumpkin. Jalen knew he should apologize, back away, and pull up his pants in shame, but seeing the glint of the knife covered in the goo, feeling the warm hand on his stiffness, it was too much, he came.

The blast of semen exploded all over his mother's gray baseball shirt, the one with the green sleeves, the one she asked him last year if it made her tits look good. The gooey white wetness, pulling along a few tiny chunks of orange with it, stood out stunningly on her shirt. His mother froze as she realized what just happened and looked down at her stomach. Jalen opened his eyes, saw her purse her lips as her chest started to heave. Suddenly her hand let go of him. His mother's rage was legendary: fourteen broken bones over the years, two hospitalizations, three visits by DCF (which she amazingly got out of), and countless scars, but she had never once touched him like this and he knew it wouldn't end well. Watching her take two steps back, he wondered what would happen next. Would she stab him? Beat the shit out of him? Kill him? Slowly and deliberately, his mother stripped off her shirt, balled it up, and smiled a sexy little smile he had only seen when she was drunk and with one of her dates. She took four small steps closer to him. She was so close he could feel the head of his penis resting against her bare stomach. Jalen knew the blood was going to start rushing back again. It was a confusing feeling, while he might have masturbated to his mother a few times over the years to great guilt, he never thought anything would really happen, but part of him maybe hoped for it and now it was happening. Jalen was having a hard time processing everything.

His mother's hand, which was now covered in a mix of pumpkin guts and bodily fluid, caressed the side of his face in a motherly yet seductive way. Finally, after all the intenseness that happened, she spoke in a sensual whisper that made his heart ooze.

"Open. Your. Mouth."

He did as he was told, he loved seeing how big the smile on her face got and he prayed in his head that she'd grab him again. Instead, she violently crammed her wet shirt into his mouth, he could have fought back, but he learned at the age of five to never do that, to let his mother do as she would. Within seconds, he was choking on the shirt. He could feel the wet cloth and gob of his own fluid hitting his uvula, making him gag. A millisecond later, that beautiful blade was against his cheek. He could feel how cold and sharp it was.

"What the fuck is wrong with you? I knew you were stupid, I knew you were fucked up from the day you were born, but to *want* your mother, to fucking cum on her? You sick piece of shit." The knife was then pulled across his cheek in one quick, long, hard movement. It left a solid four-inch slice across his cheekbone right to the top of his upper lip. Blood cascaded out. Jalen screamed through the shirt—it hurt badly, but it was accompanied by godlike pleasure shooting through him; he started to grow erect again. His mother, who had stepped back at this point, saw his penis growing, and at the sight her face filled with blood-red anger. Once again, her hand grasped his penis, only this time there was no love or seductiveness, this time she yanked on it like she was trying her best to pull it off in one hard tug. Jalen fell forward, following the motion of the tug. He tried to get his balance, but he couldn't take a proper step with his pants around his ankles. In one quick clumsy action, he was falling on top of his mother, who crumbled like a stack of pumpkins being pushed over.

The knife, which was still in his mother's hands, skidded across Jalen's ribcage, making a jagged long slice that wrapped halfway around his torso, cutting his shirt open. As his mother screamed and banged on him with her free hand, he took in a deep painful breath and rolled off her. Within seconds, her tiny frame was standing above him, her breasts heaving up and down in her lacy black bra, smears of his blood on her face and shoulder; yet she had not let go of the knife. Jalen hadn't seen her without a shirt on in a long time, he couldn't help but stare at how big her breasts were, at the tiny blue jewel in her bellybutton and the snake head peeking out from under her pant line. *God, he had forgotten about that tattoo.* She used to lay in bed with him when he was young and let him trace the snake with his fingers. It went around her hip, outlined her left butt cheek, then wrapped its way around her thigh with its tail ending right at her . . . *He used to touch that. Did she used to make him kiss the snake goodnight?* The vague and blurry memory vanished as his mother screamed and grabbed the pumpkin in her left hand. She looked back and forth at the knife, the pumpkin, and his dick, which was finally starting to go back down. Jalen was terrified at the thoughts that might be running through her head.

Without notice, she ran right past him into the living room and to the front door. He rolled onto his side, spit out the shirt, and watched her as she opened the screen and threw the pumpkin outside with such force it rolled across the front lawn like a drunk bowling ball, they both watched it until it slowed down and fell over the curb edge into a pile of leaves. Martha, that fucking nosy, fat neighbor with the yappy-ass little dog, stood holding a leash, staring at them in shock. His mother flipped her off and screamed, "Fuck you, Martha!" She slammed the door shut.

Jalen realized he should have taken the time to pull up his pants or at least assess the damage of his wounds, but he hadn't done any of that, and his mother was already heading back to him, the knife still in hand. It was only when he saw the pure rage in her face that he started to reach down to pull up his pants, but the pain in his ribs was too intense. He winced and stopped his reach, instead opting to touch the gash in his side; it was deep and wide, and blood was coming out fast. The pain made him flip onto his stomach to try and get up.

"You finally did it, Jalen, you finally did it. You pushed me and pushed me all these years. You had to push, you had to, didn't you?"

Jalen wasn't listening to his mother, he was trying to get up, slipping in the blood and in more pain than he realized. The words his mother was saying didn't really matter, she always said things like that, always threatened to kill him or feed him to the dog when they had one, but she never did, she only broke and burned him, so he focused on getting up and getting help for once.

"Ma, Ma, it hurts, it really hurts. It's deep, I need stiches, please. Please, help me up," Jalen pleaded in the best loving son voice he could muster. Looking up, he saw his mother standing above him, the knife still in her hand but now at her side, the rage fainting a bit as she looked him up and down.

"And tell them what, Jalen, tell them you made me touch your dick? Forced me to jerk you off and when you came, you jumped on top of me, so I defended myself? Because you call for help and that is what I'm going to tell them, the truth. My son is a pervert, he sticks his dick in anything, and he tried to rape me."

Jalen didn't give a shit what she said, he wanted help, fast. "Mom, tell them what you want, that's fine, I'll say that, just get me help, *please*." Jalen watched as she looked around the room and then back at him and his wounds. He had seen her do this before, when she snapped his arm and tried to figure out how to cover it up. As she did this, he tried to figure out what pain was worse, the cut or when she put him in the ICU; the ICU probably took first place in that department, but this was a close second. With a sigh, she slumped her shoulders, set the knife on the table, and grabbed the red kitchen towel that hung by the sink. She turned on the water and wet it. A second later, she was cleaning his wounds and wincing at the damage.

"Fuck, you do need stitches, goddamn it! Why did you make me do that?!" Jalen was still on his back, his pants half off, but now he was soft as his brain swirled with confusion. As much pain as he was in, he had to concentrate to not stare at his mother's breasts that were jiggling in front of his face, but it was almost impossible. Stealing quick glances, he tried to focus on her face, but all he could think of was that sexy smile she made moments ago. Shit, maybe he *was* sick, maybe something was wrong with him. A few tears started to fall from his eyes, and when his mother saw this, she shook her head and forced some of the anger out of her face.

"Come on, let's get you up. Doug has some friends who take care of things like this, I can call him and ask if any can stitch you up. You better be damn grateful, though, that fucker will make me suck his dick for a month to pay that off." Jalen had spent years listening to his mother please men, hell, almost his whole life. She wasn't a prostitute or anything, but she used her body to cover late bills and get things she couldn't afford, pretty much weekly. He was always jealous of the attention and time these men got with her, but now he was realizing it was something more, it was because they got be with her in a way he didn't have her. His heartrate suddenly started to slam at the thought of Doug's cock in her mouth. Just as he was on his feet, his pants still down, his entire torso and face covered in blood, he snapped.

With impeccable speed, he grabbed the large kitchen knife and pushed his mother away with the other hand. Then he held the blade out towards her—he had no clue what he as planning on doing.

"Fuck you, Mom, fuck you!" It seemed a fighting thing to say, even if he had no concept of why he grabbed the knife. His mother's face contorted into one that was so mocking he wanted to cut her smug lips right off her face.

"Oh, big boy with a knife, what're you going to do, fuck that too?" Jalen started to shake, his hand having a hard time holding onto the knife. He didn't know if it was the loss of the blood or nerves.

"Take your bra off." It came out of his mouth with no forethought, and once it was said he was mortified then shocked when his mother simply reached back, unstrapped it, and let her breasts fall. She tossed aside the bra just like in a cheesy porno and started to touch her breasts. For some reason, the blood that was on her hands and shoulders made it all the more appealing to Jalen, who was once again getting hard. His breathing started to hitch, and he licked his lips. Part of him wanted some water, but the other part wanted his mother like he had never wanted anything in his life.

"Jalen, take your clothing off and I'll take off mine. Why have we denied this for so long? I'm sorry, I've always wanted you, but I just, I didn't know if you wanted me." His mother's voice was almost angelic in her teasing. Hearing this, Jalen's brain started to misfire. Everything about this was wrong—it was his mother, he was bleeding and needed medical attention, yet he did what she said, wanting and needing to touch her. As he stripped naked, he made sure to not let go of the knife and more so, he made sure to not take his eyes off his mother, who was sliding out of her jeans, revealing the snake tattoo he used to trace for hours.

Standing there, both naked and a puddle of blood between them, Jalen looked his mother up and down. She smiled and made some moaning noises as she touched her body, then she turned around and grabbed the counter, putting her ass out for him.

"Take me, Jalen, take me." He did not hesitate, he threw the knife, raced up behind her, and grabbed her hips, unsure how to really go about this even though he had seen more porn than he could count. Figuring out he needed to grab his penis to get inside her, he realized what was happening, what this *really* was. His mother was slowly sliding open the cutlery drawer, and before he could do anything, she spun around with a steak knife in each hand, slicing two massive gashes across his chest. Jalen stumbled backwards and fell into the kitchen chair. His mother didn't stop, as the knives kept coming slice after slice. Jalen was horrified and in excruciating pain, but at the same time he was mesmerized. Watching each gash magically appear and blood pour out of his flesh was something he had always wanted to see, just on another person, not himself.

One after another the blades kept coming: into his arms, his thighs, his chest, his stomach, and worst of all, his face—his face more than anywhere. When she finally stopped, Jalen was bleeding so much he looked like a human-shaped waterfall of blood, and yet he still had an erection, the hardest he had ever had. When his mother saw this, she raised both knives high . . . and the doorbell rang. She froze and jumped; Jalen grunted lightly through the blood, annoyed this show might end. It was followed by knocking, then an officer leaning over and looking into the window. Within seconds the man kicked in the door and pointed the gun at Jalen's mother . . . then Jalen fainted, his blood-soaked kitchen fading into impenetrable darkness.

Two days later, Jalen awoke in a morphine haze to see most of his body bandaged like the Invisible Man. All he could think was, *Where is Mother?* Alone in the room, groggy and confused at what had happened, he stared up at the television bolted to the wall. The local news was on talking about the town's upcoming Halloween festivities. Jalen kept fading in and out, but he heard them mention something about an award being revoked when a nurse came in and smiled down at him with a large, beautiful grin. She was gorgeous and for a moment, he thought it was his mother. It was hard to hear her what she said through the gauze around his head, but he did hear a number: *thirty-eight hundred. Thirty. Eight. Hundred. Three thousand eight hundred . . . STITCHES.* Additionally, he had two hundred lacerations. Hearing this number, he started to laugh and laugh until the violent moving hurt. She didn't kill him after all, not once did she stab, every single time she only sliced him. *Slice, slice, slice.* The nurse went on about how he needed two blood transfusions, but other than some nasty scars, there was no major bodily damage. As the nurse talked, he recalled the image of his mother soaked in blood, naked and frantically slicing the knives back and forth, and once again he got hard. When the worker noticed the lump in the sheet, she simply looked away and told him more details he didn't care about. Though he vaguely heard about how when his neighbor Martha saw them when the pumpkin was thrown out, she called the cops, saving his life.

A few hours later, a detective arrived and talked to Jalen with the bedside manner of Attila the Hun. The man, who looked like he prayed for death to take him before he went to bed every night, casually mentioned how Jalen's mother was dead, as if he knew this. Jalen had to grunt and raise his bandaged arm to stop the man.

"Oh shit, kid, I'm sorry. You don't recall? No one told you? Those fucking assholes, your mom, she . . . she wouldn't put the knives down when the cops came in, she just kept at you. The patrolman—poor bastard, still a rookie—shot her three times." The man looked awkward, then patted Jalen on the shoulder as if he were a flea-ridden dog. Jalen felt numb and sick, and part of him refused to believe his mother was dead because he was finally so close to having her to himself.

Nine days passed and finally, on the day before Halloween, Jalen was ready to be discharged. Since he turned eighteen while in the hospital— what a hell of a birthday that was, only one nurse even acknowledged it when she saw it on the chart—he was allowed to go home alone and not need foster care. But before he left, there were endless hours of physical therapy and meetings with social workers, counselors, and state-appointed lawyers. He didn't understand half of the papers he signed painfully, but he did understand that he would get the house and a check for disability each month. The hardest conversation, though, was about his mother's funeral. They held off as long as they could, wanting to let him attend the service, even though his therapist said it might be best to not go. So now her body waited in a cooler for a ceremony that was to take place the day after Halloween.

When it was time to go, a reluctant social worker drove him home. On the drive home, the small old lady with wrinkly tanned skin rambled on and on to Jalen about ways he could make money from home. With his head completely bandaged, he just nodded and asked for one favor, to stop at a store to get some stuff to eat. She obliged and dropped him off at home with three large grocery bags filled with nothing but Halloween candy. When they pulled in, he saw a teen squishing the pumpkin on the side of the road with his sneaker before shaking off the rotting goo. Jalen was surprised that the pumpkin was just left there untouched for over a week, and a part of him loved the visual of a rotting gourd laying in the gutter in front of his house, but then he remembered it was that same pumpkin that started this all. Instead of feeling panic and trauma, which his therapist was worried about him experiencing if he went home, he smiled and felt himself getting hard at the memory of that glorious day.

The kitchen had been left virtually untouched—only the knives were missing. With no other family, there was no one to clean the massive amounts of blood; Jalen didn't realize that it was up to the resident of the home to clean up the gory remnants. It wasn't something he ever thought about. The blood was dried, brown, and in some places cracked like caked desert mud. It was on the table, chair, counter, and almost every tile, splattering the walls and furniture. Liking how it looked and made him feel, Jalen decided to not bother trying to clean it up. Standing in silence, the house seemed weird without his mother in it. She always made noise, whether it was playing music, singing, or just her constant fidgeting, she always made it known she was home. It would be hard to get used to, but he knew she'd be home soon, and he could wait for her to be back again. He just had to figure out when he could sneak the body out of the casket after the service or if he was going to have to wait and dig her up later.

After filling a large bowl with candy, he went into the bathroom and looked at himself. His arms, torso, and entire head were still bandaged in gauze to soak up the oozing from the stitches, but it was time to take them off for good. He pulled off layer after layer of the crusty white cotton, parts of it sticking to his dried wounds; he couldn't help but smile. His entire face was covered in long rows of stiches, making him look like a monster. There were over seventy cuts on his face still healing, and it was fucking mesmerizingly beautiful. His entire body was the same, and all he could think of was how he couldn't wait to answer the door for trick-or-treaters with no shirt on. All he had to do was say a quick "hello" to the lady across the street who called the cops, then the only thing left would be to pick which knife to keep by the bowl tonight.

The House with the Big Candy Bars

Muffin was a teacup Chihuahua mixed with some sort of mutt. She was brown with black speckles, a short stubby face, a wrinkled tongue that was always hanging out, and a deformed tail that looked like it was chewed on then spit out. Her size was cute and most people smiled at her from a distance, but at a closer look, oglers slightly jumped back in disgust at her grotesque features and loose, dry skin. To Martha, she was the most beautiful thing in the world, which is why Muffin was so damn spoiled: walks twice a day, a new toy every week, pet spa treatments monthly, the best dog food and treats money could buy, and endless affection that was almost never reciprocated. At fifty-four, childless, and single, where else could Martha focus the mountains of love she had inside of her?

It had been just over a year since Martha "retired" thanks to a back injury and a settlement from Murry and Sons Accounting. How she hurt her back at a desk job was a major arguing part in the deliberations, but at the end of the day, she won the settlement. The day she retired, she saved Muffin from certain death at the pound. It was Martha's proudest moment, saving an animal like that was just so heroic to her. So much so, she got not one, but *two* stickers saying, "Who Saved Who?"—one she put on her car, the other on her laptop. It wasn't about who saved who, she knew the truth, *she* saved Muffin from certain death. The sticker was just a subtle way of telling strangers she was a hero for saving a dog that most couldn't fathom loving. Whenever her little love acted up, she would always whisper in Muffin's ear, "Sweetie, if it wasn't for me, you'd be dead right now. Could you please not make Mommy's day any harder than it needs to be?" At times, Muffin would settle down, but the few times she didn't, Martha would put her in a crate and ignore her for an hour, no matter how much the mutt whined. It always hurt her to hear the whine, but she had to be a good mother and be strict, otherwise her baby would never learn.

While discipline was not enjoyable, there were more upsides than not. Martha's favorite thing was dressing Muffin up. The guest room, now deemed "Muffin's Manor," was filled with outfits, well over two hundred so far: sweaters, booties, hats (which Muffin hated to wear), and costumes galore. Bumblebee, ladybug, pumpkins, tutus, astronaut, cheerleader, and countless other costumes were hung on pink cloth hangers in a closet decorated with cutout dog bones on the door. With Halloween coming, Martha was excited to pick out a costume for Muffin. Last year she went as a racoon. It was adorable, every time she answered the door, holding Muffin in one hand and the candy bars in the other, kids and parents alike would all gasp in unison and let out a collective "*awwwwww*." This year, she was thinking of going with a spookier costume, something like a zombie dog or Frankenweenie, but so far her search for the perfect costume had come up empty.

Going for walk number two one morning, she strolled down the street and thought about different costume ideas. The idea of making one was strong in her head, but she had zero talent went it came to sewing and stitching. As the leaves crunched underfoot, she took in the houses, most of them already fully decked out for the holiday, but a lot of the ones that went full out were still being put up piece by piece, as they didn't want to reveal everything until it was the big day, that way the judges would be shocked. Martha was indifferent about the holiday, but she loved the season and the excitement it brought to their town, and she enjoyed seeing the creativity all her neighbors put into the displays. One house in particular she had been watching all week, at times even stopping to chat to the owner, who she found out was named Ruben. He was a bit awkward and a bit frumpy like herself, but she found herself blushing at his compliments and admired his enthusiasm over his house and how "epic" it was going to be. He begged her to come see it. She blushed and said she would, even though she knew her nerves would probably stop her from going. One day he asked if she wanted to come have a coffee with her. She panicked and lied, saying she had to get Muffin her morning medication, but maybe the next day. Since then, she had avoided his street, but she thought about Ruben obsessively.

Martha never did well with men or boys or women, or people in general. She could put on a smile and fake politeness, but she just never felt like she belonged with other humans, to the point where she wondered if she was ever one to begin with. Animals suited her just fine. Within arm's distance, she made it through life. Her mother, who never once hugged or consoled her, died when she was twenty, leaving Martha enough money to buy herself a house. She even skipped college, even though she was ranked ninth in her graduating class, simply to avoid being stuck in a dorm room with another young woman and having to go through four more years of hormonal people ranting around. The thought was just too much to bear. Instead, she did a correspondence course and got a certificate in accounting. She was always great with numbers and got a job at an accounting firm almost instantly. Then the next thirty years went by in a flash. Wake up, work, go home, TV dinner, movie, take care of current dog, bed. Repeat. Not one physical or emotional relationship, nor a single vacation. Every penny saved, every meal ate at home, it was tidy and consistent, just like she liked.

Then she hit fifty and suddenly, Martha didn't want to work anymore. Numbers got boring, the routine got stale. When her back went out trying to fix the leg of her desk that had gotten wobbly after the janitor moved it to clean the carpet from her spilt minestrone soup, she decide that was her way out. Sure enough, after countless meetings and paperwork, which gave her an ulcer from all the human interaction, she was given a good-sized settlement and took an early retirement so she could, so she could . . . do nothing.

Some days, she regretted waking up and having nothing to do, and other days she slept in—one day she slept so late she got scared and had a panic attack. She had never slept past eight before and she thought something might have been wrong with her. But after a quick online therapy session, she was assured that nothing was wrong. It was after that incident that the panic attacks started to pop up regularly. Most of the time they came out of nowhere, but other times they were triggered by pure boredom and loneliness. Muffin only gave her so much company, and while she wouldn't admit it to anyone, even herself, Muffin was the first dog she had that seemed to truly *not* like her. Sure,

Muffin would listen and obey, but she never wanted to sit on Martha's lap without being forced. She didn't beg to sleep in the bed, and most of the time Muffin was trying to get away from her rather than being by her side like other dogs. At times she wondered if she was losing the ability to connect with animals as well.

With Muffin leading the way on their walk, Martha had to pull the pink leash hard to stop her baby from going down Ruben's street. Muffin wanted to go that way every day since Ruben gave her some bacon off his breakfast sandwich he was eating while putting up some tarps on the side of his house. Martha was furious that he gave Muffin food without asking, but she let it slide when Ruben gave her a smile that for the first time in her life made her . . . feel something. It was a warm feeling inside of her chest and she liked it. Regardless of how interesting it felt, Martha dragged Muffin away from Ruben's street and kept walking down her new route, past the woman's house who planted a full pumpkin patch in her yard. Martha had gotten a kick out of it at first, watching pumpkins pop up overnight, but now the woman was just letting it get insane. The vines were crawling all over the house, it was like they were taking over. It would look awesome on Halloween, but she hoped the woman would cut it all down well before December. No one wants to see pumpkins during the jolliest time of the year, after all.

With her walk stretching on, Martha came back to her street and gave a dirty look at the Tranche house. It was the yard she encouraged Muffin to piss on every day. The creepy-ass teen that lived there and his fussy mother were the epitome of trash. They had no right to be living on such a nice street, especially across from her own house! Part of her wondered if Cathy squatted the house or blackmailed the last owner because the woman never worked, she only had men come over night after night, and usually they were drunk and partying. There was no way she could afford the mortgage. It wasn't just her that hated them either. The town shared her sentiment, as they were the only house for miles that didn't decorate for the holiday. The street even offered to pay for and set up decorations last year, but that bitch refused, saying she didn't want anything messing up her lawn, which was already yellow and full of weeds. And Jalen, her sick son, that boy was going to be a menace one day. Watching him through binoculars with the lights off in her living room, she had seen him do things in that house that made her skin crawl. She couldn't wait for the day she could call the police on . . ..

Martha couldn't believe what she saw when the door flew open. There was Cathy, half naked with blood all over her. With rage, she threw a pumpkin out the door with all her might. Martha watched in awe as it rolled across the yard, right past her and Muffin on the sidewalk. When it landed next to the curb, Muffin growled at it as if it were a nemesis.

"Fuck you, Martha!" She heard as she turned back just in time to see the door slam. It wasn't the first time that Cathy had told her off, but Martha knew it would be the last. Scooping up Muffin, she raced across the road and back to her house. Within seconds, she had her binoculars in one hand and the landline in the other. For the next five minutes, Martha watched breathlessly while Muffin whined for her lunch. Through the lens she could only see some movement in the house. Her heart raced as she wondered what was happening. *Was she killing the boy? If the cops came in time and the boy lived, would she have saved his life?!* She would be a hero again, not just for Muffin, but for Jalen as well. Maybe he would turn his life around after that and see the world in a whole new way. She could become a surrogate mother of sorts and help him to . . ..

That's when the police suddenly arrived.

It all happened quickly after that. The cop knocked, looked in the window, and kicked the door down. The three shots fired off after that sent Muffin into a frantic barking fit, but Martha didn't hear it. The panic attack that washed over her shut off all her senses. Her body froze with the binoculars to her face, and then she wet herself as her body lost all control. When she awoke, Muffin was licking her face and there was pounding on her door. Seeing she wet herself, she started to cry and didn't want to answer the door, but the officer wouldn't stop pounding and pounding and pounding, and Muffin kept barking and barking and barking. It was driving her mad. In a ball on the floor, she covered her ears and let out a scream. Then her door was kicked open. The frame splintered, sending shards of woodchips all over her; Muffin ran and hid in her crate. Opening her eyes just a bit, Martha saw the orange-and-black wreath she had just bought for full price lying next to her in a twisted heap.

The whole time the officer talked through to the time the medic came to check on her, all Martha could think about was how much it would cost to fix the door and that she had to now go back to Michael's to get a new wreath. She hardly heard anything they said to her and only responded in nods and monosyllabic responses. When they finally stood her up, she dared a look outside and saw a man who looked to have been made of pure blood being wheeled out of the Tranches' house. The site made her dizzy and she started to faint again. Whoever the people were around her grabbed her by the arms and set her on the couch—the one that faced the picture window, the one she sat on to spy on the house she despised. There she sat, watching the scene unfolding in front of her as they took her vitals and gave her a shot of something to "calm" her down.

Several hours later, Martha showered and fed Muffin, all while the front door was wide open. She had to keep Muffin on her leash and tied to a chair while she ate so she wouldn't wander off. Clean and able to breathe normally, she sat on the front steps and stared at the house across the street. The police tape was up still and a few people were still coming in and out, but the main crowd of gawkers was thinning down. That is when she noticed Ruben standing by the tape, his hands on his hips. This made her nervous, she didn't want to talk to him, not like this. But before she could get up, Muffin noticed him too and tugged on the leash so hard, she broke free and ran across the street, going right up to him. Martha was starting to feel faint again as he watched him pick up Muffin, then look around until he saw her. Martha smiled and forced a tiny wave. Ruben pet Muffin—who looked happier in his arms than Martha had ever seen her in her own—and walked over to her house with a huge smile on his face.

"Hey, Martha, so this is where you live." Martha just nodded at his awkward comment.

"Hell of a thing, huh? Never thought we'd have something like this happen in our little town, let alone a murder. Wait, can you call it a murder if the cops are the ones who killed . . ." Ruben noticed the tears in Martha's eyes. Without hesitation, he sat down next to her and picked up her hand and held it in silence. Martha's heart skipped, rolled, then danced her chest before it settled down to a heart rate that matched the calming purr of a kitten. Ruben's hand was so warm, her hand felt so wonderful inside of it. Fifty-four years and this was the first time anyone had held her hand longer than a shake. It was glorious.

They sat this way in silence, Muffin curled up in his lap, her hand in his, until the last of the crowd moved off. The sun was down and only the porch light lit them up. It had to have been almost two hours that they sat like statues, just being in the moment. When Ruben spoke and broke the silence, Martha wanted to cry, for she never wanted the moment to end.

"I'm going to get my tools. You can't have your door left open all night. I'll be back in twenty minutes and I'll have it fixed in half an hour." With that, Ruben stood up and gave Muffin to her and shuffled off. Muffin immediately tried to run after him, but Martha held on tighter to the leash this time. Suddenly her head was filled with thoughts of Ruben and a life with him, she pictured him in her house, sitting on her couch, eating dinner with him, watching movies, going for walks, playing with Muffin. The thoughts made her heart start to race again. Knowing she only had a few minutes, Martha darted to the bathroom and freshened up. Mouthwash, a bit of blush—which she hadn't worn since she retired—and a fluff of the hair, and she was back on the front steps to wait.

Ruben showed back up with a set of tools and bacon for Muffin. Over the next hour, she sat and watched as Ruben sawed, hammered, sanded, screwed, and did various other "manly" things, all while his short round belly jiggled. Martha thought it was adorable. She offered water, which he drank. They chatted mildly, but mostly he worked and worked at fixing the door. When it was back up and closing like new, Martha clapped, waking Muffin from her bacon-induced happy slumber on the living room floor. Ruben smiled shyly and then suddenly looked sad that there was nothing left to do. Looking at his watch, he finally looked up at Martha.

"It's pretty late and you had a stressful day. I should be going." He hesitated, then shrugged before continuing. "But I, I'd like to leave my number in case anything happens, well not that nothing is going to happen, I just mean like, if you need something." Ruben pulled out a piece of paper and set it on the coffee table. Martha smiled, realizing he had written it down before he came back.

"Need something, like . . . coffee?" Martha asked, surprising even herself. Ruben smiled and nodded. Picking up his tools, he started out the door.

"Ruben, I can't thank you enough for this. I would have left and gotten a hotel room and paid a ton to get someone to fix it. It means the world to me. I don't have anyone to look out for me like you just did, I never have." Martha instantly flushed and regretted the last line. Ruben smiled, looking at the floor.

"I have a brother who I hate, but other than that, I've been alone for thirty years myself. So I get what you mean. Coffee soon, like really soon, okay?"

Martha had to hold back tears as Ruben suddenly rushed out, her newly repaired door closing gently behind him.

The next morning, Martha was up early and found herself whistling, which she couldn't ever recall doing before. She ate a quick breakfast, took Muffin for a walk—though she still avoided Ruben's street, as she thought it would be too soon to rush by—then headed out to the store. She needed to get a new wreath, Halloween candy, and a thank-you card for Ruben. When she arrived at the strip mall, for once she didn't obsess about the idiots parking crooked or the slobs who shouldn't be using the handicap spots, instead she whistled the "Monster Mash" over and over again as she pushed her cart around, Muffin sitting in the child seat in her custom hot-pink cushion. Getting the wreath was easy, she just grabbed the same one, but picking out a card took her over twenty minutes. She couldn't decide between one with puppies on it saying, "You Are the Dog-Gone Best," or the one that was more professional with just flowers and a simple "Thank You." When she asked Muffin her opinion, she barked at the one with dogs, of course.

The barking reminded her that they still needed a costume, so they went to the pet section to peruse what was new. Going there every week, there was very little that was new, so she was not hopeful, but low and behold, in the small costume section was a new one that made Martha gasp out loud at her luck: a muffin! A silver cupcake liner went around the body with the words "Stud Muffin" written on the side. On top was what looked like a blueberry muffin top. It. Was. Perfect. *A muffin for Muffin*. Martha squealed with glee and put it in the cart without hesitation, she couldn't wait to tell Ruben about it. Then she paused. The thought of telling someone about something that she found or happened to her never came through her head before. She never had anyone to tell. It made her smile once again.

Martha was in such a good mood, when she got to the candy aisle, she bought *full-size* candy bars for Halloween, an expense she would have never dared in the past. Over half her cart was filled up with entire boxes of all the name brands—none of the generic stuff or cheap bags, nothing but full-size bars. It was going to cost her a few hundred bucks, but so what? The kids would go nuts and she didn't spend the thousands like Ruben and the others did on decorations. She could bring a smile to some kids' faces. It was going to be a great Halloween.

When she was home, she unpacked all the stuff and had Muffin try on her Stud Muffin costume. When she saw her little baby running in circles, trying to bite off the costume, Martha squealed with joy as her baby looked perfect. Seeing Muffin run and yip, she felt the bubbles of excitement run through her stomach again as she thought about Ruben. Martha realized she had not been this happy since her mother's funeral, which felt like a lifetime ago. Picking up the little piece of paper with his number, she looked at it and felt a wave of nausea wash over her. There was only one time in her life she called a boy. When she was seventeen, her mother got a phone number of some college guy named Micha whom she met through a friend. Her mother was obsessed with the young man and desperately wanted Martha to meet him, as he would "make for a good husband." Martha refused to call, so her mother refused to let her eat any food, she unplugged the television, and she wouldn't let Martha out of the house until she called. After a two-day standoff and desperately needing some food, Martha called Micha and introduced herself. Twice she gagged, and vomit stung her throat as the nerves coursed through her. She could hear that Micha was confused, but then she heard a woman in the background encouraging him. After two awkward minutes, they made plans to meet.

Before the date, her mother took her on a shopping spree and spa day, the one and only time in her entire life her mother took her out for anything like that. The next day, Martha was dropped off at the mall. She was set to meet Micha at the fountain in the center of the atrium. There they would share an orange cream from the stand at the food court and then, if it went well, they would go to the bowling alley or movie theater in the mall. It was a plan devised by both of their mothers that made Martha feel sick. Sweating profusely and feeling itchy in her fluffy new sweater that she hated, she sat "sexy-like" on the fountain edge, just like her mother taught her. Then, she waited and waited and waited. Ten minutes past the time she was supposed to meet, she heard arguing behind her—it was a loud, angry whisper, but she could clearly hear the words.

"No fucking way, she looks like Porky Pig got shot in the face by Elmer Fudd. I wouldn't be caught dead in public with a heifer like that." The hurtful words were followed by what sounded like a hard slap to a face. It was hard for Martha not to turn and look, but she knew it was the boy's mother giving him a backhand.

"You go over there, or you will not get the car for your birthday." Martha heard more whining as she felt woozy from the heat and the panic. Sitting on the fountain was a good and bad thing. When she fainted and landed in the water, it kept her from hitting her head hard on the ground. On the other hand, she almost drowned in front of hundreds of people, including a dozen from her school, two of whom took Polaroids of her soaked body on the stretcher as she was carried away. When she called her mother from the hospital and told her what happened, she got hung up on. Three times she called back, using the last of her dimes. After waiting an hour, she walked four miles home in the dark along the highway. Her mother didn't talk to her for months afterwards, she didn't even show up to her graduation.

Now, decades later as she looked at Ruben's phone number scrawled on the paper that shook in her trembling hands, she did her best to ignore the memory that was crawling up her spine like an evil parasite.

This is different, I'm not being forced. He wants *me to call him.* Martha calmed herself and picked up her landline, then she glanced at her flip phone. She had never sent a text before, but maybe that would be an easier first step. She plugged the number into her cellphone, then typed, *Hey, it's Martha. Thanks again for fixing the door.* She wanted to add one of those emoji things, but she didn't know how. Setting the phone down, it instantly chirped—a sound she had never heard before. Picking it back up, she saw there was already a reply from Ruben: *You can pay me back with a coffee anytime! Actually, I'm free now if you want to meet at Kat's Cafe? If not, anytime except Halloween is good for me.*

Martha dropped the phone in shock and panic, but at the same time, happy tingles ran up her legs, through her body, and spread to her groin, another new sensation. She desperately wanted to meet him, but she wasn't sure she could handle it. *Was it too much, too fast?* For the next five minutes she talked out loud to Muffin, who was still trying to bite off the costume, asking her opinion about going. Muffin did not care. With trembling hands, she picked up the phone and typed *yes.* After hitting send, she looked at the phone in shock, as if she didn't realize she had done it.

Ten minutes later, she was walking down the street with Muffin, who was now changed into a sweater rather than the costume. Martha was doing deep breaths, trying to calm herself. She was partially amazed that she was going, but she was also proud. As she rounded the corner to Parker Street, she bumped into Frank and Tammy, who stopped and said "hello." Tammy quickly bent over and rubbed Muffin's head while Frank commented on the weather like he always did. While more than twenty-five years older than Martha, she considered the couple her only real friends, even if they had never done more than talk when they bumped into each other on the sidewalk. Like her, they took two walks a day "to keep these old bones moving," as Frank would always joke. They had invited her over for tea and pie several times, but Martha was always too nervous to go to their home. Realizing she was going to have coffee with someone else and always turned them down, she knew she had to make a lie to get away, as they always talked for at least twenty minutes.

"I'm so sorry, guys, but I have to get to the pharmacy. A prescription I need is ready, and if I don't take it in a few minutes, I'll be a mess. My nerves are still on edge from the other day," Martha blurted out, surprised a lie came so easily.

"Oh my, you go right ahead, dear. If you ever need to talk, you let us know," Frank said with that smile that always made Martha wish he was her father.

"Martha, Frank is going to make you a pie this week, it's his . . . specialty. We will drop it off, if that is all right."

"Or we can leave it on your step," Frank added to Tammy's chipper statement. Martha smiled and said either would be great before rushing off, wondering if her and Ruben would be taking walks together in twenty years.

"Ruben, Ruben, Ruben, *Ruuuuuubeeeeen*," Martha sing-sang to herself on the walk back. Two hours—two straight hours of talking. It was the longest and best conversation in her life. They enjoyed the same movies and books, they both hated their families, they had the same ideas on politics, and they thought a God existed, but they didn't worship Him because He was a bit of a dick. It was like they were twins. Martha didn't want to leave but kept it to herself, and Ruben echoed her thought out loud, but the shop was closing for the day and their conversation had to come to an end.

It was fine, though, they made a plan to meet the next day at the same time, which turned into the next and the next and the next—eight days in a row, all the way until the day before Halloween. Each time they spent over two hours yapping and yapping and yapping and smiling and laughing. On the second day, he brought her flowers, and on the fifth he held her hand. On the last day, he asked her on an official date, but it had to wait until after the holiday because Ruben had so much to set up and besides, he wanted to take her out to celebrate his win for the "Scariest House." Well, his *hopeful* win. Martha could not wait. She was on a high like none she had ever experienced or could have imagined.

It's Halloween! Martha was conflicted—she was excited for the holiday but also sad she wouldn't see Ruben, besides a quick walkthrough of his haunted house. After a light breakfast of a bottled shake and one piece of toast with marmalade, Martha headed out for the first walk of the day with Muffin. The plan was to walk by Ruben's and hopefully get a glimpse of him, but when she got to the house with the pumpkin patch growing, she gasped. The entire house was covered in vines and pumpkins hung like giant Christmas lights all down the sides and over the roof. You could not see a single inch of grass, driveway, or the house, yet not one leaf touched the sidewalk or went off the edge of the property. Martha could not believe it was real, but if it were fake, it would cost a fortune. Curious, she leaned over and plucked a green leaf, brought it up to her face and rubbed it between her fingers—it was real, all right. As she looked at it, she heard a yelp from Muffin, the sound making her heart sink.

Looking down, Muffin was not at her feet, instead she was surfing across the ropey vines as if being carried away by a current. In shock, Martha looked at her hand. She still had the leash in it, but somehow the latch had silently been unhooked, which had never happened before. Seeing the vines slither away, she understood that they, whatever *they* were, must have released the clasp. Her parental instincts kicking in, Martha dropped the leash and ran blindly into the thick of the vines to rescue her Muffin. It felt like a thousand prickly snakes wrapping around her ankles, each one doing its best to hold on and stop her from moving. After only four steps, she was stuck, the vines climbing her torso, ready to devour her. When they grabbed her arms and started pulling her down, she screamed and cried out. Muffin yelped in reply, her furry body completely hidden beneath the vines.

"Enough!" Martha instinctively looked up at the sound. There in the top bedroom window, which had magically appeared as if the vines created a cutout for her to see it, was a woman who looked down at the yard with a powerful posture. The vines started to loosen around Martha, as if scared of this woman.

"Let them go, they mean us no harm. You know that," the mysterious woman said into the air. Suddenly, the vines let go of Martha and a path cleared like the Red Sea in front of her to reveal Muffin, who looked just as confused as her. For the first time ever, Muffin sprinted towards Martha and jumped up into her arms. Looking around, she held Muffin tight and slowly backed up to the sidewalk. Once there, she grabbed the leash and reached into her pocket for her cellphone.

"I wouldn't do that if I were you," the lady of the vines said. "They will just think you're crazy. Vines don't move on their own." Martha nodded, as if the words deeply resonated with a truth that she somehow understood. Keeping an eye on the house, she backed away.

"Ma'am, try to enjoy the day. And don't worry, Muffin will be just fine," the woman said, waving from the window.

Martha was confused and scared, only turning her back on the yard and its living vines when it was no longer in site. Cutting the rest of the walk short as fear, panic, and confusion coursed through her, Martha marched home in a state of confused panic. As she got to her house, she saw a car in the Tranches' driveway. Curiosity momentarily paused her fear. Maybe someone was coming to empty it out to start the selling process. Standing on the sidewalk, she squinted, wishing she had her binoculars, but when she saw the heavily bandaged person get out of the car, she knew she didn't need them. It only took a second for her to realize it was Jalen . . . coming home.

The faint feeling was coming again. Martha rushed over to her front steps and sat down. She clutched the railing and took slow breaths. She desperately wanted to call Ruben, he said she could call anytime she had a panic attack, but he was just too busy today, she couldn't take him away from the thing that meant the most to him. Opening her eyes, she saw Jalen brining in groceries—he was here to stay. *She* called the cops on them. *She* is the one who got his mom killed. *Did he think of it that way too?* Martha fought against the raging panic that wanted her to faint, while Muffin fought to get out of her tight grip. This was all too much, so much in fact, that she started to wonder if the violent vines had been a hallucination. Was her brain just stopping her from finally being happy? Was the creepiness of Halloween mixing with her own anxieties? What was going on?

Easing herself up, she finally forced her way inside on stilted, weak legs. With a cold glass of water, she sat on the couch, breathing and staring out the window at the Tranche house. After a few moments, she thought she saw a tiny vine peeking into her window. Closing her eyes tight, she counted to fifty, because ten and twenty were not enough to relax. When she opened them two beats after fifty, she screamed. Looking into the window with a crooked and grotesque smile was what was left of Jalen. It was now a monstrous version of him, sliced and cut to the point of not being recognizable. He no longer had hair, only tiny tufts stuck out between the red gashes and thick dark rows of stitches. She had never seen anything like it before and worst of all, he was smiling and waving to her.

"Hey! I, I just wanted to thank you for . . . saving my life." The voice came out gurgled and muffled through the glass. Martha closed her eyes, counted to three and opened them again, but he was still there. Part of her felt silly, the poor boy was just abused and, wait, did she save him too? Just like she saved Muffin? This sudden thought sent a burst of adrenaline into her, making her weak legs strong, making the dizziness fade. Jumping up, she raced to the door and unlocked it. Thinking of Ruben as she saw the freshly sanded marks on the door, she smiled— she could not wait to tell him that Jalen thought she saved him.

"Jalen, right? I'm so, so sorry for what happened to you. I felt awful, I couldn't sleep at all for days. I'm glad you are home. Is anyone going to take care of you?" Jalen's face was so messed up, it was hard to look at, let alone tell what his facial expressions were trying to convey.

"May I come in? The sunlight hurts the cuts." Martha nodded and moved out of the way. A second person in her house that month—that was more than there had been in the past few decades.

"You poor thing, can I get you something?" Jalen shook his head "no." When Martha turned around and saw the knife in Jalen's hands, she laughed, thinking it was a Halloween prop.

"You killed my mom. We were about to be happy together and you had to call the cops. Now I have to sneak her out of the morgue. Do you know how pissed she is going to be at you?" Jalen screamed with a slurping stutter caused by the stitches on his lips.

Martha, shocked at herself for not fainting, slipped her hand into her pocket and pulled out her phone, but before she could dial, the knife breezed by her wrist, slicing it open like it was wet paper. She yelped and dropped the phone as she grabbed the cut that already had a waterfall of blood cascading out of it.

"Hurts, huh? Imagine having this many!" Jalen said, gesturing to his face.

"Muffin, sic him, sic him, Muffin!" Martha screamed as she backed up, hoping her spoiled little pup would attack and give her enough time to escape. Muffin looked up from the couch, then put her head back on the pillow, bored as could be. Martha was stuck behind the kitchen island, the only way out was past him. She could grab a knife herself, but with her hand aching and blood making it slick, she was helpless. Her only weapon was words.

"Jalen . . . Jalen, I'm so, so sorry about your mother. I thought I was protecting you. She would have . . . killed you," Martha said with as much truth and heart as she could muster over her tears.

"*No*. She loved me and *wanted* me. She still does. She just gets, mad at times."

Hearing this, Martha suddenly felt an odd tidal wave of relief wash over her. It was like someone reached down and pulled a weighted blanket off her that she didn't realize was on her body her entire life. She felt light and free, all her anxieties and fears in life were gone. She wasn't scared, she wasn't worried, and she didn't feel the pain anymore.

"Thank you, Jalen," Martha said, her voice nearly a whisper. Jalen looked back at her confused and almost angry that she wasn't scared anymore.

"Can you please just do me a favor? Well, two. Please make sure Muffin is okay. Maybe you could take care of her? And, could you tell Ruben Sidel "thank you" for me?"

Jalen lowered his knife a bit as bewilderment took him over, Martha saw this and saw a way out, but she was tired and ready.

"Just tell him he made me happy for the first time in my life and tell him I hope he wins. He deserves it."

Martha finished her sentence, closed her eyes, and put her arms out wide as if ready to accept a hug for the first time ever. Instead, the knife came faster than she expected.

"OMG! That house has big candy bars!" The teen in the homemade Jason Voorhees mask screamed to a group of three other knockoff horror movie killers.

They all whooped with excitement and ran up to Martha's house, but as they got close, they slowed down with caution. There in front of them, set out on the steps, was a scarecrow sitting in a lawn chair, at least it *sort of* looked like a scarecrow. The body was frumpy as if it were stuffed, but instead of hay coming out of the sleeves, there was what looked like pumpkin poking out in spots. In its lap was a huge bowl of massive, full-sized candy bars. The dummy's gloved hands were wrapped around the bowl, holding it tight to its belly, which was covered in cuts and fake blood. A big silver knife stuck out of its chest that stabbed through a sheet of bloody paper that read: *Take Just One . . . or Mr. Slice Will Get YOU!* It looked sickeningly real to the mini-Jason, but what scared him the most for some reason was the head. The head was stuck into some giant muffin costume. He had never seen a scarecrow that looked like that, and it scared him.

"I don't think that's a dummy, guys," the fake Jason said. "I think it's a person and they're going to jump at us when we take a candy bar."

"Yeah . . . that's why these are big bars—everyone will try to take more than one, then it will jump up at us. I'm not getting one," said a laughable-looking Freddy Krueger.

"Don't be a wuss, just take one," a chubby Michael Myers egged on. Jason nodded behind his mask and slowly stepped up to the body. Reaching ever so slowly, he grabbed a full-sized Twix, then jumped back like a scared cat trying to get out of the way of nothing. The dummy didn't move, and he laughed.

"See, it's fine, unless they are going to wait until like the third one to really get us." They all laughed as one by one, they each snuck a big candy bar and bolted away from the house.

"Hey, let's go across the street," said the mini-Jason. "I heard someone say the guy with a little dog has some sick makeup on!"

Clare's Pumpkin Patch

The gooey, creamy orange-and-white strands slid between her fingers, eager to escape her clutch. It was as if the innards were alive as gravity pulled them down, making the long entrails slide across her skin like a living creature. The slithering she felt reminded her of the time she picked up a fistful of nightcrawlers at a bait shop when she was a child. Her father had yelled at her before apologizing to the owner—it was a mere moment that was all but forgotten until the sensation of the pumpkin guts took her back to that time. Unlike the worms, though, with this gooey mess, she could close her fist tightly, squeeze, and watch as the orange juices shot out; it made her giggle.

With all the guts falling back into the pumpkin, Clare—spelled without an "i," just like her nana—shot her hand back inside the open cavity and grabbed another handful. She couldn't stop smiling the whole time, it had been years since she carved a pumpkin. At one point she tried to do the math, but she gave up and said it had to have been when she was a child. At thirty-one, she never had the need or desire to carve a jack-o'-lantern, why would she? With no kids and no desire to spend her hard-earned money on candy to hand out to ungrateful children, there was no need for pumpkins. But this year, living in a new town that celebrated the holiday as if it were the most holy day of the year, made her change her mind. Well, that and she feared the dirty looks from neighbors if she didn't participate at a hardcore level.

It took her ten years, but she was able to finally afford a real house of her own, not some apartment with a perverted landlord or a cheap room in a basement with a man living above her who did nothing but play Meat Loaf's albums on a constant twenty-four-hour loop, she finally had a home to call her own. When she moved in during the summer, things couldn't have been more perfect. The neighbors were overly friendly, and they didn't care that she was unmarried or had no kids—in fact, they seemed relieved to have someone who would be quiet next to them. As she met the townsfolk, little by little they all asked her if she was ready for "*their* Halloween." Clare thought it was an odd question to be asked in the summer, but she quickly found out that *everyone* on her street, hell, the whole town, went all out on All Hallows' Eve. Her street alone estimated that they gave out four thousand pounds of candy every year. She could not fathom that. The town even had all sorts of contests and a fair every weekend of the month leading up to the big day. After doing some research, she found out they were becoming the second-most popular city in the country for the holiday, just behind Salem. Having never cared about the holiday one way or the other, she simply replied to the constant questions with "oh, that is interesting" and "maybe I'll do something small this year to start off," only to forget about the comments until the next time Halloween was brought up, which was *every time* she saw a neighbor.

When September rolled around, she was shocked when she went for her morning walk. It was cool and a bit foggy, and the leaves were just starting to turn, making for the perfect walking weather, something that Clare even said out loud.

After passing only three houses, right at the bend in the road, Clare almost fainted when she saw a dead body hanging from a tree, right in the path of the sidewalk. With the fog and her quick pace, she didn't see it until it was almost five feet in front of her. It was a full body, stuck inside of a yellow beat-up, bloody sleeping bag, tied to a branch by a rope. The bag was tied up tight, showing only a pale ghostly face obscured by a mess of blonde hair. The scream Clare let out was beyond anything she knew she was capable of, in fact, it was so guttural, she had to sip tea and whisper for four days afterwards as her throat healed.

On her knees, fumbling for her cellphone to call the police, she cursed the world for ruining her perfect new life in the town she loved, on the street she adored. *She just wanted to be left alone and happy, was that too much to ask for?* She cried to herself as she tried to unlock her phone with her shaking hands. Just as she was about to hit the second number one, a hand slammed down on her back. She screamed again.

"Oh my, Clare, are you all right? Did you fall? I heard the scream and came out right away. Do you need help?" Realizing it wasn't the killer about to string her up as well, Clare spun around to see Ms. McCarthy from two doors down. The cherubic-faced old lady had her hair up in curlers and was wearing a dingy bathrobe like an '80s sitcom character.

"There . . . there's a body," Clare stuttered as she got up and backed away, grabbing onto her neighbor's shoulder at the same time. That was when she heard the laughing.

"My goodness, darling, the fright you must have had! That is part of Phil's Halloween display, he is always the first to put his stuff up. I forgot that you are new here. You better get ready because every house will have a thousand spooky things! Though my house is a Disney Halloween theme, so it's not as frightening. I won the "Not So Spooky" award twice!"

Clare was trying to understand everything through her adrenaline-confused mind as her neighbor rambled on.

"I complained to him once that the dead bodies were too scary for the little ones leaving my house, but he won the argument by saying it was like a stop sign warning parents to cross the street if they didn't want to be spooked, like you did." Ms. McCarthy laughed again as she reached out and offered a hug that Clare accepted without hesitation. It was the first hug from an adult she had received in years, and it felt so good she didn't want to let go—it made her miss her nana deeply. With her heart rate slowing, she finally moved out of the warm embrace, thanked her neighbor, and then dared to poke the hanging body. Sure enough, it was fake. Now it was her turn to laugh.

From that point on, more and more things appeared on her morning walk every day. Giant skeleton animatronics, howling dog statues, kid-friendly dioramas, and of course, more pumpkins than she could count. On October 1st, she realized her house was the only one that didn't have at least a handful of decorations. Not wanting to be ostracized for being the boring house on the street, Clare headed off on a mission to find out what she wanted to turn her yard into. At first, she thought about creating a graveyard, but there were already two of those on her street. Then she thought about giant blow-ups, but she hated how they looked like melted freeze pops still in the wrapper. Finally, after making a spreadsheet of each house's theme, she realized that no one had done a spooky pumpkin patch. Over two thousand dollars and a week's worth of work later, "Clare's Pumpkin Patch" was born. And she was more than proud of it.

Two giant pumpkins, over five feet high and ten feet around, stood on each side of the house with small spotlights to showcase them. They were custom-bought and the most expensive showpieces, and she had no clue where she would store them when the season was over. There were twenty hay barrels, fifteen bundles of dried cornstalks, and over 100 *real* pumpkins. She had to flirt with the farmer to talk him into giving her all of them at a discount and to drive them back to her house for her, but he was a harmless, kind old man who looked like an extra on *Hee Haw*, the old show her nana used to make her watch on VHS tapes when she was a kid. Although on the day he dropped them off, he sort of trailed off in thought, the smile sliding off his face like a glacier calving. It dropped so quickly she thought he was having a stroke. As she reached to him to see if he was all right, the man gasped in some air, then gave her a large smile as he looked at her with tears starting to build in his eyelids.

"Missy, I'm going to get you my very best pumpkins, ones that I grew extra special this year. I held on to them until I found the right person, who is, well, you."

Clare laughed and swatted him on the shoulder. She figured he was just covering up from his glitch, so she just smiled and did her best to blush and thank him. Though all the pumpkins had been unloaded, he went back into the cab of the car took one out that was absolutely beautiful. It was a cover-of-a-magazine-worthy pumpkin. He handed it to her with pride and a bit of hesitation, as if he was sad or maybe concerned to see it go.

"Missy, you treat this one real special and it will take care of you as well," the old farmer said with a wink and what looked like a tear in his eye. As she thanked him again and offered a tip, which he declined, she watched him look at the pumpkin with longing, as if he was saying goodbye to something he loved. It gave her a bit of concern, but by the time he drove off, she had forgotten about the incident and set the pumpkin in a prime spot on the steps.

With all of the stuff in place, the yard was a beautiful, seasonal display of pure fall and Halloween spirit that rivaled any store or public display she had seen. Best of all, it was family-friendly. Clare even special-ordered pumpkin candies from a wholesaler in Detroit and she got herself a scarecrow outfit and a real tractor seat that she stuck in the ground to sit on as she handed out candy. By mid-October, she couldn't wait until the big day.

It was five days before All Hallows' Eve, the day after she carved that perfect pumpkin, when things started to take a turn. Heading out to work early in the morning, Clare stopped next to her car to blow out a big breath of steam. It was the first time that season that you could see your breath, and she wanted to take a moment to enjoy the crispness of the air. Looking around the yard, she was happy, but then she noticed something was different. There looked to be more pumpkins than she had before. Looking closer, she noticed the orange gourds seemed to have multiplied for sure. Clare had painstakingly placed every pumpkin and now there were ones in areas she never put them, a lot more, in fact.

Holding her keys tight, she left the side of her car and walked towards her pretend pumpkin patch and looked around. Counting, she quickly got to one hundred, but then she kept going. When she finished the count, there were 167 pumpkins—over five dozen more than the one hundred she bought originally. Scratching her chin, she looked around, wondering who the hell would prank her by putting out more pumpkins—they weren't cheap, after all. Then she wondered if it was the farmer, what was his name? Could he have done it, thinking he was being kind, dropping off leftovers from the season? She wanted to look into the matter, but it was harmless and maybe someone just had extra pumpkins and was being nice. Besides, she had to get to work. As she pulled out, she drove slowly by the house and admired the extra pumpkins. They looked nice, but just as she was about to pass, she noticed something else that was off. All the new ones seemed to have vines attached to them, as if they had *grown*. Not wanting to stop the car, she shrugged it off, but the rest of the day she couldn't help but think of the new additions to her display.

The sun was down when she got home from work, but the spotlights she put out to shine on the display gave her enough illumination to see, and what she saw, she didn't believe. There were now well over two hundred pumpkins. With a quick glance, they seemed to have grown. *It was scientifically impossible for a full pumpkin to grow in a mere eight hours, right?* All the new pumpkins were attached by an intricate network of vines. It was hard to see where they all came from, but something in her gut knew they stemmed from the one "special" pumpkin. Tracing the vines, she saw there were even more sprouting up. There were bright yellow flowers and small green baby pumpkins all over the vines. Grabbing a flashlight from her house, she tried to follow the twisting and curvy greenery to the source, but it was a knotted mess that was impossible to detangle and decode. When she went to look at the special pumpkin that she had set next to the tractor seat, it wasn't there. The oddest part was that the vines also reached out and attached themselves to the pumpkins she already had that were cut from their stems, some of which looked to be growing even more as if they had fused back together, which was another impossibility. Clare was confounded and had no clue what was happening or what to do.

Sitting on her front steps, looking out over her pumpkin patch, she took deep breaths and thought hard. It was completely impossible, yet her yard begged to differ. Regardless, they were just pumpkins growing, so did it even matter? Even if she wanted to do something, what could she do, call the farmer to look at it? He would just say, "It looks like you grew pumpkins." Besides, it looked pretty cool, so why not just leave it until Halloween, and then she could worry about the cleanup. She'd probably have to hire someone, but she could afford the cost.

Heading in that night, she locked her doors like normal and did her nightly routine of showering then reading exactly three chapters of a romance novel, but there wasn't a second she didn't think of the pumpkins growing in the yard. The thought of the vines spreading weaved into her every breath, just like they had weaved through the yard. On several occasions she looked outside to see if more had grown. It was hard to tell from the upstairs window, but she was almost positive that there were more pumpkins than three hours earlier. Finally, sleep won over and Clare fell into an unrestful slumber filled with dreams of vines wrapping around her body as a smiling jack-o'-lantern watched with glee. It was terrifying yet slightly erotic, which made her feel even more confused.

In the morning, she jumped out of bed as if it were on fire, having just bolted awake from another nightmare of vines grabbing her legs. Realizing it was a dream, she closed her eyes, took a deep breath, then turned and looked at the bed. *It wasn't a dream.* The entire room was filled with pumpkins and vines. They snaked up under the bedposts, right under the comforter. *They were in bed with her.* Throwing back the blankets, she saw that the entire bed was covered in green ropy vegetation. The only place there wasn't any was the left side of the bed, where a white outline of her body was. Though the whiteness quickly disappeared as the vines slithered over the spot, claiming it for themselves. Closing her eyes tightly again, she slapped her own face, demanding that she wake up out of this nightmare. Instead of waking up, though, she felt the prickly vines caress her feet before working their way up her legs like some sort of plant-based snake.

Everything about her wanted to scream and pull away, to run and grab a machete (not that she had one) and to start hacking, but for some reason she didn't move. Maybe it was because there was nowhere to go, but it was more so because the vines touching her leg felt, good, almost *loving.* It was like she could tell they were *praising* her. Licking her lips, she took a deep breath and spoke out loud.

"I have to go to the bathroom now. I'd like privacy." Like a pair of pants ripping at the seam, the vines suddenly moved aside, exposing the cream-colored carpet, leaving a solid path around the bed. As the splitting seam reached the bathroom door, she let out a laugh as the door opened and the light turned on, courtesy of the slithering greenery. The way the vines worked like hands reminded her of Audrey II from *Little Shop of Horrors*—she used to be obsessed with that movie, she even rehearsed several songs from the musical and performed them for her nana over and over one summer. Swallowing hard, she nodded in approval and walked on the carpet between the writhing vines. Inside the bathroom, she heard the door shut behind her. Looking around, she saw there wasn't even a single leaf in the room, she was alone. Sitting down on the toilet, she peed on autopilot as she wondered if she were having a mental breakdown or if this was all really happening.

In a fog, she washed her face and put on deodorant, both of which she did harder than normal to make sure she could feel things, to ensure she was awake and conscious. Ready to leave the bathroom, she took a deep breath and wondered if all the greenery would be gone, maybe it was just some vivid waking dream, but her gut knew deep down that her baby—*why the hell did that word come into her mind?*—would still be dutifully waiting for her.

When she opened the door, she saw a thousand tiny leaves and tips of vines turn to look at her like eager puppies. As she took a step out, the vines moved, once again clearing a path. Her bedroom door was opened for her in a manner that seemed elegant. In the hall, she watched as the leaves slithered and moved—there wasn't one spec of her wall, ceiling, or floor that wasn't covered. It was clearly the layout of her house, only it was now all lush green. It was fascinating, watching how every one of the thousands of stalks seemed to be alive and breathing. As she stepped, they seemed to anticipate her every move, they even cleared the railing for her to hold on to. As her hand slid down, she giggled to herself watching the vines unravel, clear the way, then recoil around the white wood as she walked. Arriving in the kitchen, she found that the table was clear and already set with her daily breakfast: a container of cottage cheese, a banana, and a small orange juice. The chair was even pulled out for her. *How did they know what she ate?*

Ignoring the impossible and surreal world around her, she sat down and started to eat when the television remote suddenly appeared in front of her face, a vine wrapped carefully around it.

"No, thank you," she reflexively said, only to see the vine place it down gently.

"You guys can understand me?" All the leaves on the vines shook in unison as if with a small laugh, but the one in front of her waved gently up and down as if nodding a polite "yes." As if everything that happened up until that point wasn't already insane, Clare let out a huff of disbelief.

"Why is this happening? I mean, why did you all pick my house . . . or me?" The vines wiggled and moved fluidly like they had been, but they didn't respond to the questions. Just when she was about to ask another question, the lead vine reached out and wrapped itself around her hand and squeezed it so gently, she almost cried. Without a thought, she whispered with a tear coming to her eye.

"Can I see you?" The vine let go of her hand and pulled back. The entire room started to ripple and pulsate as vines pulled to the center. First there appeared feet, then legs, then a torso and arms, until suddenly there was a full body in front of her. A complete human shape made of . . . vines. There was even a vague mouth, eyes, and nose. The thing nodded to her before more of them grew behind the first one. Two more figures appeared, only these did not have human heads like the first one; instead, these ones hoisted up large pumpkins to represent their heads, which looked odd being smooth and uncarved. Looking at the main figure, she understood it was the leader, the one who knew how many others there were.

"Is, is there one of you for every pumpkin?" The endless leaves all fluttered as if saddened. One of the creatures in the back actually raised an arm like an appendage and covered an invisible mouth on its smooth orange flesh, as if it was upset. It was then that she understood there were once many more of these creatures, but there were now only a few left of what had been an army. She didn't understand how she knew this, but she did. It was like they were somehow communicating with her telepathically.

Something made Clare stand up and walk toward the, vine-man. He stood, staring at her. Even without eyes, she felt like he was looking at her in a way that no one ever had before. She could tell he was seeing right into her, that he knew and accepted everything about her. Without a word, she hugged him. It hugged back, wrapping vines around her back and then all over her. The fauna against her cheek was prickly, but it also caressed her. It was the greatest hug she ever had and the most love she had ever felt. After a few seconds, there was a tickle in her ear—there were no words, it felt more like tiny pulses of air hitting her eardrum in a pleasant rhythm that she understood clearly.

As she pulled back, she felt a few tears run down her face. "Until dawn on the first of November?"

The man nodded sadly to confirm.

"What about next year? Will you all be able to come back?" The man stepped back, all the vines did. They seemed to recede away from her, leaving a clear five-foot space around her. The man reached out and offered three seeds to Clare. She took them and closed her hand around them hard, as if they were precious stones she was scared of losing. An image of a young woman, not much younger than herself, came into her mind. She saw the girl's entire life and tragic end in one brilliant hot flash. Her death and the pain the poor thing must have felt made Clare sob, but instantly she also knew it was unavoidable. In order to get these seeds, the ones that were hot and tingling in her clenched fist, sacrifices had to be made. It was all becoming clear.

Suddenly the creatures all took a knee and bowed to her. She didn't need to hear them, she understood. As long as she planted her pumpkin patch, they would be here every October, but just that one month and only as long as the darkness was kept at bay.

"Can't I have you longer?" They didn't shake their head "no," they didn't move—she knew the answer. She would get thirty-one days a year until she picked someone else to take over for her. As the thought rang in her head, she wondered, *Why her? Why was she picked?* She was nothing special, she was less than special, in fact. As if reading her mind and concern, the man stood up and placed his viny hand over her heart. An almost electric warmth rang through her. In that second, she knew she would never question why again.

"There are only four days left, we have work to do, gentlemen," Clare said, placing her hand on his as the entire house vibrated with cheer.

After calling in sick to work for the rest of the week, Clare put out her hand and let a vine wrap around it. She felt an odd sense of being one with them. Any time she was touching them, she could sense what they wanted to say. She didn't hear words in her head, she just suddenly and intuitively understood things. She knew she had to carve two dozen jack-o'-lanterns, but before carving, she also knew she had to bless each pumpkin with a kiss, as if the touch of her lips told them it was okay and to be brave. After carving, the vines would grab the seeds and split them evenly—half were put into jars and half were brought to the yard to plant. When she was done with a particular carving, she stood, held it high, and let the vines form a body. When the figure was in front of her, she would hold the pumpkin up like a crown and set it on top. The vines would grab and hold onto it, then the green creature would lean back and the face on the pumpkin would come alive with the ability to make small facial gestures. The most amazing part to her was the light that started as a small spark, then turned into a flame. She knew the fire was kept burning by an ancient spirit.

One after another, she created this army. And while she knew she had to do it, she didn't really understand the reason why or what they would do on Halloween night, just that they were *essential*. So much so, it was like her life, maybe the town's survival, relied upon it. While she made these carvings, taking breaks only to eat, stretch, and use the bathroom, the one figure, the one with a human-shaped head, stayed by her side, silently guiding her. Every once in a while, she'd turn to him and feel that warmth and comfort that made her feel so at ease, so loved. After the tenth carving of that day, her hands hurt and she was tired.

"You guys can make me a sandwich and do everything I can do, so why don't you help with the carving?" The figure next to her put a sinewy hand on her shoulder. She nodded, understanding that they had to come from her.

"Okay, we can keep going tomorrow. I need sleep." When she got to the top of the stairs, she saw her bedroom was filled with candles, all lit and flickering like a romantic movie. She had no clue where they came from, as she only owned two overly expensive Yankee Candles that she never lit, but she had learned to not question anything. It was beautiful, but it also made her uneasy as she wasn't too sure she wanted to be seduced by vegetation. A bath was also drawn and the vines ushered her in there, shutting the door and leaving her be. In flickering candlelight, she laid in the warm bubbles and smiled to herself, feeling like a queen, knowing she was important for once.

An hour later, she was lying in bed. Everything around her was green and writhing except the white of her comforter. Not a single leaf touched the top of the bed—they were holding back like polite gentlemen. She knew that with a mere thought, they would all leave her room and let her sleep in peace. But instead, she breathed out and thought of what she really wanted. A second later, the vines were under the blankets and wrapping around her. Lying on her side, she could feel the figure forming behind her to spoon and cradle her like the most enduring lover of all time. With her body embraced like never before, Clare cried salty tears of pure joy. Though a few tears were also shed knowing this would only last a few days, and then she would have to wait an entire year to have it again.

The next few days were pure bliss: carving, being held, and being treated like royalty. On the third day, when taking her daily pills, she briefly wondered if this was all in her mind, if she had some sort of psychotic break and this was her delusion of grandeur. Then, as fast as the thought came, it went because she didn't care, even if it was perfect. With less and less pumpkins to carve, Clare started to go to her bedroom more. Lying in bed and being held was so extraordinarily gratifying, she wanted it every second she could. And while it started to get . . . satisfying, it never became overtly sexual, just sensual. By the day before Halloween, the vines had wrapped around every inch of her body except her face when she laid down. They slithered between her legs, held her groin tight, but they never once tried to enter or please her. Though she knew they would if she asked. She didn't need it, though, just the presence of their prickly touch, was enough to bring her to a full-on release of pleasure unlike anything should had ever imagined could exist. About to feel that pleasure once again, she heard screaming in her front yard.

Within seconds, the vines lifted and brought her to the window. They were still working on this, but they started carrying her so that she didn't even have to walk. The day before, they took her in the backyard and wrapped her up into a giant monstrous being that rose high above her house. She sat in its chest like a small alien controller. If she moved her arm, it moved its arm. And while she had a limited view from her cockpit of fauna, she could see what it saw in her mind, it was surreal and it made her feel powerful and most importantly, safe.

"Enough!" She screamed out loud even though she didn't have to, but she needed to show the woman with the little dog in her front yard how *she* was in control. The frumpy woman and little yappy dog had somehow wandered onto her yard. The vines didn't know what to do with them, but Clare told them to let her go. They obeyed, but then a sudden sadness fell over Clare as the vines told her that the woman was going to be one of the sacrifices tonight and they wished they could protect her. Clare felt a bit of sadness and spoke to the vines in her mind. *You know your jobs, and you know they require a minimum of one sacrifice from each decade. You can only save so many. I just wish they didn't have to take a child.* As the woman rushed off, Clare thought about the ancient rules that had seeped into her soul without ever being told to her.

The costumes were meant to scare and make the darkness think the above world was already ruled by another of his ilk on the one day when they could cross over. But when the costumes became too friendly, the ancient seeds came back and picked sacrifices of real horror to show the darkness it was just as awful here. Clare stopped her thoughts—she had all year to research and find out the history of the battle she now led. For now, she just wanted to be held a bit longer, as tomorrow the fight would begin, and she would lose her loves.

As the sun set on Halloween night, Clare sat in a massive throne in her backyard, all of her pumpkin warriors kneeling before her, their heads bowed slightly. Like always, she spoke to them through her thoughts. The speech that came out echoed the hundreds of queens and kings before her, one that reiterated their purpose and the importance of defending the living from the dead. She reiterated that they could not save any of the chosen ones, that they were simply guardians to push the darkness to see what they wanted it to see, then make sure it went back to where it came from. Observe and guide in peace—nothing more. As she spoke, as the lines got more impassioned, she found herself standing. A giant staff made of vines appeared before her, which she grabbed. She felt like William Wallace giving his last speech, only to a bunch of pumpkins.

Bowing her head with the last line, she felt the hairs stand up on the back of her neck as every inch of the thousands of vines vibrated with a cheer. Seconds later in unison, her warriors reached down, pulled up the main vine attaching them to the house, and snapped it, freeing them from the nest. Seconds later, one by one, they jumped over the back fence and went on their way. Clare watched until the last one disappeared in the dusk. With a sigh, she sat back down and let the chair glide around the house to take up a spot in the front, so she could give out candy and smile and enjoy the wonders of the night, all while knowing that Curcibita—she knew his name now—would stay with her for one more night. She understood that he was her diwan and soulmate, and that he would be here by her side every October until the end of her days.

"Trick or tweet," said a little girl, no more than five years old and dressed as a zombie, holding her bag out to Clare.

"And why, my dear, are you not a princess?" Clare asked in a sing-song tone. The little girl scrunched up her face.

"Because they aren't scary."

Clare smiled and let a vine reach into the bowl, grab a big wad of candy, and drop it into her outstretched bag. The girl watched in amazement, her parents behind her obliviously looking around at the house in awe.

"Do me a favor, young lady: don't change, stay scary." The little zombie laughed, then forced down her smile and did a low guttural growl as she shuffled off, doing her best *Walking Dead* impression. Grinning and feeling good, Clare watched the little girl walk past the line of princesses and superheroes waiting for their candy. There was still hope for this night and for every Halloween.

Meet Mr. Tricks

I was fourteen when Ted Bundy was executed. I watched the coverage on the evening news with my family over a dinner of greasy pork chops, yellow rice, and a bland salad with just vinegar and vegetable oil for dressing. My father, who was a massive pile of a man, usually shoveled in his dinner, finishing his first plate before most of us finished a quarter of ours. That night, however, he kept pausing to look up at the television in the corner of the dining room, directly behind my older sister but right in my dad's view. I spent more of the time watching my father silently shake his head in disgust as they talked about Bundy's crimes than I did the television. Being young, I was confused at the emotions I had. I thought what Bundy did was exciting and amazing, it was hard for me to understand how upset and disgusted my normally stoic father was.

The next day in the bitter cold I rode my bike, slipping on patches of ice, to the local mall that was four miles away. I raced inside and went to Waldenbooks, where I usually spent my allowance, slush melting off my boots, leaving slippery footprints across the tiled mall floor. It took me a mere one minute to find two books on Ted Bundy; they were on display in the front of the store. When I bought them, the Madonna wannabe behind the counter brought up the execution and how damn happy she was that the "evil bastard" was gone, I said I couldn't agree more and gave an empathetic smile—at least I hoped it was.

I devoured the books and made notes in the margins. I read them so much, the pages ended up getting worn and torn. Keeping them under my bed in a box that had "Baseball Cards" written on it in black marker, those books were pretty much my bibles. As I got a little older, I burned them in the backyard when my parents were not home one afternoon, for I was finally understanding at the age of sixteen that my feelings and thoughts were not normal and certainly not accepted. If someone found dog-eared, heavily marked-up copies of books about serial killers hiding under my bed, well, it wouldn't go over well.

In high school and right through college, I took all the psychology classes offered and asked an immense amount of questions, but I made sure to never allude to why I loved it. Everyone just thought I wanted to help people, no one realized I was trying to diagnose myself and figure out how to blend in with regular people. In all the school classes, they shied away from talking about the "deranged" people who killed others and focused more on other common illnesses. Though the few times they came up, almost every professor liked to quote the Macdonald triad, "Well, all serial killers have had three things in common: they wet their bed into later years in their life, they had an obsession with fire, and they abused animals." It was like this was the mandatory statement from everyone who wanted to act like they actually knew a lot about killers. For a while I believed it, and since I never wet my bed, could care less about fire, and couldn't contemplate killing an animal, I thought I was safe and that something else was wrong with me. But it turns out, that one fact everyone knows about killers is wrong. Dead wrong.

By the time I started my residency as a psychologist at a local hospital's mental ward in the late '90s, I had come to accept what I was: a sociopath. The idea of killing was the most beautiful and attractive thing in the world to me. I read over four hundred books in a ten-year span about serial killers and psychology and realized I fit petty much right in with all of them. I didn't have a lot of the so-called "markers," but in my research, neither did some of the most famous ones. We aren't all abused or suffered some trauma that made us sick, our brains are simply wired differently. I won't go into the details about my own psychology here, but if you want to read that, you can get my book, *The Killer Psychologist*, which will be out six months after I'm incarcerated or after my death, whichever comes first.

Killing for me is simply a thrill, a power trip, and really a necessity. The day I killed my first victim, Mark Wallace, a twenty-three-year-old bipolar patient being held for observation, my life truly began. I walked through the halls with this sense of power and wonder like I had never felt before. I looked at every person and smiled, knowing I had the unique power to kill any one of them I wanted—it was a rush to say the least. On paper, Mark died of a suicide, I just happen to be the one who found him. He hung himself with a bedsheet, which was a tricky task in a suicide ward. There were no doors on the rooms, the walls were hard foam, the showers had no curtains or rods, and pretty much everything was made in a way so you couldn't hurt yourself. As the report stated, somehow Mark was able to take his sheet, wrap it around his neck, tie one end to the leg of the bed, and then pull as hard as he could until he collapsed. He did this within the ten minutes of his last check-in. In reality, I slipped into the room, choked the shit out of him with the sheet (he didn't fight back at all, I think he was happy to have death come, he was suicidal after all), and then walked out of the room and entered again to "find" him. No one ever suspected anything.

Why did I choose Mark? I was just simply ready to kill and figured I could get away with him as he had no family, so it cut down the chances of someone pushing for an investigation or anything. Regardless of the reasons, it was a wonderful, exhilarating rush. It was like winning the lottery and knowing that for the rest of your life, you will be free, or as people like to say, "It was like my life was black-and-white and suddenly it became Technicolor." That and many other cheesy lines were true. My life was changed forever, plain and simple.

After two years of killing patients, I got bored and didn't like the idea of being called an "Angel of Death" if I were ever caught. I was so much more than that. In my research, those kinds of killers (usually nurses) who killed scores of sick people were sick themselves. They were a different breed of serial killer. They didn't have passion, charisma, and brains. No, they typically thought they were "saving people" or doing the work of God or some other shit. I was definitely not like that; I was just honing my craft. Making sure I covered up the kills to look like suicides, overdoses, and accidents was exhausting, and I truly wanted to enjoy the kills in a much more flamboyant way. When I left in 2001, the mortality rate for patients at my facility suddenly dropped shockingly, and yet I was never suspected of a thing.

When I started my own practice in a medical building right outside the hospital I was working at, I felt free, away from the watchful eyes of other staff and higher-ups. While all I had was a tiny reception area with room for a desk and four chairs and an even smaller office to see patients in, it was heaven to me. I made my own hours, paid an overweight retired woman to work part-time as my receptionist (mostly she just did scheduling, I usually received patients alone), and saw clients all day long. It was beyond tempting to want to kill my own patients, but I was not an idiot. I merely did my work, helped them the best I could, took case studies on people I thought were interesting, and lived a normal "bachelor" life. I visited my parents once a month and they were truly proud of their "doctor" son, even though I told them over and over that I was a psychologist, not a doctor. Being a young, single "doctor," every relative and casual acquaintance tried to set me up on dates, most of which I would refuse, but here and there I would take one and be the perfect gentleman, just to keep up appearances and to create character witnesses just in case.

At night, I stalked women and planned my killings. I admit, I was obsessive and did this almost every night. I was rarely home and at times I had to get myself in check to make sure I didn't go overboard or be careless. Don't get me wrong, I was not killing nightly, I was too smart for that. I had a routine. I would find my victim, which was rather simple, I would go out to a public place—a park, mall, grocery store—and just watch people until I found one that gave me butterflies. Then I'd follow them until they went home. If they were married or lived with a lot of people, I usually backed away for the sake of ease. If they were alone or just had a roommate, then they were easier prey. Natalia was my first non-patient kill, and she was stunning.

I saw Natalia coming out of a local gym one afternoon and my jaw hit the floor: in perfect shape, wearing painted-on yoga pants and a pink sports bra, a mint-colored towel over her shoulder. Making myself wait for her was torture, but I held out for three weeks. When I knew her schedule and everything about her (thank you, social media), I pulled a Bundy and put on a cast and acted like I couldn't get a box in my car when she came out of the gym one afternoon. I parked with my trunk facing the wooded side of the parking lot and made sure I had plenty of cover. When she fell for it, I could feel Ted looking down at me and nodding with approval. The crack of the baton on her skull was so loud I thought anyone in the lot would hear her. I then tossed her in the trunk and drove off in my "kill car," a vehicle I stole four states away with plates from another car two states away that I used only when stalking. I always wore gloves and a disguise while driving it and only filled it from gas cans I filled at the station using my real car. I avoided all toll roads and as many cameras as I could when I stalked. With Natalia safely in the trunk, I drove to the storage unit I kept the car in—you guessed it, a storage unit rented under a fake name. It was hard finding one that wasn't a chain and that didn't have gates, but I found a locally owned place with only thirty units, no gates, and no cameras on the side mine was on. It was perfect.

Yes, I had my own *Dexter*-style "kill room." It was an extra-large storage unit, enough to fit four cars. The front half I'd use to store the car and other "normal" items like boxes and old furniture. If anyone walked by, that is all they saw. Right behind the car, I made a fake wall out of cardboard boxes (that had wood frames inside of them and were secured with iron rods through them and were bolted into the floor). One stack I had on a swivel, so I could lock it to the wall. I'd always open the door, back into the spot, shut the door, and lock it from the inside, then go through the secret door into the back area, which as you guessed it, was coated with plastic wrap, had a table, a chair for myself, and lots of tools and other items I could play with. When I picked the unit, I purposely chose one that backed up to the woods, there was even a small stream about twenty yards away. One night I blared loud music and acted like I was working on the car, when in reality I cut a hatch through the sheet metal in the back wall that I could escape out of if I ever needed to. While I could sneak bodies out in the car trunk to dispose of them, I could also go out this little door and wash up in the stream when needed, which ended up being a lot. With the advent of wireless cameras, it was easy to see if someone was ever coming. If they did, I'd put on my overalls and slap some grease on my hands and face, grab a tool and they'd meet "Grease Monkey Carl," restoring his old Buick. Although that had yet to occur—no one cared that I spent hours on end in this dumpy old storage facility.

That first time with Natalia . . . Christ, I can't even explain and really, it was so magical and private, I don't want to share the beauty with you. It would be like telling every fine detail of the time you first made love and came with your partner—it's private and it's mine. Let's just say she was there for several days, and we only finished our romance and fun when the news started to really focus on her disappearance. Feeling nervous, having never committed a murder that police would look into, I killed her, cut her into six pieces, placed the parts into three large plastic tubs, and dissolved as much of her as I could with sulfuric acid I bought at local hardware stores. With a "Joe's Plumbing: You Drip, We Dry" T-shirt I stole, I would visit store after store buying gallon tubs of the stuff in bulk with cash. The stuff worked like a miracle. It turned Natalia's body into enough of a slush that I could pour the vast majority of her out into the stream. As I watched the goo wash away in the moonlight, I cried. I didn't want to give her up, but I knew there would be others. I packed her bones into a small cheap suitcase, drove six hours away, and dumped them into a lake. They would dissolve in the acid, but with some tests, I found they take over ten days, making it too much of a risk to leave a bin of bones in the storage unit for that long. Though in the future, it was probably the better bet, as taking the time to ensure there was zero evidence was worth the wait.

After she was gone, I felt an emptiness and longing for another victim, but something interesting happened: I became more obsessed with how the media and world reacted to her being missing. She was young and sexy, so the media picked it up and ran with it. Her disappearance made national news on day three of her being missing, and it stayed in the spotlight for weeks as search parties set out and family and friends did countless interviews. I never thought I would ever enjoy anything more than the kill, but the media sensation it caused, *Jesus*. It was intense. Seeing the massive ripple in the world that *I* caused, *holy shit*. There were hundreds of people searching, dozens of officers looking, families devastated, and thousands upon thousands watching the case and talking about it around the water cooler. It gave me a sense of power and wonder that stroked both my fascination with psychology and my ego. It was then when I realized that causing a media stir was going to be my main priority, not just the kill.

Almost a decade went by, and I was rather satisfied with my killings—you know a lot of them, trust me. After that first one, I almost never took someone from my state. The search and closeness was too intense. I always took drives, upwards of four days each way (when you ran your own business, there was no one to wonder where you were) to get my prizes. I was clean, precise, and never suspected by anyone, but after thirty-three of these kills, I was getting bored. About half of the disappearances got major coverage, four of which went on to have *Dateline* specials and more. Though without any evidence or bodies and with them spread so far out, no one ever linked them together other than a superficial theory. All that time, I kept my same routines and used my same storage space, though I went through several cars, but otherwise it was like clockwork.

When the boredom seeped in, I started to think about what to do, how to spice it up and bring new life back into my work. That is when I came up with the idea of something grand, something that would be a headline on national news, not just the third or second story. Something so gruesome and awful that it would become the stuff of legend—books would be written about it, movies would be made based on it. Hell, Bundy has had well over a dozen movies and forty books made about him and people wear T-shirts with his face on them, and yet I've already killed more people than him—he just happened to be more famous because he was gruesome and in-your-face about his kills.

It just happened to be around Halloween-time when this boredom crept in and started to make me plan. Night after night I racked my brain trying to figure out what to do. What could top anything and everything

I'd already done? I needed to do something that would make the entire world quake, something they would make movies on and cause kids to whisper rumors and stories about . . . and then it came to me.

While watching a horror movie marathon on some cable channel, I started to become enamored with the Halloween spirit. It is the only time of the year when everyone loves horror and likes being scared, and as my brain worked, I realized it was the only time of year I could get away with things you could never normally do, like walking around covered in real blood. Muting the television right as a masked man was about to stab his umpteenth teen girl, I stared at the dark ceiling in my apartment and a plan came together, one so horrific it even made *me* get the chills.

The plan revolved around the idea of "the survivor girl." All the great horror movies had them. Look at Jamie Lee Curtis, hell, she was still the survivor girl and fought her boogeyman forty years later. They were the stuff of legend, all the horror movie killers went up against them—Jason, Leatherface, and Victor Crowley: they all had a girl who got away (once in a while a guy lived, but no one really cared about them). That was the key: let one get away. Let one see something so horrific that the world won't even believe it. Taunt her, let her build a story and myth around a monster so surreal and terrifying, it grows into an urban legend. The idea of becoming the boogeyman filled me with such joy, I giggled.

Killing a teenager was never something I wanted to do, but it was something I knew would make national attention, something that would cause the world to cringe and recoil in fear and disgust, so it was going to be necessary. Not that I cared about killing a kid, it just didn't do anything for me, so why bother? All I had to do was pick a town, then a house. It was really that simple. Of course, I would prepare methodically, but who became the victim would be a surprise, even to me. The idea of not knowing, of killing in the moment, brought a wave of nerves and excitement in me that I had never felt before, and it was intense.

Of course, like before any kill, I made sure all my affairs were in order in case I got caught or in the astronomical chance that I got killed.

Really, all I cared about were my writings. My studies of my own mind alone would change the psychology world forever—they needed to be released no matter what. I ensured they would be too. Of course they would be held in evidence, but my will is ironclad and requires them to be released with all monies going to charity to avoid the notoriety-for-profit law. While I have many more years to do research and, have fun, if anything ever happened to me, I'd become the most important psychologist ever as well as the most legendary serial killer of all time. There would classes about me in colleges, FBI recruits would study me extensively, television shows would be made, books written, and maybe I'd even end up on a T-shirt. These ideas were intoxicating, but I had an entire year to plan and wait and practice.

The town was easy enough to pick. It was an hour and a half from where I lived and the classic all-American place. The reason I decided on Haven, Massachusetts, or "Halloween Haven" as their advertising called it during the month of October, was because it was semi-famous for its Halloween festivities. They filmed a crappy made-for-TV movie there about witches and ever since then they took the theme of the season and ran with it. They had house decorating contests, dances, costume contests, sales, and even a parade every Friday leading up to the big day. The town, and more so the country, would be rocked to its core by what I planned. Again, I kept giggling with the idea and how perfect the place was. No one, and I mean *no one* would even expect what I was doing and would laugh at what they thought was fake.

The house was a random pick. All I needed was a home with bushes a bit overgrown by the door to give me some coverage when I took my victim inside. There were several candidates, but I picked one with a backyard that touched another street—that way I could park there and leave out the back, making for a clean getaway. With the town and house picked and the plan in motion, I had the last few days before Halloween to relax and enjoy the season, as well as set up an alibi in case

I needed it. Again, that was rather easy and very ironclad. Things were good and I was about to become a legend. Just an elderly couple in their eighties stood in my way, one Frank and Tammy Worthy. At 3:15 p.m. on Halloween, just before the little kids started trick-or-treating, I rang their doorbell and Tammy, in her bright pumpkin sweater and pointy orange witch hat, answered the door with a large bowl of candy and a smile on her face. I couldn't help but smile back. If only she knew she was about to become a part of my legend.

Frank's Famous Pumpkin Pie

Frank first tasted pumpkin pie in the eleventh year of his life. When his teeth first pushed their way through the soft spicy filling, his entire world slowed. Telling the story to customers, he always said with a cheesy but fun bravado, "I saw fireworks and angels and a tear fell down my cheek." Frank would then go on about how his aunt from Georgia taught him right then and there how to make the pumpkin pie and he has never changed a single ingredient since that day. While there were no angels or real fireworks, the story was true and that was how Frank recalled it. That pumpkin pie changed his entire life several times over, and it would until the day he died.

In 1966, at only twenty-three years of age, he opened up Frank's Southern Pies and Chicken in downtown Lockport next to an old-timey gas station, though back then it wasn't being nostalgic. Business was good and got better. He went from a ten-seat train car diner to a new construction restaurant that could hold fifty people. Regular business was good, but during the holidays, it was impossible to keep up; people drove hours just to get his pies. The week before Thanksgiving, he'd sell over six hundred on average. That one week could keep the place afloat for over half a year. Things chugged along and couldn't have been better.

Then, three years after opening, a beautiful young woman came in and applied to be a waitress. When he offered her a slice of pie and saw the happiness on her face as she bit into it, Frank fell in love. A year later they started to date, and in '71, they got married. As a wedding present, he officially changed the name to Frank and Tammy's Southern Pies and Chicken. She was against the name change, insisting that the restaurant and food were his creations, but he did it anyway, saying that she was the face the customers wanted to see when they came in, while he was just the man behind the food. Besides, there was no more "I" anymore, they were an "us."

Business grew year after year as customers became loyal and brought in their friends and family, it was a domino effect that didn't stop. There were even offers to open franchises and one persistent offer from a frozen food company to mass-produce his pumpkin pie and sell it nationwide, but Frank could not fathom the idea of not being able to make the pies himself. Being able to check and make sure they were all just right was too important to him. The ones he sold to the local stores were just fine, he made them after all, but the idea of machines making them, no way. And so Frank and Tammy turned down the offers and just kept their booming business to themselves, slowly socking away money so one day they could retire and have their future children take over. It was the American dream, but dreams only last until you wake up.

In the late '70s, they found out they could not have children—that was their first blow, and it was a hard one. One night after closing up and sending all the staff home, Frank sat in a booth and looked around, thinking of all the good times—the food served, the parties thrown, and the friends made in that room—and he realized that one day, when he and Tammy died, it would all end. There would be no children to take it over, no grandkids to spoil with giant dripping ice cream sundaes at the counter. He sobbed and sobbed as Tammy held his head, but he vowed it would be the only time he would dwell on that pain, and he never did again . . . on the outside, at least. On the inside, a piece of him died. For a few years they toiled with adoption, but their hearts were too broken, and they pushed it off until one day they no longer brought it up. Instead, they focused on the business and worked seven days a week, hardly taking time off.

The years flew by, then on Halloween in 1984, a middle-aged woman wearing a plastic bonnet came in from the rain. The entire night was filled with bummed-out children eating meals with their families, their masks drooping around their necks, paint streaking all over their sad faces. The rain was awful and no one was trick-or-treating, but Frank did his best to make everyone welcome. He had Tammy run to the store and gave out half-gallon-sized bags of candy to every kid who came in, their faces were shocked at the sizes and it made him feel good, but in his gut, it hurt looking at those kids, as he wondered what a child of his own would have looked like. While pumpkin pie was a staple at the restaurant year-round, he always changed the pastry design on the top for each holiday. When there wasn't a holiday, the top would sit bare like a normal pumpkin pie, but during holidays he would make elaborate crust designs. An egg or rabbit would sit on the burnt orange goodness for Easter, a dyed green shamrock for Saint Patrick's Day (while everyone teased him for making pumpkin pie that day, people still ordered it), decorated pine trees for Christmas, turkeys for Thanksgiving, and of course on Halloween, he made jack-o'-lanterns. That night in '84, he gave a slice free to everyone who came in, because everyone deserved a treat after all, but it was that kindness that destroyed his life.

The lady, who was prissy and alone, took off her plastic bonnet, placed it next to her on the table, and snapped her fingers to get a coffee. She ordered a turkey club sandwich and ate it while reading some cheap paperback novel that had a cross on the cover. Keeping to herself, she huffed and made a face every time a child was loud. When Tammy cleared her plate, she brought over a slice of pumpkin pie and placed it down in front of the woman with a large smile and said, "Happy Halloween, ma'am, it's on the house."

The woman scrunched up her face and replied, "I'm not paying for that." Tammy smiled and reiterated that it was free because of the holiday and the rain and all.

"It's a sick holiday and it's getting worse every year. Damn kids dressing up in disgusting costumes, women dressing up like sluts. It should be outlawed."

Tammy, being her ever-pleasant self, smiled and replied, "Well, pie makes everything better. You enjoy now." She then turned and walked away.

Tammy went behind the counter and told Frank, who was cleaning the griddle, what the woman said. Frank frowned and kept an eye on the irritable old woman. He was not surprised to see the cantankerous lady poke at the slice like it were an alien autopsy, disgust on her face. When the woman took a mouthful, he waited for the look of happiness that typically followed or what he called the "*oh* pumpkin face." Instead, the woman scowled, swallowed hard, then sighed before quickly taking two more bites, each time with a grimace. At this point, Frank realized he was no longer cleaning, he was just staring at the woman with fascination. The woman then dug her hand into her purse and grabbed something small—at the time Frank assumed it was a mint or aspirin. The woman turned her head, shoved it in her mouth, and swallowed hard. This would later become a major part of the trial.

What did she swallow? According to the plaintiff, it was just an antacid.

A few seconds later, the woman started coughing, harder and harder. Tammy brought over a water, but the woman knocked it out of her hand, shattering the glass. Then, in a dramatic flair, the woman stood up and waved her arms, knocking over stools until she finally dropped to the ground.

An ambulance came and took her away. Frank was so concerned that he went to the hospital that night, but they refused to tell him anything. Two days later they were served papers, the woman was suing for giving her an allergic reaction with their "free" pie. The suit claimed that she did not "want or ask" for the pie, but that she felt "obligated" to eat it as the owners stared at her, making her feel pressured. Frank thought it would be over quickly and that all he had to do was apologize, but the woman was nasty and filed another suit of "harassment" for him showing up at her house when all he did was bring her flowers and a nice card. The two-year ordeal was the worst time of Frank and Tammy's life, and it almost ruined their marriage. In the end, while they stayed together, it destroyed everything else.

The woman won the lawsuit, flabbergasting both of them and even the lawyers. Between the legal fees and the settlement, they had to sell the restaurant, their dream house they custom-built, and pretty much everything that mattered to them. They ended up filing for bankruptcy and had to downgrade to a small ranch home in Haven. Tammy took a regular job as a waitress and Frank worked in a bakery where he was not allowed to cook his own items. It was crushing, humiliating, and deflating.

The hardest part of it all was that when Frank sold the restaurant, he had to sell away his pie recipe and sign a contract stating he would *never* share how it is made with anyone, nor could he ever make and sell it again. To Frank, it was like losing a child. The years that followed were the hardest. Being just an employee, barely making it by on the checks they made, living in a small house, and sharing one car—it was a challenge. They went from having the American dream they fought so hard for to hating their jobs that gave them just enough to live. But as the years went on, the restaurant years started to seem like a past life, one that wasn't even theirs. Their new life wasn't much, but they managed and did their best to not be bitter every day. Although things got bad when Frank found out that the woman sued someone every five years like clockwork. He knew all along it was a scam, but by then there was nothing he could do.

By the mid-'90s, Frank was all right with his middle-class baking job, and in fact, he enjoyed not having the stress of the restaurant. Sitting home and watching television and having nothing to do on the weekends was nice at times—at least, that is what he told himself.

After a few years of their *new* normal, Tammy tried to build up the courage to ask Frank to make her a pie, as he hadn't baked a single thing at home in a decade. Her nerves were intense as one Sunday morning, while sipping coffee and watching a sappy morning news program on CBS, Tammy took a big swig of her coffee and said, "Frank, would you make us a pie for dessert tonight?"

Frank paused, swallowed hard and set down his coffee mug. A full ten seconds of silence droned on as Frank looked across the room, a blank gaze on his face.

"What type?" He finally asked, almost in a whisper. The moment felt like a Hallmark made-for-TV movie scene, with her saying "blueberry" and then the two talking and laughing about the time Frank accidently dyed his hands blue mixing a batch of blueberry filling without gloves. It was a nice moment that Tammy would fondly recall as a turning point.

That night he made a pie, and it was wonderful. The two smiled and sighed as if it was a massive release being able to eat a pie in their house again. From that day on, Frank made a pie every other week, every flavor *except* pumpkin. A few years later, they discussed selling pies on their own again, but at this point they were almost sixty and the thought seemed too big, so they let it go and just made pies for themselves and the few friends they had. It was nice having pie back in their lives, but it didn't change much.

Of course, the one holiday they both tried to ignore was Halloween, but it was impossible when your doorbell rang every ten seconds—it was just their luck to move to a town where the main economy revolved around the day, though it wasn't that way when the moved in, a year before that damn kids' movie about the witches was filmed there. Two years after they started to eat pie again, without saying a word to Frank, Tammy went and bought bags of candy, decorations, three pumpkins, and a festive shirt for the big day. Before Frank came home one afternoon, she put out the pumpkins, set up the decorations, and then patiently waited in the living room. She watched *Ellen*, but she was too nervous to really pay attention to any of it. When Frank came in, her heart started slamming. Before he could even enter, he had to see the decorations on the porch, so she knew there would be no waiting for a response.

"Place looks nice, you buy candy this year?" Frank asked so nonchalantly that it made Tammy's heart melt. A quarter of a century later, they were finally able to let everything go, but cooking pumpkin pie was probably never going to happen again, and that was just fine with her.

And yet, a few more years later, Tammy was coming home from her scratch club, in a bad mood because they only won thirty dollars—

stupid Halloween-themed scratchers, the holiday ones never win—and almost fainted when she saw Frank in the kitchen with several gutted pumpkins on the counter. When he saw her shocked face, he just smiled, a warm and happy smile that made her want to hug him, and she did just that. When she let go, she wanted to address the situation but was scared of sullying the moment. It was Frank who chose to speak.

"I missed it, Tam, I missed it so damn much, but last time I made it . . ." Tammy looked up at him and wiped a tear from the corner of his eye. He didn't have to say anything more.

"I can't wait to taste it," Tammy said, unable to smile any bigger. They laughed and hugged a bit more, then Frank went about making the pie that once had made him famous and was now in thirty percent of all grocery store freezers across the country in a bastardized form, his name and old logo emblazoned on the box in red lettering. Tammy watched Frank spin around the kitchen and felt a happiness she hadn't felt in decades.

When the gorgeous pies were cooling on the table between them on the kitchen table (he apparently made one for Martha as well), both of them staring at them as if they were newborn children, the doorbell rang. They looked at the clock—it was just about 3:15. Tammy made a comment about how early the trick-or-treaters were that year before slapping on her witch hat and grabbing a bowl of candy.

Swinging open the door, she was expecting to see a few toddlers in some cute store-bought outfits—they always came out the earliest—but instead there was a small round man with a bad toupee holding a sheet of paper, a backpack slung over one shoulder. The man was preoccupied with kicking off a vine that seemed to be attached to his leg. Tammy, still holding her bowl, frowned a bit but then smiled and made a joke about not knowing what his costume was. They both laughed as the man finally got the greenery off his leg, then she asked what she could do for him. The sight of his lips curling back to show a sickly and menacing smile made her stomach drop.

"Man, those vines are grabby. Anyway, I'm part of the census, ma'am, I just need to ask you a few questions." While the man's story sounded fake, slamming the door in his face, even if it was a scam, was not in Tammy's DNA. Besides, Frank was here, he'd step in if the man got too pushy. Regardless of thinking she was at ease, she could feel her fear creeping into her facial expression. The man seemed to notice her sudden change in demeanor, as he snuck a quick look behind him around at the street. Tammy looked too. She saw a car drive by with a boy covered in bandages. Her heart sank a bit, she heard a rumor that Jalen would be coming back today, but she didn't believe it. Then the anger at that damn woman came bubbling up again—it was all she could think about since the day she heard the awful news. How could a woman treat a boy like a curse when she had no clue how lucky she was? Just as the car turned the corner, the man lunged.

Tammy was on the floor in a flash, her hat flown off her, the candy strewn about the floor. The door slammed shut as she looked at the Smarties and Warheads on the yellowing linoleum that Frank promised to replace next year. Her brain was not processing what was happening. Nothing like this had ever happened to her—she had never been attacked physically, and it was scaring the shit out of her. As she started to get up, she saw Frank run into view and point a kitchen knife at the stranger, but the man was laughing because he had something worse: one of those tasers that shot out the long tentacles of electrifying pain.

As the tiny metal strings went into Frank's chest, Tammy thought of his pacemaker, and she screamed. Like a three-hundred-pound pile of bricks falling off a truck, Frank was suddenly next to her, his eyes rolling in the back of his head. Without thinking, she grabbed the wires and yanked them out—the tiny harpoons were decorated in blood and this scared her more. Just as she was about to let go of them, the man pulled the trigger again, sending God knows how many volts into her arm, knocking her out as well.

Tammy woke first, she had gotten less of a shock and didn't have the heart issues, after all. It took a second for her to realize she was on the couch, her hands and feet tied, mouth gagged. As she caught her breath, slowing her breathing through just her nostrils, she realized she had wet herself, but she also didn't care, she needed to know if Frank was all right. Through blurry eyes, she saw Frank next to her—he was out of it but still breathing. *The man. Where was the man?* Tammy scanned the room and saw that the man was in the kitchen . . . cutting himself a slice of the *pumpkin pie.* She had wet herself, she was tied up and sore, a man had attacked them and come into their home, and yet seeing that man touch that goddamn pie she had waited decades to taste again set her off more than all of those things combined. She screamed through her gag and thrashed like never before. It was enough to wake up Frank, who was also gagged. Seeing Tammy, he choked back a cry. She nodded for him to look at the man, and they both screamed through their gags.

Yelling and thrashing, however, was exhausting when you were overweight, tied up, and gagged, let alone when you were in your eighties. After a few seconds, they both settled down and breathed heavily as the man walked over with a plate, fork, and a beautiful slice of pie on top of it.

"Do you have whipped cream?" The man asked as if he were over for a casual dinner. Tammy watched as Frank nodded, then she saw the man's face light up with delight before he raced over to the kitchen and went in the fridge. Seconds later he was back with a can of whipped cream. He squirted out the most perfect dollop and smiled even more.

"My mother used to make pumpkin pie, but it was awful. I fell in love with it in my twenties, though, I was shopping and found a frozen one at the store and bought it after a celebratory night. "Frank's Famous Pies," that was the name, and wow did it change my life. I was hooked, I bought it every few weeks and ate a slice every day. You ever eat that brand? It's amazing, harder to find nowadays, though, which is a shame. This . . . this, though, looks like the real deal."

Frank's eyes were dead cold as he stared at the man taking the fork and stabbing off a small piece. The man had removed his toupee and was bald as could be, and his face also looked slightly different, as if he had changed his nose. Watching the man put a bite in his mouth, Tammy cried out. Frank and Tammy looked at each other as if their own child had just been eaten; they both felt the pain of that bite. The pie that had made them, then destroyed them, and was about to heal them one last time, was now, being stolen once again.

The man chewed once, closed his eyes, chewed some more, and moaned. He slowly swallowed, smiled, and then opened his eyes.

"Oh my God, it's still warm. Christ! That was the greatest bite of dessert I have ever had, hands down. This is like a spiritual experience. Wow, did I pick the right house. Man, it's so much like the Frank's one I used to get, it has that certain flavor I never tasted in other pies, but this is even better." The man set down the plate on the coffee table, got up, and took the gags off both of them with quick excitement.

"Don't be stupid," the man warned. "It's Halloween, you can scream all you want and no one will think anything of it. Now, which one of you made this? You *have* to give me the recipe!" The man looked back and forth at them, again acting as though he were a kind guest at their dinner party.

"What do you want?" Frank asked, slowly and calmly.

"The recipe," the man said with glee. Frank closed his eyes and tried to stay calm.

"You came here because you knew I created Frank's Famous Pies? Is that what this is?"

The man looked confused. He looked down at the pie, then back to Frank.

"No freaking way. It's impossible, you aren't Frank from Frank's Famous Pies . . . are you?" With excitement, the man got up and ran around the room, looking at the pictures on the wall. While they had put away almost all the memorabilia from the old days, they always kept up the picture of them under the restaurant sign—it was where they met, after all. When the man saw this, he started to get giddy.

"Holy shit! What are the odds of this?! I did so much research on you guys, and I never came across that." Picking up the plate again, the man shoveled another bite into his mouth. "Crap, I'm sad I'm going to kill you now. You have given me such pleasure over the years." The man frowned and looked around the house. "Wow, you must have gotten screwed on the rights to your pies."

Frank let out a big breath hearing the man say this. "Listen, we are old, we don't have kids, we don't have family, we are all we've got. So, either take all the shit you want and leave, and we won't call the cops, or kill us both quickly." This made Tammy gasp. Frank turned and looked at her. "I can't stand the thought of you dying first, let's just die together. I'm tired," Frank said with a sigh.

"Frank . . ." Tammy replied with a soft cry.

"Tammy, you know how much I love that damn movie you make me watch every year—they both die in the end at the same time. I can't imagine a happier ending. My worst fear has always been living without you."

Tammy and Frank looked at each other, whispered that they loved one another, and then leaned over for a quick and awkward kiss. The man burst out cheering and clapping.

"This is a first for me! Seriously, I'm so used to everyone fighting so hard. I'm truly impressed." The man looked around and took a few more bites of the pie.

"You know what, you guys are sweet, if you hadn't seen my face, I'd let you go, but you have, so how about one last request?" After the man said this, Frank looked at Tammy. She smiled and nodded.

"Could we just each have a slice of pie?" Frank asked in a whisper. "Our entire world revolved around it." The man gave them a big grin and ran into the kitchen. He cut two slices, put them on plates, ran back over, and squirted dollops of whipped cream on top. The pieces were beautiful. They all looked at them in awe as the man set them on the coffee table.

"The answer is 'no, I'm not going to untie you guys to eat it,' I'm not that stupid. I'll give you a few bites each, then we all say our goodbyes, all right? And seriously, this is unprecedented for me, so don't try anything."

Frank nodded; Tammy just started to cry at the man's words. Then, just as he said, one by one the man forked a perfect-sized bite, making sure each forkful had some cream, and fed them. Having not tasted the magical concoction in years, they both smiled and cried, and for a beautiful moment, they forgot they were tied up by a madman and about to die.

On the fourth mouthful, it happened. Instead of gently putting the fork into Frank's mouth, the man rammed it in, forcing the prongs into the back of Frank's throat. The pointy metal tips, covered in the soft filling, pierced through Frank's uvula and stabbed into the back wall of his throat. Not only did the fork start to choke him, but the blood pouring out made it even harder to breathe. The chunk of pie, sitting on the back of his tongue, however, still tasted wonderful.

Tammy wasn't stupid enough to open her mouth for her own pie, yet she did open it to scream, which was cut off quickly as her own fork was jammed right into the wrinkled flesh of her neck, two prongs hitting an artery. The pain they both felt was brilliant and terrifying, yet they both did not fight it, they simple looked each other in their eyes as they lost blood and gasped for air. Frank let go first, dropping face-first on top of the coffee table, his forehead an inch from his famous pie. Tammy went seconds later, though she opted to fall back into the couch as she slowly bled out. As Frank died, he spoke in his mind, hoping Tammy could somehow psychically hear him: *I only loved two things in this world, my pies and you. At least I got to leave with both of them.*

The man picked up his plate and ate the delicious pie as he watched them both slowly die. When they finally faded from existence, he smiled warmly, then reached over and grabbed Tammy's plate.

"You aren't going to eat this, are you?" He said, snickering to himself. Taking a bite, he rolled his eyes back and moaned in pleasure.

"You make a hell of a pie, Frank." Just then, the doorbell rang. The man smiled giddily.

"Well, this had been lovely, but if you will excuse me, I have some work to do." Reaching into his bag, the man pulled out an apron, put it over his head, then set the wig back on his head and set a fake nose on his face before grabbing a large knife and striding to the door, humming a soft tune of excitement.

Below the Window

Its slumber was disturbed by a slight rocking of the Earth. Every time it felt that slow, gentle nudge, its limbs started to ache and unlock. Having not moved since it was last called upon, it always took some stretching and unthawing of joints before it could move freely. Though in the complete darkness, it never ventured farther than two steps to the right or left—there wasn't much space where it was, but it was all it ever knew. Darkness, sleeping, and waiting. Awake, it knew what would come next: the sound. It waited stoically, without thoughts, as it was incapable of them, it was only able to take orders and run on instinct. *Climb out, see, report, kill, return.* Century after century, it did exactly what it was designed to do, nothing more. It was simply the eyes of something much more advanced than itself, a tool used to keep the balance.

Now. It wasn't so much a whisper it heard—it didn't know words, after all—it was more of an instinct of exactly when it should go. With the time starting, it began to dig and dig. It didn't understand time, nor did it feel exhaustion or need breaks for food or water, so the exactly thirty days it took to make its way to the surface felt like nothing to the beast. Just before it reached the surface, it was always ordered to stop inches before breaking through. There it would sit stoically until the sunset on the 31st, then it would climb out and stretch once more before starting its tasks. While it didn't have thoughts or feelings, when it was above the ground, the cool breeze on its shape would always make it shudder and howl before starting its work.

Four of Clare's warriors, standing over ten feet tall, were positioned around the all-American backyard, watching the ground as it stirred slowly. Unlike the thing about to rise, these creatures had a consciousness, thoughts, and feelings. They understood their job and the severity of it. They knew that they had to make the thing oozing through the dirt think that the earth was infected by creatures like them. When it was fully out, they could only stalk and watch it, monitor its activities, and push it to see the planned deaths, but they could not touch it until the last of the sacrifices had died, all eight of them. When the last heart stopped beating, it was time for them to make sure the thing went back into the earth, where it could slumber until the next time it came to check on the status of the surface world.

Even though these warriors were created each year with freshly carved pumpkins from the sacred seeds, and while they had different carved faces each year by whoever their chosen queen was, they were the same spirits they were when they volunteered thousands of years ago. Though when they did so, they did not fully understand the definition of eternity, but not one of them regretted being the warriors who kept the dark from taking over the world. It was a duty and honor that saved their tribe; they would all do it again without hesitation. It was the most important task ever done, and they would keep on doing it for eternity, or until something worse happened.

Martin rubbed his eyes, looked, and then rubbed again. Shaking his head, he stepped over to the sink, turned on the cold water, splashed his face four times, then dried it off and looked again. Walking over to the door, he snapped the light switch off and walked back to the window, and with his right hand—the one he just obsessed over for having a liver spot on it—he wiped the steam off the glass and looked once more. Sure enough, they were still there. Four gigantic vine monsters with jack-o'-lantern heads glowing softly in the darkness were standing in a semi-circle in his backyard. At first, he thought it was a prank, that someone had bought those big-box store decorations and put them in his yard. The street gave him enough flack about his "lackluster display," so maybe it was them trying to spice it up. Only these were in the backyard, and they were, moving.

Animatronics, they had to be some sort of crazy new robotics run by AI—that crap was going to take over the world soon, so that was what it had to be. The window kept fogging up, so he shuffled out of the bathroom just as the doorbell rang. It had rung every one to two minutes for the past three hours. Answering it was not his thing. He hated the awkward chitchat and having to fake excitement over cheap, crappy store-bought costumes, so he made his loser son, Rick, who pathetically still lived in the basement at twenty-seven, answer the door and give out the absolute cheapest candy he could find. Rushing into his own bedroom, he kept the lights off and looked out the window—it was much clearer and sure enough, there were the four animatronic pumpkin monsters wandering around the yard.

Part of him wanted to rush down there and unplug the damn things. If they were using his power, he'd make whoever did it pay his electric bill that month—prices had gone through the roof recently and he was not giving free power to anyone. But something in his gut stopped him from going down, something that told him they might *not* be robotics. With a deep breath, he quickly got dressed in the dark on autopilot, sneaking looks out the window the entire time. The things stayed staring at the dirt the entire time. *The dirt.* Realizing they were looking down, he cupped his hands around the glass to take off the glare and stared down at the ground, trying to see what was there. *It was moving.* The ground was *moving*. There was a flicker of anger about his lawn getting ruined, but then his heart sank—no one cared about him that much to do an over-the-board prank like that.

The door kept ringing. He could hear the faint "trick-or-treat" being giggled by kids over and over again as he kept his face glued to the window. Part of him made a mental note to have Rick clean the upstairs windows tomorrow as they were going to be covered in fingerprints, but the rest of his brain focused on the dirt that was bubbling up through the grass. He had never seen dirt move that way. It was as if there were a giant air tube beneath the ground shooting up bubbles that pushed their way through the soil. It looked almost liquid, and it made no sense. Gobs of dirt came up through the lawn—grass that he paid damn too much to have mowed and fertilized every year—all while the monsters watched. He couldn't tell if they were summoning the thing that was coming up or if they were just watching as he was.

After six more doorbell rings, the dirt bubbles stopped and a . . . *thing* started to emerge from the ground. It was vaguely reminiscent of a giant bear, but it was also shapeless, almost like an aqueous substance. The shape was darker than black, it was such an intense density of dark that Martin had no clue what to even call it. If it wasn't for all of the light pollution caused by the massive Halloween displays, he didn't think he would be able to see the morphing shape as it emerged. As it got bigger, he saw the monsters around it tense up, as if they were ready for battle. He found himself doing the same. He got stiffer and felt his heart race more as the thing took the shape of a . . . what exactly, he couldn't tell. It wasn't a blob, but it certainly wasn't a human shape either, especially since it was so massive. Though it had vague limbs and while it didn't have any defining features, the shimmering blob was the most horrific thing he had ever seen.

Martin had no clue how long he was standing there, but it suddenly occurred to him to grab his phone and to record whatever the hell was happening in his yard, not for fame or attention, but simply to show someone he was not crazy when his mind snapped. Grabbing the phone off the charger, a sense of understanding washed over him. He knew he would never be the same after tonight, that his mind would slowly melt in his brain, as if seeing the coal-black thing was a forbidden poison akin to Medusa's snakes. Yet knowing this, he still turned on his phone. The light of the screen was all the way up, instantly sending off a flare of light reflecting in the window. Two of the pumpkin heads snapped to look up at the window as he did his best to lower the light, but before he could swipe it down, the window shattered.

A vine wrapped around his hand, grabbed the phone, and crushed it like it were a baby bird egg. His phone almost disintegrated. Feeling his heart start to quiver and skip beats as it raced, a new worry came into his mind: a heart attack. Martin always knew he would have a massive one someday, he just didn't know how or when. But if it didn't happen now, he'd live to be a hundred. Another vine shot through the window and grabbed his other hand. Both vines started to slither down his body like playful snakes, tying him up like an old-time damsel in distress who was about to be left on the tracks. The things lifted him off the soft plush carpet that he always enjoyed on his bare feet. Pain shot through his chest.

It had been over twenty years since Martin had been to a theme park and rode a lying-down roller coaster. He hated the feeling of being zipped around above the ground so much, he never took Rick back to a theme park again, not even when he begged him and begged him. "It wasn't worth the money," he told him. And now, all those years later, he was lying on his stomach and flying out of his own window, heading right towards the ground at a rapid speed. If only Rick could see him now!

Just as his face was about to smash into the ground, he stopped moving, hanging upside down. It only took a second for the blood to start rushing to his head. Sucking in air, he forgot he had the powerful tool of screaming, Rick was just inside, he would certainly hear him yelling. Though he wasn't sure what that imbecile would be able to do. Opening his mouth, he instantly knew what a pumpkin vine tasted like: bitter. A vine found its way into his mouth and around his head, stopping him from making anything more than a gurgled, grunting sound.

Trying to calm down and assess the situation, he looked around and saw a jack-o'-lantern looking at him. It slowly raised a viny finger to his face, giving him a classic "*shhhhh*" look. Martin nodded, then looked at the black beast which had finally made its way out. The constant fluctuating made it hard to figure out where to look, so he just stared at one spot that resembled a pointy bone sticking out. That is when it, *roared?* The sound was unexplainable, it was like every living creature on Earth all screamed at once, but it was muted through a filter that made it muddy and jumbled. The cry lasted a solid twenty seconds, then the thing stopped moving altogether and seemed to settle into our world, forming a head-like appendage. It was a mess of a blob, but it morphed its mass in such a way that Martin could tell that was what it would use to lead itself through the town. What did it want? Was it going to eat everyone in Haven? Martin started to panic, but then he realized he didn't care—he didn't like anyone from town, hell, he hardly liked his own son. It was through this distraction that he realized his chest was not hurting anymore, in fact, it felt fine. If he were capable, he would have laughed in that moment, but the vines were still squirming around in his mouth like tiny prickly tongues trying to French-kiss him. *He was going to live forever!*

The shape started to move, lumbering slowly as if figuring out how to use legs for the first time, even though it didn't have any. It headed slowly toward the back fence, but instead of jumping or climbing it, the shape simply just pushed itself through the slats. It reminded Martin of the titular creature from the movie *The Blob*, only this thing was more solid. When half of it was gone, the vine monster that was holding him lifted him up and carried him to the picnic table that hadn't been used in ten years. Setting him down on top of the wooden surface, the vines started to unwind and remove themselves.

"What the fuck, Dad!" Rick screamed from the upstairs window, breaking up the peaceful moment of extraction. The four vine monsters snapped up their pumpkin heads and looked at a bewildered Rick. They readied their vines like weapons, then looked toward the shape that suddenly pulled back from the fence and stood tall, doubling in size. It now towered several feet over the vine creatures. Martin thought about screaming, to tell his son to run, but if he did that, the thing would focus on him. He couldn't risk that. Instead, he stayed still, lying on his back as if he were already dead.

"Dad! Are you all right? What do I do?" Rick hollered, his eyes moving frantically between the vine monsters and the growing blob.

Martin gritted his teeth and shook his head—he couldn't believe his son's stupidity. Daring a look, he turned to the black mass, which was slowly gliding toward the window, moving right past him. Martin was confused at why the vine things didn't try to stop it—they were acting almost like zookeepers keeping their distance from a dangerous animal while letting the creature do what it would normally do. Slowly moving his head back to the window, Martin saw his son still standing there like the idiot he was. The mountain of a black stain was now right in front of the window, its vacillating head-like thing reaching out towards Rick, who was starting to cry. Martin could do something, he could save his boy—hell, he even thought about it—but in the end, he did nothing.

Rick's mouth dropped open in terror, but then he seemed to gather himself and nodded, bending over and grabbing two large shards of glass. Martin watched, confused and inquisitive. Then, in horror, he saw his son slam the pieces of glass into his eyes, then pull them out. Even from this far away in the dark, he could see that they were covered in bloody chunks of viscera and white ooze. Martin turned and threw up instantly, while out of the corner of his eye, he saw his son slam the glass back into his face over and over and over. Trying to catch his breath, he heard glass break, followed by a whooshing sound and then a slam as his son's body hit the pavers of the patio that he wanted to replace next year. For a split second, he wondered how hard it was to get blood out of concrete, but then he remembered the mass was only ten feet from him. He had to be silent, especially since the vine monsters did not seem to want to protect him anymore as none of them were close and no vines were on him.

In a daze, Martin sat up, wiped the vomit from his mouth with his forearm, and stared at the black thing that was once again morphing back down to its original size. Once there, it turned towards him. The site of it made the pain in his chest come back with a vengeance. The head formed again and seemed to examine him. Then he heard a laugh in his head, only it wasn't like a traditional laugh, it was like a thousand souls in pain all mocking him. As the thing cackled and got closer, he felt his chest clench and tighten and let go, then clench and tighten again. His arms went numb and his vision blurred. Reaching out to the vine things, he saw them shake their heads no and recede. Then, like a wet paper bag popping, his heart exploded in his chest.

Dropping back onto the picnic table, the laughing faded as the thing started to move away, the vine creatures following in its wake. As everything went black, he felt a vine caress his cheek and heard a whisper in his head. *There has to be eight. Be proud that you are one of the chosen.*

Sloshing through the last dying remnants of his consciousness, Martin understood the words were meant to comfort him, but all he could think was: *Fuck you.*

The Halloween It Happened

The sun was setting; an uneventful, boring sunset, as Molly took Chet from house to house. His pillowcase was getting full of candy and her feet were getting tired. Being a nurse, she had worked a twelve-hour shift before starting off on this night of trick-or-treating. Being a single mom, she had to do what she had to do.

"Only a few more houses, Chet, then we have to go back before it gets too dark and cold, all right?" Molly sighed.

"Mom! Don't call me Chet!"

"Sorry, I mean . . . Captain Flame!" Looking down at her son, she could tell he was smiling behind the plastic mask. At first, she was upset to dress him up in a store-bought costume—*her* mother always custom-made a costume for trick-or-treating, but after realizing how easy it was to just take something off the rack and have Chet jump into it, she was fine with the lazy decision.

Being rather early, there weren't too many people on the streets yet, only other groups like her: moms with the really young kids. Though the houses were scrambling to decorate to the tee, she always got a kick out of how the town turned into a mecca for the holiday, all because of that silly movie that had been filmed in Haven years ago. Though it was "silly," she loved that film dearly and watched it every year because it was her one claim to fame. They had wanted locals to play trick-or-treaters, even though it was March when they filmed. Her mother signed her up and before she knew it, she was on the set of a real movie, watching her crush, James Kinkade, ham it up with a group of other teen actors. Several times she had to be told by some producer to stop looking at James and do what she was supposed to, but even when she skipped down the street with her Little Red Riding Hood costume on, she still watched James Kinkade out of the corner of her eye. One particular take, he ad-libbed as she passed and said, "Hey Red, you could blow my house down any day!" Molly giggled but kept walking. She waited a year to see if that line made it into the movie, but it didn't. In the final version, you see her for only three seconds, and sadly only from the back. It was her fifteen milliseconds of fame, but the experience always made her smile and wonder what life would have been like if she had been brave enough to pursue acting.

With her feet screaming, she chased behind Chet and looked at her watch. Chet himself was only four. His bedtime was 8:00 p.m. and it was already almost 7:30, which meant with all the candy he would eat at home, he would not be going to bed on time. She needed her own sleep, so she was going to have to bribe him with the offer of a few extra pieces tomorrow to make him go to bed quicker.

"Mom, that lady gave me Reese's Cups!"

"Your favorite! Awesome!" Molly answered on autopilot as they walked away from the house and headed for the next one, which had a creepy-looking scarecrow holding a bowl of candy on its lap. There looked to be fake blood everywhere.

"Let's skip that one bud, it looks too scary."

"But Ma! I can see from here she has full-sized candy bars! And I'm not scared, I'm a superhero!" Chet said in a voice that was so cute, it made her smile.

"Fine, but I'll grab it, stay on the sidewalk." She could tell he was pouting, but the last thing she wanted was for that scarecrow to jump up and scare Chet, giving him nightmares for weeks. The freaking makeup on the guy across the street had been terrifying enough—thankfully, she had seen it from the road and ushered Chet past the house.

No one else was around when she walked up to the scarecrow. It looked a bit too real, and it was also an odd choice having a muffin head. She just knew it was going to be one of those jump-scare animatronics, so she grabbed a candy bar, turned, and ran all in the same movement, but nothing happened. Looking back, she shrugged her shoulders and handed the full-sized Hershey's bar to Chet, who looked at it like it was a gold bar. Down the street and around the corner they went, accumulating candy at house after house.

"Last house, buddy." Molly sounded a bit sad herself that the night was almost over, but she was thankful that Chet didn't fight back this time—he must have been getting tired himself. The last house had some rather high bushes by the front door, but other than that, it looked just like any of the other houses, fully decked out with the porch light on, which meant it was fair game.

"All right, Captain Flame, are you ready to go get that last piece of precious candy?!"

Chet nodded and marched up to the door with his faux heroic walk.

The routine was for Molly to push the doorbell so Chet could do a good superhero pose while waiting for the door to open. Using her pudgy finger, Molly jabbed the glowing orange circle. The same instant that the bell chimed inside, the button sent a shock up Molly's arm. She let out a yelp, scaring Chet. It frightened her more than it hurt, but she'd still have to make a point of telling the homeowner about it: it could be dangerous, especially for the little kids.

With Chet in position and Molly rubbing her finger, the door opened to reveal a small round man with odd-looking hair, glasses, and a sweater vest on. He had one of the most pleasant smiles on his face, a smile that Molly rarely saw in her line of work.

"Trick or treat!" Chet said on cue with his best deep voice impersonation, which sounded more like a chipmunk losing his voice.

"Wow! Captain Flame! I love your comic book. And look at that! You're covered in flames." The man reached out and touched one of the cloth flames on Chet's shoulder, then quickly brought it back with a yelp, pretending it was hot. They all giggled. Molly thought about how this man must be a good father while she tried to keep thoughts of Chet's dad out of her mind, *the bastard*.

"Well, a superhero gets to pick whatever candy he wants!" The man said as he produced a bowl filled with an assortment of candies. Chet immediately dug his hand in and searched for another Reese's. As if he had a Reese's magnet in his hand, he found one instantly.

"Thank you, mister," Chet chirped, forgetting to use his deep hero voice. The man smiled and nodded back as he placed his hand on the door to close it.

"Oh, sir!" Molly said, "I should tell you: when I ran the bell, I got an awful shock. You might want to cover it up with tape or something so no kids get hurt tonight."

The man's face scrunched up with concern. "I'm so sorry, I had no clue." He leaned out of the door to look at the bell and the bowl of candy slipped from his hand, dumping dozens of sugary delights everywhere.

"Oh, darn it!" The man cried, looking down at the candy. Chet instantly started to pick them up for him.

"I'm sorry," Molly chirped, as if it were her fault, then bent down to help. With both of her hands full of candy and her head facing downward, it happened. The man, out of nowhere, grabbed Chet's tiny body and threw him into the house like an old duffel bag. Molly's motherly instincts didn't hesitate: she rushed after him. She ran right past the man to Chet, who was crying and starting to get up, not realizing she fell right into the man's trap. The second she passed the man, the door slammed shut and several locks snapped into place.

Picking up her son, she felt a blast of pain slash through the back of her head before darkness took over her eyes.

When Molly's eyes opened, she felt the type of pain she had only ever heard about before. She had no clue how much time had passed, though she assumed it wasn't long, for she could hear the doorbell ring and child after child scream "trick or treat!" Hearing the door slam shut, she shook the fogginess from her head and looked down at herself. She still had her pink scrubs on, but that was it. She was naked from the waist down. Her legs were spread wide and tied to the legs of a chair she was sitting in. Her arms were bound behind her back so tight that she knew if she struggled too hard, her shoulders would dislocate. Her mouth was also gagged with what tasted like a dirty dish rag that gave off a vague pumpkin spice scent that filled her nose. She attempted a yell but could hardly hear it herself. It was also Halloween, screams were everywhere on this night. No one would think twice. Looking around, she realized she was in a hallway and the lights were off. It seemed normal enough, though, with a few pictures on the wall.

Seconds later, the man she had thought was so nice walked past her and flipped on the lights. He looked *much* different now. He still wore the same outfit, only now he had a white chef's apron over it, and it was covered in blood. Both his hands had rubber gloves on and they, too, were spotted red. His glasses were also gone. Without them, he looked evil and menacing, as if the glasses had kept all his secrets buried inside.

"Oh, you're up! How wonderful! If you remember, your son asked for a trick *or* a treat. Well, I'm giving him a trick. Would you care to see it?" The thought of this man touching her child, in *any* way, filled Molly with feelings of vengeance she had never felt in her life. She wanted to kill this man and rip his beady little eyes out, even if Chet was fine, even if this were all some sort of joke. The man walked behind Molly and pushed the chair. It scraped against the hardwood floor but moved smoothly on the tile through the doorway into the kitchen.

As her body passed through the threshold of that room, the world stopped spinning and everything in her universe ceased to exist. In that room, Chet's tiny body was lying on the kitchen counter, stripped naked, his stomach splayed open. Instantly, Molly vomited into her gag, sending the bile out through her nose and back down her throat, almost choking her. The man quickly removed the gag, allowing her to expel the early dinner she had eaten with Chet at Friendly's an hour earlier.

With all of it out of her, she wanted to scream, to thrash in the chair and run to Chet's body to try and put him back together. She was a nurse, she could do it. She could get him to the hospital in time. Subconsciously, though, Molly knew there was no way for him to be alive. Instead of doing anything, she just stared at Chet's face, which was pale and sickly looking. His eyes were open, staring at nothing, cold and dead. Her own eyes moved a few inches to look at his pillowcase full of candy on the chair next to him. He was so excited to get home to eat and eat until the treats made him sick. Instead, she was the sick one, physically and mentally.

Realizing the situation, Molly understood that at that moment, no matter what was about to happen, she, too, was dead. Whether the man killed her or not, her life had ceased the second Chet's heart stopped.

"Please . . . kill me. Quickly—so I don't have to look at him anymore," Molly mustered in a barely audible voice void of any emotion or feeling.

The man looked at her with a smile of pure joy. She could tell he was loving this, as if he enjoyed killing her slowly without ever drawing blood.

"Oh, dear, no. You and I are going to be friends for a long time, but we can talk about that later, I have a lot of work to do. You can watch while I get to it!" The man left her side and headed for Chet's lifeless body. He took up a position on the other side of the counter, facing Molly as if he were about to give a cooking demonstration. And in a way, he was.

"Don't touch him," Molly barked through gritted teeth. The man ignored her and went about his work as she screamed until her voice went hoarse. Cut by cut, the man pulled chunks of meat and organs out of Chet's stomach, placing them on the counter next to his body. The man giggled as he watched Molly shut her eyes and hum to herself, though she couldn't help but take peeks to see what was happening to her baby. The man joined in with a hum of his own as he pulled out Halloween goody bags: small orange bags with pictures of black cats, pumpkins, and bats on them. One by one, he blew each bag open, placed a chunk of Chet into it, and tied it shut with a twist tie. After filling two dozen small bags, he placed them into the same bowl that Chet had taken the Reese's from. The doorbell rang.

"Let the festivities begin!" The man said, as if he were about to host a party.

Molly was just far enough to the side that she could see the door, but the people on the other side could not see her. She didn't have her gag on, so she knew she could scream for help. This was her chance! Hearing the door open, she started to scream.

"*Help!* For God's sake, he killed my son! Help me, please!" Over and over again, she screamed. The man was obviously planning on this; he did have a blood-splattered apron on, after all. As the children asked for their treats, he cackled.

"Want to come in? Ha ha ha ha! You guys can be my next victims! Ha ha ha!" After laughing over and over, he dropped the goody bags of Chet's still warm body parts into four different orange buckets held out before him. He even winked at the parents standing a few feet behind, who were trying not to laugh at their scared children.

"Now, don't open your treats until you get home! It would ruin the surprise! Besides, chunks of liver taste better with salt!" The man laughed again. Molly could hear the kids say, "Thank you," and then he shut the door.

"That was fantastic! Now we only have to hope they actually don't open those bags until they get home. If all goes well, we'll have another two hours of this before I have to take off. Even if they do open a bag, they'll think it's fake." Molly just stared at him, not believing what was going on. At first everything was real and her child was dead, but now she didn't know. This couldn't actually be happening. Things like this didn't happen in life, and if they did, it was certainly not to her, let alone in her town or hell, even in her state. She started to laugh.

"This isn't real! Ha! I can't believe this. I must have fallen asleep at work. Or maybe I got into an accident and I'm unconscious, but this isn't real!" Molly was laughing and crying. The man walked over to her, leaned over, reached between her legs, and pinched as hard as he could. Molly threw her head back and cackled even harder.

"You feel that, bitch? It's real all right! Hell, take a look at them." Spinning her chair around, Molly could see the other side of the room for the first time. An elderly couple sat on the couch next to each other, holding hands. Their chests were covered in blood, forks sticking out of them in odd angles, a dirty pie plate on the coffee table. They looked like they were posed for a beautiful picture, if it weren't for the blood. After taking it in for a few seconds, Molly realized that their heads were on the wrong bodies. The man had cut both of their heads off, then swapped them when he put them back on the bodies. She laughed some more.

"Well, we'll see how much you laugh at this." Pissed she wasn't believing him, the man stomped over to Chet's body, dug around in a few drawers until he found a large cleaver, and slammed it down on Chet's neck. It took four solid whacks to remove the tiny head. The realization started to seep into Molly, and she got dizzy as she watched. Having already bled out all over the counter, the decapitated head bled very little as he carried it over to her. She wasn't laughing anymore, but the smile was still on her face. As the man held Chet's head right to her face, she leaned back from it a bit; her lips quivered, but she forced the smile to stay on her face.

"Kiss your son! KISS HIM!"

"This is fucked up. This is one messed-up hallucination. I want to wake up now."

"There is no waking up. And if you're not going to kiss your own son's adorable face, I guess he'll have to go back to where he came from." The man lowered Chet's head to Molly's bare thighs and rubbed the boy's cold lips against them, slowly teasing her into reality. Molly could feel Chet's cold nose—the nose she had just made him blow a few minutes before—on her thigh; she knew this was all too real. Just as the head started to move forward, the bell rang again.

Leaving Chet's head on her lap, the man walked back to the door, whistling. Molly just stared straight at him: no longer crying, not smiling, and not laughing. She wanted desperately to wiggle the head out of that place, to get it away from her, but at the same time it was . . . Chet. She couldn't let his head fall to the floor and then see his eyes staring up at her, as if asking, "Why didn't you protect me, Mom?"

Over the next two hours, the man handed out sixty-eight bags filled with parts of Chet's body. All the while, Molly didn't move an inch, didn't say anything, and hardly blinked.

A few minutes before ten, the man grabbed a plastic shopping bag, walked over to Molly, and picked up Chet's head. He placed it in the bag, tied a knot with the handles, and leaned over to whisper in her ear.

"I'll make you a promise. I know you'll want nothing more than to kill yourself after tonight. After all, you did let your son die, you could have stopped me, but you didn't. But let me ask you this: how could you let your son be buried without his head? If you kill yourself, I'll personally piss on your son's head every day for the rest of my life. But if you stay alive, I will give you his head back next year . . . on Halloween. Don't worry about finding me, I'll find you when it is time."

With that, the man walked over to Chet's body, dunked his hand inside him, and it came back wet and red. Using the blood, he wrote "Mr. Tricks Was Here!" on the bare white wall next to the door. He then turned, winked at Molly, and walked out.

The man was right, she wanted to die. She wanted to *die, die, die*. But there was also a nuclear explosion of rage inside her that was slowly building, telling her that she would do anything to stop this man and get vengeance for her son next Halloween.

The Last Slice

As the trick-or-treaters dwindled down, Jalen shut his door and snapped the lights off. Clicking on some music and dancing around his house, he couldn't recall ever being in such a good mood. Slicing a real person other than himself felt beyond anything he could have ever imagined. Especially with it being Martha, she got what she deserved for getting his mother killed. Thinking about the knife going in, slicing ever so effortlessly through her fat, he started to get hard. It made him wonder what he could do to the holes in Martha—they'd be cold by now, but that wouldn't bother him, so were pumpkins.

Grabbing a hoodie, he zipped it up and pulled it over his face. He gave Muffin some food, petted her, then headed out the back door of his house. He snuck through a patch of woods, then through two neighbors' yards. It was a path he had taken a hundred times when he didn't want to be seen sneaking out of his house. He knew exactly where to walk to not set off motion-sensor lights or be seen on security cameras, and he had never once been caught, not that he was doing anything wrong, he was just taking a shortcut. The path he took exited out onto Pine Grove, the street behind his and closer to the main road that left the neighborhood. With it being almost midnight, it was rather silent, though he could hear a few teens out causing mischief, or at least what he thought were teens—it sounded like glass shattering and some rustling in the woods.

Just as he was about to walk behind the back fence of the last house, he saw movement in front of him. It was dark but still light enough to see basic outlines, so when he saw massive stringy legs step over a fence, he stopped, having no understanding of what he was seeing. Stepping back behind a tree, Jalen watched with more intrigue than nerves. Two giant creatures made of vegetation were climbing over the fence, and he could see a faint glowing behind the branches that seemed to come from where their heads were. As he tried to figure out what they were, a black mass oozed through the fence like a floating amoeba. He reached down to his knife and grasped it, just in case. The creatures started to head away from him. It was hard to see them fully, but they made no sense. Just as he was about to follow, two more of the giant tree-like monsters stepped over the fence and started to follow the others, though one stopped and turned back and looked in his direction. It was then when Jalen saw the pumpkin face.

Seeing the glowing orange head, Jalen smiled, then laughed to himself. He wasn't scared, he wasn't in disbelief, he was *thrilled*. When he was bleeding out in the back of the ambulance, when he heard the paramedics saying they were losing him, he truly thought he saw a pumpkin looking through the back window at him. At the same time in his head he had heard a voice, as if a conversation about "choosing" him was happening, but then he slipped away into unconsciousness and forgot all about it until this moment. He swallowed and took a step right out into the path, showing himself to the creature. As he did so, he expected his heartrate to shoot up and to sweat and feel the tingles of fear, but instead he felt like a warrior with nerves of steel. It was like he knew he was facing his destiny. The creature took four quick, massive steps towards him and leaned down, putting its orange glowing face right in front of his. It was so close, Jalen could feel the heat from the flame burning hot inside.

The creature lifted a fist, then shook his gourd. Jalen heard a voice, but it was in his head, not coming directly from the thing's mouth. *You . . . are . . . one of the . . . infected.* The voice was echoing gravely in his mind, yet they had a faint and light sensation—it was more like Jalen was just understanding the words rather than hearing them. *You are tasked with one more . . . they must . . . be in . . . their fourth decade of life.*

Jalen nodded. Understanding, he responded out loud. "Yes, and I will make sure it happens before midnight." He didn't even know when he heard that part, but he understood that it had to happen before 12:00 a.m., otherwise it would be too late.

The monster backed up, and as it did so, Jalen got an overwhelming sense that the viny creature wanted to kill him violently, that it despised him with every fiber, er, *leaf*, in its body. Yet it could not touch him and in fact, *needed* him to complete the task. Jalen looked at the time on his phone as the beast walked away, joining the others and the blob-like thing. It was already 11:40 p.m. He only had twenty minutes to find a person in their forties to kill. It was exciting to accept the mission and the thought of slicing once more tonight made him hard. Martha's cold body would have to wait.

Walking in the same direction as the creatures while racking his brain as to who he knew in their forties, he took a peek over the fence of the yard where the monsters had gone, and he could see two bodies that made him tingle with excitement. He wanted a closer look, but there was no time. He frantically searched the recesses of his mind to find a victim in their forties whom he could get to on foot within the next few minutes. There were plenty of middle-aged people on the street, but he had no clue if they were in their thirties, forties or fifties—he was never good with ages. Then it hit him: Ms. Marshall. He knew she was forty because last year in school the other teachers surprised her with black balloons and cake. She also lived in the neighborhood. He had seen her jogging many times, and a few times pleased himself to her breasts jiggling when she ran by. He only knew where she lived because he had followed her home once, and the jogging to keep up with her almost killed him. It was three streets away. He could make it if he ran. As he picked up speed, he realized the last time he ran this hard was when he followed her. The thought made him giggle.

After one block, he had to stop. He could hardly breathe, and all of his stitches were starting to pull, ache, and ooze. One particular slice above his right eye was dripping so much blood that it blurred his vision and he had to wipe it to see clearly. From then on out, he ran one minute then walked the next. When he got to Ms. Marshall's pristine two-story house, which he knew was blue but couldn't tell in the dark, he looked at his watch and saw he had twelve minutes left. Plenty of time. Only he didn't know if she had a husband or some sort of attack dog or alarm or anything that would stop him. Panic and fear started to set in. Martha was one thing, that was revenge, and he knew he could get away with it. Wait, why did he even think he could get away with it? She was his neighbor. She got his mom killed and he now had her dog—there was no way he could get away. Jalen felt nauseous and dizzy as the realizations set in, it was like his brain got T-boned by a Mack truck going ninety miles per hour. Just hours ago, he was a million percent positive he would be free and no one would ever suspect him. Was he delusional? Was it the painkillers messing with his thought process? He fell to his knees and started to hyperventilate.

Then he realized, it was *them*. The pumpkin things. They somehow chose him, pushed him, and manipulated him into killing Martha. He probably would have done it without any encouragement, but to do it so brazenly, with not a care in the world, that was *them*. Why did they push him to do that, why were they pushing him to kill again if they despised him? With both hands on the cool grass, he gasped for air. He was going to have to pack up and run, and he better start now before someone found the body—forget killing Ms. Marshall. Just as he was about to lift his hands to turn and run away, vines shot out of the grass and grabbed his hands, pulling him back down. The ground between his fingers started to shake and crack open, allowing a fiery jack-o'-lantern face to rise up. It was the most sinister-looking pumpkin he ever saw, and the fury on its face was boiling hot. Jalen screamed and writhed in the vines' unyielding grip.

Do it. DO IT OR WE ALL DIE. The words exploded in his head like a thousand air horns all sounding off at once. Jalen fell to his side, and the vines let go. He covered his ears and sobbed.

Opening his eyes, he saw a light snap on in an upstairs window of Ms. Marshall's house.

NOW. NOW. NOW. The words were like gunshots in his head. He just nodded "yes" in response and got up. Walking to the door, he rang the bell over and over, not caring if Ms. Marshall called the cops, only caring about slicing her to death. After excruciating long seconds ticked away, Ms. Marshall, wearing a bathrobe—*was she naked under it?*—came down the stairs hesitantly and looked out the door. She jumped and covered her mouth at the site of Jalen's mangled face.

"Ms. Marshall, please. It's me, Jalen, I had your class last year. I got attacked by some assholes, I'm bleeding everywhere." He watched through the glass, he could tell she was thinking but scared, then she came closer. *Yes.*

"Jalen, I'll call the cops and get you help, all right? You can stay on the porch and wait for them." She said, having to be fucking smart.

"Ms. Marshall, they're still out there, they're going to kill me. They stabbed me twice. I don't want to die, I already almost did that," he cried in his best acting voice, knowing she would have heard what happened to him—everyone in town had. There was a pause, and then he could see her picking up the housephone and dialing. She was calling the police. *Shit.* Jalen stepped back a bit and looked at the door, wondering if he could break it down.

Suddenly, the power went out. As everything went black, he knew it was the vines helping him. Taking the opportunity, he prepped his shoulder and slammed into the door. It didn't budge, but he heard the scream and saw Ms. Marshall running upstairs. As he backed up to try again, he felt vines wrap around his body. They encased him, instantly giving him a faux green tendon-like muscle suit over his scrawny frame. The door broke with ease that second time, and as soon as he was in, the vines shot back like elastic snapping. The help of the vines made him feel invincible. With a new rage and lust for a few more slices, Jalen ran up the stairs two at a time.

With only one door shut in the hallway, it was clear what room she was in. The bedroom door splintered with ease and this time with no help from his viny friends. Jalen saw Ms. Marshall standing next to the bed, a bat in her left hand, her cellphone in the other—she seemed to be having a hard time getting it to work with how much she was shaking. He took out his knife and threw it at her without hesitation. It did not stick into her like he'd seen in movies, instead the knife cut her arm and fell to the floor alongside the phone. With one arm bleeding, she swung the bat blindly. Jalen raced at her, dove, and tackled her on the backswing. The struggle was quick, Ms. Marshall was in shape, but her fear made her muscles into a mess of uncoordinated mush. Jalen and his adrenaline easily overtook her.

Sitting with all of his weight on her chest, he used his knees to pin down her arms and picked up the knife. Realizing his crotch was so close to her bare chest that was falling out of the robe, he got hard, but then he looked at the time: it was two minutes before midnight. Raising the knife above his head, he paused.

"Ms. Marshall, I apologize for this. It isn't personal, I just have to do this. I'm saving the world, after all. Thank you for being a great teacher." Then he brought the knife down once, twice, three times . . . then twenty more times. When the clock slipped over to midnight, he heard a collective sigh in his head, though he didn't know if it came from him or the vines.

Standing up, he desperately wanted to play with the body in so many ways, but part of him knew he had to get out of there fast, and besides, he had one more thing to do that night. As he walked down the stairs, he checked to make sure he didn't bleed or ooze on anything. He didn't notice any of his own bodily fluids left behind, and he hadn't touched anything other than his knife, so he felt pretty good about not getting caught for this one. Then, as he walked out the door, he saw carved pumpkins on Ms. Marshall's front steps—they were dark and cold, having been blown out long ago. It wasn't Halloween anymore, but he suddenly had an idea of how he could pay homage to the creatures that had pushed him to commit his Halloween atrocities.

The second time he walked out of the house, he giggled to himself. The site of Ms. Marshall propped up in her bed with the pumpkin on her head and candy strewn all over the sheets made him smile bigger than he had in days, maybe in his whole life. With the cool autumn air on his skin, soothing his throbbing cuts, he whistled as he walked towards the funeral home to get his mother.

The Day After Halloween

Haven Gazette – Online Edition
BREAKING NEWS: Updated November 1st, 9:37 a.m.

Throughout the night and into the early morning, six bodies have been found on four different properties in the idyllic town of Haven, known to most as "Halloween Haven," the town made famous by the 1998 film *A Witch's Wish*. Haven Police have issued a warning for residents to shelter in place until they do a search of the entire town while they figure out if the situation is active. One suspect has been arrested, but he is believed to be connected to only one of the murders. While the police have yet to comment, rampant online posts and comments have been exploding with stories about children receiving baggies full of "human parts." These claims have not been confirmed by the police at this time, but numerous photos have been posted online that all but confirm the claims. The police had no comment on these claims but said to reach out to them if your child received anything suspicious in their bag. All three crimes were within walking distance in an area of the town known as "The Woods" due to all the streets in the neighborhood being named after trees.

The first body was found around 11:30 p.m. at 34 Oak Terrace. No names have been released, but the police have stated that the homeowner, who was competing in the "Scariest House" contest, was arrested in conjunction with a body found on his premises. Details are still emerging on this case.

The second body was found around midnight on the steps of 57 Maple Lane. The body was posed and decorated as a scarecrow holding a bowl of candy. Two teens out after-hours vandalizing property hit the body with a bat. When it fell over, they realized it was real and they called the police. Officials have not confirmed this, though the teens, which will remain unnamed in this article due to their age, posted the entire incident, along with a ten-minute live feed as they waited for the cops, on their TikTok page. Their video has since been removed by the site.

The third body was discovered at 12 Birch Lane by the victim's husband, who came home after working a night shift. No details have been released other than it is a suspected homicide.

Police have confirmed that the last three bodies were found at 71 Cedar Lane, along with one survivor bound to a chair. The police have not given any other details other than that a neighbor saw the door was open and called the police. This site has had the highest amount of police activity, though the media was pushed back several streets, allowing for no further information to be gathered at this time.

Police Chief Jack Pisano made a brief statement to the press just before dawn: "I have been working in this town for over forty years, well before we became known as Halloween Haven, and I have never once had to attend the site of a murder, let alone five in one night. We are a small, loving community that welcomes in strangers and tourists this time of year in an effort to show our passion for the holiday as well as bring in commerce to our wonderful town. Maybe we opened some doors we shouldn't have by doing so, maybe we invited this evil into our town, maybe this is our fault and we should . . ." At that point in the speech, Mayor Drumbold stopped the press conference and apologized to reporters, saying there is "far too

much to be done" and that "outside
help would be sought to deal with
the mass amount of casualties." At
that time, all press and onlookers
were ordered out of The Woods
neighborhood. Each street was
closed off and residents were
ordered to not leave.

All residents are to shelter in
place until further notice. No
further information is known at this
time.

Haven Gazette will have updates
as things progress.

BREAKING NEWS: Updated November 1st, 2:14 p.m.

Residents of "The Woods" neighborhood
of Haven are no longer under a
shelter-in-place order. The ban was
officially lifted at 1:59 p.m.,
though it is highly suggested that
all residents stay indoors and away
from all crime scenes to help ease
the investigations. The police did
not give an in-person update, but
they did post the following on their
social media accounts:

*Anyone who received an orange
Halloween bag the size of a snack
baggie with black cats, pumpkins, and*

bats on them, please do not open it and contact the police immediately.

There are reports that officers and detectives from over half a dozen towns have shown up in Haven to help with the investigations. While unconfirmed, there are reports that the FBI has been contacted as well. No further information is known at this time.

Haven Gazette will have updates as things progress.

BREAKING NEWS: *Updated November 1st, 6:41 p.m.*

At this time, the police have not issued an update, nor have they responded to calls from the media.

No further information is known at this time. *Haven Gazette* will have updates as things progress.

BREAKING NEWS: *Updated November 1st, 9:16 p.m.*

The Haven Police have held an official press conference, though Police Chief Jack Pisano did not participate. Detective Bernard read a written statement and took no questions. The statement reads:

First off, we want to say our hearts and thoughts are with the families of the victims. There are five confirmed deaths that occurred on Halloween night. One murder was an act of rage by a homeowner who got mad at a teen for ruining his decorative display. We will release more information on that once families are notified. There are two other crime scenes, one with one body and another with three as well as a surviving victim. At this time, while it is a preliminary investigation, we do not believe these two crime scenes are related and no suspects have been found.

Folks, that means we have two killers who got away last night. We do not think these murders were committed through rage or by accident, we do believe they were planned and purposeful, which means that all residents should be diligent and cautious until arrests have been made. However, we do believe that the kills were directly related to the Halloween holiday, so we do not believe there is an imminent threat . . . as of now. The FBI as well as surrounding local task forces have been called in to assist. We are going door to door interviewing residents, and we invite anyone who has any information to contact us at the dedicated hotline. That is all we can say at this time.

Haven Gazette will have updates as things progress.

BREAKING NEWS: *Updated November 2nd, 8:00 a.m.*

Haven Police have updated what social media is calling the "Haven Horror" and the "Halloween Haven Massacre." While victims' names have still not been released, police have released a sketch of the suspect of three of the killings, a man who has eerily called himself "Mr. Tricks." They have also confirmed that one of the victims was a child of only four years of age and that over fifty children received baggies full of suspected human body parts. The contents are being tested at this time. They reiterated that if you or your child received a bag of any suspicious contents on Halloween night to please call the police immediately. They are also advising that all candy received on Halloween night should not be eaten. All contents received should be placed in bags and labeled with your name and address. Teams of police will be going door to door to collect all Halloween candy for inspection.

Haven Gazette will have updates as things progress.

BREAKING NEWS: *Updated November 2nd, 10:39 a.m.*

Two more bodies have been found at a residence on Pine Grove, but no address was given. The police have stated that while the situation is suspicious in nature, it is believed that it is a possible suicide and heart attack, and that they do not seem to be linked to the other murders, although the investigation has just started. More details to come.

Haven Gazette will have updates as things progress.

BREAKING NEWS: *Updated November 2nd, 12:09 p.m.*

The *Haven Gazette*, along with other news outlets, has received a letter from one of the suspected killers, who calls himself "Mr. Tricks." After consulting with the police, we have been allowed to post the letter in full, as it has already been posted in several outlets. Reader discretion is advised.

Dear Halloween Haven,

I hope you all enjoyed your Halloween! Yes, such a shame that a poor child had to die, but talk about the ultimate trick! Opening up a goody bag and getting something messy . . . I hope it gave you all a good fright. Now that I introduced myself in a bloody way, I just wanted you to all know that this was just my opening act. Every Halloween from now until the tricks are over, you will be getting treats from me, your very own Mr. Tricks! Though I do have to apologise for having only killed three this year. I wanted to start off gently. Though now that we know each other, I promise to double, if not triple those numbers next year. But, at the same time, don't be surprised if I come to visit a few times during the year. I don't want to get rusty now, do I?

Can't wait to kill your loved ones soon!

PS: Whoever killed the others, I like your style, but bugger off, Halloween Haven is mine.

Yours Truly,
Mr. Tricks

No further statement has been made by

local police or the FBI at this time.

Haven Gazette will have updates as things progress.

BREAKING NEWS: *Updated November 5th, 7:44 p.m.*

Things have been quiet on the "Halloween Haven Massacre" front. In conjunction with the FBI, the local police have been holding a daily news conference, but no new updates have been announced. We will keep you up to date as they come in.

Haven Gazette will have updates as things progress.

BREAKING NEWS: *Updated November 6th, 1:21 p.m.*

During today's afternoon briefing, the FBI made a statement that they believe Martha Wilkes was killed by Ruben Carter, who also killed Nick Cotter in his own home during the "Scariest House" contest. Mr. Carter was romantically linked with Wilkes before her death. While the suspect is denying the claims that he killed Ms. Wilkes, there is evidence that puts him at the scene, including fingerprints and DNA. Mr. Carter will be charged for both murders in court tomorrow morning.

The deaths of Rick and Martin Aster have been deemed to not be suspicious. Rick's cause of death is being listed as suicide while Mr. Aster's is being listed as a heart attack. It is not known if Rick found his father dead and committed suicide or if Mr. Aster found his son dead and had a heart attack. An investigation is underway, but they are not sure the order of deaths will ever be determined.

While Mr. Tricks has taken credit for three of the deaths, due to evidence at the scene, the FBI believe he also committed the fourth murder on Birch Lane. They believe his letter was written to purposely try and throw the investigation off by suggesting another killer. The police are still asking for anyone who has any information to call their tip line. A police sketch based on one of the victim's mother's firsthand account will be released shortly.

Haven Gazette will have updates as things progress.

NEWS UPDATE: March 31st, 2:25 p.m.

As the six-month anniversary of the "Halloween Haven Massacre" approaches, the FBI is nowhere to be seen. No updates have been given since their last press conferences were held back in January. Each request for an update from our reporters has been met with the same comment: "There are no substantial new updates. When there are, we will update you." While they have not given us any further information, sources say that only one agent has been left in town to work on the case full-time, but they are still adamantly trying to find Mr. Tricks.

Meanwhile, the town of Haven has been decimated with over one hundred homes going up for sale in the past several months, with more going on the market every day. Yet not a single one has sold. The thought of a serial killer who has not been caught, who has stated they will be back, has destroyed what was once a quaint community full of love and pride. It is now a community on edge, its citizens either fleeing their homes or investing in security systems and personal protection.

Numerous community watches have been formed with upwards of twenty people walking the streets at night with bats and weapons. Though most say they are doing more harm than good, as over two dozen complaints of harassment and assaults have been reported to the police. Local authorities have begged citizens to stop the watches, assuring residents that they have stepped up patrols by over five hundred percent in the past six months. Though some locals say they have not seen a cop drive down their street once.

Haven Gazette will have updates as things progress.

BREAKING NEWS: *June 10th, 8:23 a.m.*

A body has been found in the Haven town green. Little information is known at this time, but eyewitnesses have said that the body was posed in the gazebo and that there was a pumpkin in the center with "Mr. Tricks" carved into it. The *Haven Gazette* is working to confirm the facts.

Haven Gazette will have updates as things progress.

NEWS UPDATE: June 12th, 12:53 p.m.

The FBI encampment is back. In a statement this morning, agents identified the victim as Cheryl Montagna, last year's "Ms. Pumpkin" winner. With this latest murder, more residents are leaving town. Over three hundred homes are now sitting empty in the city, all with "for sale" signs and seemingly zero potential buyers. Tensions are running high and the town is on edge. A proposal to ban all Halloween activity is on the table for the next town meeting.

Haven Gazette will have updates as things progress.

NEWS UPDATE: July 14th, 1:32 p.m.

In light of the recent events and with still no suspect in the horrific murders, the Haven City Council has voted to cancel all Halloween activities in the town and ban trick-or-treating this coming October. If Mr. Tricks is caught, they will have an emergency meeting to reconsider the bans. Many residents have protested, stating that the vast majority of their annual income comes from tourists during the month of October.

"An entire season without an income will be detrimental to most shops and vendors, and could alter the landscape of this city forever," argued Councilman Max Dermondy, who was the only councilmember to vote against the ban.

Haven Gazette will have updates as things progress.

NEWS UPDATE: *August 2nd, 9:02 a.m.*

Night Watch, the nationwide true crime ratings king, will be in Haven next week to film a special two-hour episode on the "Halloween Haven Massacre." While some residents are against sensationalizing their pain, others hope it will help bring attention to the murders and possibly create more leads. The world's fascination with the crimes has already spawned six podcasts, two self-published books from locals, five books from major publishers, a slew of websites, and a cottage industry of "I survived the Halloween Haven Massacre" T-shirts and paraphernalia that is being sold at some of the dying gift shops in town that are now catering to the true crime tourism boom.

"It is sick to see people profiting off our pain," said one local who wished to be anonymous.

Ten months of Haven being in the constant spotlight is putting most locals on edge and at odds with each other. One city councilmember is even promising to change the town name and to auction off the vacant houses for pennies on the dollar to rebuild the town, but with Halloween approaching and a promised visit from Mr. Tricks, the proposal will have to wait until November.

Haven Gazette will have updates as things progress.

NEWS UPDATE: September 27th, 11:40 a.m.

With the Halloween season only days away, police from six different cities have arrived in Haven to help patrol the streets to keep it safe. The town that once embodied the fun of the fall season is unrecognizable with virtually no decorations up other than a few houses with pumpkins. An estimated 60 percent of residents have either moved out of town or plan to be out of town for some or all of the month of October. Hundreds of yards are unraked, unkept, and becoming derelict, causing countless complaints from locals as property values have already dropped over 70 percent.

Police will also be cracking down on the true crime tourists who have plagued the town all year, including a major spike after the *Night Watch* episode aired. While they will not be banning tourists, all cars are subject to search at checkpoints coming and going from the town, and there will be a nightly curfew. With no festivities planned and trick-or-treating banned, authorities hope to have the city in a safe semi-lockdown on Halloween.

Haven Gazette will have updates as things progress.

The Next Halloween

Clare - October 1st

Clare sat next to her prized pumpkin, a loving hand resting on it as she waited for the vines to grow. The past year waiting for them had been torturous, but she knew it was worth the wait. Over the year, she dedicated her time to studying and finding out all she could about them. She even took trips to Europe and interviewed countless scholars to understand her warriors more. At the end of the day, while she learned a lot about history and traditions, what she knew in her heart was much deeper than any written history.

Knowing she was the only human connection to ancient warrior spirits who kept evil from spilling into the world on the one night it could, gave Clare an air of confidence. When an asshole in the canned goods aisle at the shopping market cut her cart off, she spoke up, louder and with more confidence than she ever had before. She stood up for herself now, and she didn't back down from anyone. She was a queen, after all, one who helped save the world and would again this year . . . she just wished it didn't require a sacrifice of one of every decade age group in the chosen town. From what she could gather, the deaths used to be much more subtle and discreet. Heart attacks, strokes, slips, falls, choking, and other seemingly natural causes . . . just pushed a little by some vines and the chosen vessels. Even though they weren't bloody per se, the evil saw that death was there and taking the life without discretion for age. It saw the morbid and scary costumes and it was tricked into thinking evil ran our world, keeping it satisfied. But after decades of costumes getting sexier and cuter, the darkness was finally catching on that the world wasn't pure evil, requiring extra special and extra *gruesome* sacrifices—just like last year. She just hoped this year could be much more subtle again. Though after the media storm, even a stubbed toe in their town was going to be scrutinized, so she wasn't sure what would happen or how enough people could be sacrificed when almost any family with kids had moved far away.

Just after sunrise, the first leaf started to move on its own, like a tiny baby finger reaching out to their parent for the first time. Clare smiled and a tear ran down her face. Part of her had been so scared that they wouldn't come back this year, but now she knew they were coming.

Jalen/Mr. Slice - October 3rd

Life was good. Jalen had gotten away with the murders by simply saying that Ruben came to his house and asked him to watch Muffin on Halloween night. Jalen even took the stand in the trial and pointed right at Ruben's red, sobbing face and stated, "That man, I saw him walk away from what I thought was a scarecrow. He walked right across the street and knocked on my door. He asked me to watch Muffin for Martha. He said she had to go out of town on an emergency and he just couldn't watch the dog himself. I've always loved her dog, so of course I said 'yes.'"

The investigators, the lawyers, the judge—they were so sympathetic towards him. They treated him like he mattered and they truly believed his story. The stupid news program even asked if they could interview him, but he turned that down after preliminary talks with the reporter, as he wanted to paint his mother as evil, and Jalen would not tolerate that, especially because things had been so good with her lately.

Jalen and his mother had a beautiful relationship that he got more and more fond of every day. Things really took off after taking online embalming classes to stop the smell. She no longer verbally or physically abused him, and she was now a perfect, loving—in two different contexts—mother. But most importantly, he got away with the murders he committed, and although the pleasure he got from them awakened an addiction that was hard to satisfy, he was smart and did all of his new killings far outside of Haven. For the past eleven months, what he was calling his practice year, he only killed the homeless or prostitutes. The total over that time came to nine kills, not counting Martha or Ms.

Marshall. He was doing his best to keep it to one a month, if not less. If he could, he would do one every day, but getting caught would mean no more slicing, and besides, with the way he looked, it was hard to go unnoticed. So he did his best to abide his time with mother and Muffin, whom he had grown to love tremendously.

Over the year, his own cuts healed beautifully, to him at least. His face looked like a peeled potato that got thrown into a fan blade. It was impossible to not be noticed and looked at in public—there were constant whispers and points and disgusted faces, and Jalen loved every one of them. Before the scars, he was invisible. Being noticed made him feel like he existed, and he liked that. The more he killed, the more he walked with pride and confidence, as he was leaving a mark on the world. Life was good, though the only thing that bugged him was Mr. Tricks. Jalen wanted to get away with his murders, but it was frustrating seeing the attention Mr. Tricks received instead of Mr. Slice, who hardly ever got mentioned other than in a few media outlets claiming that Ruben used the name to cover up his crimes. He wanted that attention, he wanted to be the one terrorizing the town, and this year, after working for months on a plan, Jalen was certain that the whole world would be talking about Mr. Slice on November 1st.

Mr. Tricks - October 5th

Oh happy day! What I did worked, and it worked spectacularly. Not only did it get worldwide attention, but it also got the podcasts and the news shows and there are even films in the works. Killing a child caused a cottage industry of outrage—it was brilliant. I have heavily documented the entire year in my book. I'm actually shocked, there was so much more to write about, I'm going to have to split it into a series. Book one will be my biography and thoughts on the mind—in a way, my origin story. Book two will be about the media and the world's utter fascination with death and murder, which will be showcased through the "Halloween Haven Massacre." And book three will be the continuation of the killings and how everyone condemns it… yet eats it up more and more and more and more and more and more. They all want to hate a killer, but they all want to know every gory detail even more. Knowing that I get to keep doing this for years, and that when I one day get caught, this will all explode in a much bigger way as my books and the truth come out, it is orgasmic. It's like winning the Super Bowl and the Oscars all at once.

Of course, the pièce de résistance is Molly, my beautiful and angry Molly. What a perfect and unexpecting victim she was. I absolutely love that she refused all media interviews and basically went into hiding. It has made the public's obsession with her much more intense. It leaves so many open-ended questions and will create such a satisfactory ending. Though I have to admit, this all blew up even more than I could have ever imagined, it is going to make this Halloween extremely hard to pull off. There is no way she won't be watched by the FBI, local police, and even podcast sleuths. But I have planned for that all year long. Houses are dirt cheap and plentiful in Haven—in fact, there was one right next door to Molly that I got for a song.

Clare - October 30th

This year was different, something was wrong. The vines were loving and caring like the year before, but this time they seemed scared. Clare kept asking but got no answers. Finally, on the day before Halloween, she screamed in the kitchen with her arms out, showing she meant business. All the leaves quivered and bowed to her anger. She demanded an answer as to why they were scared and finally it came to her in a tidal wave of horror. They showed her that a man, a "Mr. Slice," could potentially disturb the thousand years of peace the vines had kept. Hearing this, she simply asked them to kill the man, but they just bowed their heads. It was then she understood their code was not just one of honor, it was one they physically could not break. They could guide and encourage the bloodshed that was needed, they could protect the innocent and keep the monsters at bay, but they were banned from killing or interfering with the chosen.

"So, if you can't kill him, just tie him up until the day is over, that wouldn't break the codes, right?" She asked out loud. They seemed to confer with each other before showing an image in her head, it was awful. It was a man she knew, more so a boy, the one with the nasty scars: Jalen, that's who it was, the kid whose own mother had almost killed. *Jalen was Mr. Slice.* The image they showed her was of the potential future, of what he was ready to do. Jalen had stockpiled weed killer and bought a makeshift flamethrower. He knew about her vines and he was ready to kill them for good. In the vision, she saw her babies dying, one after another. The thought crushed her in ways she had never felt before.

The rest of that day, she couldn't get the thoughts out of her mind: her vines being cut with a machete, sprayed with acidic chemicals, burned—it was awful. Then she felt even more guilt as she saw the images of the other dead people, the ones Jalen sliced and burned alive in their homes—they didn't give her as much grief as the thought of her vines being destroyed, but they were still awful.

When her warriors were busy getting ready, she called the police to leave an anonymous tip, but they didn't take her seriously. In fact, the woman on the phone got angry and said the poor boy had been cleared of all suspicion and even volunteered at the hospital reading to injured children and giving talks about overcoming trauma, *the boy was a damn saint!* Clare cried and pleaded, but she had no evidence as nothing had happened yet. They hung up on her. Clare cried, but then she was quickly embraced by her vines, giving her a bit of comfort, although she couldn't relax knowing some of them might die the next day and that more than the allotted eight sacrifices could be killed as well. She had to do something.

Molly - October 31st - 7:15 p.m.

After two months in a mental health facility, Molly got out with a clean bill of health and went back to work the next month. The entire time, she refused all media interviews and took back door exits and various routes home to avoid unethical podcasters and vicious reporters trying to get exclusives. As if her life wasn't hard enough, now she had to go through it like a scared cat trying to get by rabid dogs every day. Through the process, she lost all contact with the little family and friends she had. She merely showed up for work and left. She was never seen outside of her house other than for work, and did she did virtually all of her shopping online after being ambushed one day in the grocery store by some teen YouTubers trying to catch her off guard.

They trapped her in an aisle with a small camera crew rushing from each end. The greasy little man-child held a phone out in front of him and talked a thousand miles an hour. It took Molly a few seconds to realize he was talking to the people watching his livestream and not her. Every time she tried to step away, the cameras got in her face. Not having it, she grabbed a glass jar of matzo ball soup and smashed it into the bleach-blonde hair of the kid, who hadn't looked away from his phone. With chunks of matzo balls and carrots stuck in his head, blood started to flow out. Two of the cameramen, or rather *camera boys*, ran away, but one stayed and filmed it all. Molly didn't know it, but the video went on to have over thirty-two million views and she became a meme called the "Matzo Ball Mama." Thankfully, the local cops threatened the kids with stalking and kidnapping for not letting her out of the aisle, so they did not press any charges. Since then, it had been all online shopping for Molly.

Slowly but surely, as the stress of the media storm simmered down, she became the strange lady that lived on a dying street in a poisoned town. The woman who dwelled in the house where children would dare each other to ring the doorbell, the lonely woman whom parents pitied and felt bad for. The only person who was ever nice to her was the slimy new neighbor who always said "hello" and tried to start up conversations. Even after telling him off and to leave her alone, he still said "hi" and offered a hand anytime he saw her—it was frustrating, but as long as he stayed out of her way, it was fine. Besides, she didn't have long to live. In August, she quit her nursing job and more packages started to show up on her doorstep regularly.

If she had told the investigators one of the last things the man had told her—*I will give you his head back next year . . . on Halloween*—they would have had a full sting operation going on at her house at all times. Instead, they just had a patrol car do drive-bys and park in front on certain nights, like Halloween. It was nice having them there, as they kept chasing off the scrupulous journalists—they never gave up, especially the damn podcasters. They constantly tried to get shots of her doing anything. They even had the balls to walk right up and knock on her door in search of an exclusive. But she got it, an exclusive with the mother of the only child victim on the anniversary of the country's most gruesome Halloween murders would be massive for any of them. As the sun set that Halloween, the neighborhood was eerily quiet with the no-trick-or-treating ban in effect. Even with the cops outside and the ban in effect, just as Molly expected, someone still showed up on her door for a trick of their own.

Watching on the small security monitor in the kitchen, she saw a man at her door. He wore a tucked-down baseball hat and a heavy coat and carried a bag. She couldn't see his face, but she knew it was him. For the past year, Molly had purposely not trimmed her bushes, leaving the front door invisible from most of the street. Grabbing a wire next to the door, she gave it a hard tug. Instantly, an axe swung from the bushes and right into the back of the man's left leg, sending him toppling towards the door. She pulled it open just in time for him to fall flat on his face inside the house. Facedown, the man tried to pull a gun out of his belt, but Molly, with another axe already in her hands, swung it down on the back of his head. The blade went halfway through his skull, splitting the back of the baseball cap in two. The man twitched a few times, then stopped moving; Molly pulled the axe back out with a wet squelching sound and swung it down again with a guttural scream. This time the steel exposed the inner workings of the man's brains.

Satisfied he wasn't going to attack her, Molly dropped the axe and dove for the bag on the floor next to him. The small pool of blood spreading across the floor was already touching it. She fell to her knees and clasped the bag in her hands. She thought about Chet's funeral and the closed casket—his headless, organ-less body sitting in the ground forever. At least now he would be whole again, and then she could put an end to her misery with a lone bullet to her head. All she wanted was to be in the ground next to her baby, but she needed his head to do that first. She felt relieved, almost happy for the first time since that day. Not wanting to see what time had done to her son's beautiful face but needing to be sure, she opened the bag. Inside was a Frank's Famous Pie with note on top.

That bastard, did he . . . cook Chet? She grabbed the note, flipped it open with rage, and read it.

From the detectives at District 12: We want you to know that our thoughts and prayers are with you tonight. And that we will not rest until this case is solved.

Molly dropped the card, grabbed the body, and pushed it over. It only rolled halfway; the axe sticking in the back of his head stopped him from making it all the way over. It wasn't the man from last Halloween. It was the lead detective on her son's case.

Mr. Tricks - October 31st - 7:46 p.m.

Holy shit. I mean, *HOLY SHIT.* Talk about taking a turn that I did not expect! Three months with me living next door, waving to her, trying to start up conversations, and offering help without her ever once knowing who I am, all of that time and effort put in for nothing, *fucking nothing.* Months and months and months of planning, it was foolproof! I had a perfect way into her house, I saw all her traps and how she planned to catch me, I could get past every one of them with ease—it was going to be so perfect. I was going to kill her, cut off her stupid head, and put Chet's head on her body instead, all before leaving a note and slipping out with her head. Now, now that will never fucking happen. Fuck me. There are thirty cop cars, ambulances, fire trucks, and the media all swarming over Molly's house. Fuck me. Fuck, fuck, fuck. This is not the scripted ending that would have sent chills down the entire world's spine.

Why did that damn cop have to walk up the porch? There's absolutely no way for me to get to her now. And worst off, I can't even leave the house. I tried to go outside to be a gawker, but I was told that I had to stay inside and keep my shades shut. Fuck them. I can't believe I have to revert to the emergency plan. At least I have one.

Jalen/Mr. Slice - October 31st - 8:01 p.m.

Kissing his mother goodbye, he felt like a four-year-old who slammed down a million Pixy Stix and then was told he was going to Disney World; he was bursting with excitement. The planning was exhausting and he was methodical, but it was enjoyable. Those damn vine creatures were going to be sorry if they tried to stop him. And as for the black ball of evil, or whatever the hell it was, he wasn't worried about that thing. In fact, he wanted to meet it, to touch it, because something told him he should. Ever since seeing it, there was a tiny, tiny voice in his head that would whisper *touch me* every once in a while. It was always accompanied by the image of the black mass. Jalen knew that tonight there would be some sort of spectacular fate, whether it was his ending or a new beginning, he just didn't know yet, but either way it would be brilliant.

Strapping on the last tank, he slid on the fireman mask he bought at an Army surplus store and headed out his back door. It was hot, heavy, and exhausting carrying two tanks on his back and another in his left hand, but he had practiced this walk a thousand times. His body had gotten harder and stronger over the last few months as he rehearsed and rehearsed the plans. Now it was time to ignite them, literally. He just hoped those vine bastards showed up quickly after the fires began, so he could get in as many kills as possible.

Four streets over from his house, he pulled out the nozzle attached to his right leg, flipped the switch for the igniter, and started the flamethrower, well, he liked calling it that, but in reality it was a butane flame weedkiller that he altered to have a longer-lasting tank. The three-foot orange flame screamed out of the end of the canister-like tube. Jalen smiled at it, then brought the torch to the house. It took less than a minute for the outside wall to be engulfed. Then he sprinted to the next house and the next and the next and the next. Within five minutes, five houses were fully on fire. By the time he slipped into the woods to the path he had worn down over the past few months, he heard neighbors screaming for help. Now it was time for the hard part: the long jog.

Running through the woods, he scanned every inch in front of him, knowing the vine monsters would probably show up around this time. But he was ready for them. And he would not let them stop him from getting the full mile away from the fires. On the other side of the neighborhood, while the emergency personnel panicked, he would be free to break into house after house, slicing his way through town. Sure enough, halfway to his destination, a giant viny leg stepped out in front of him. Jalen stopped, quickly grabbed the nozzle attached to his left leg, and sprayed. This nozzle was attached to a tank filled with Kill All weedkiller concentrate—he did not water it down. He was going to use the pure concentrate—the strongest, most poisonous mix he could find after testing hundreds. Pulling the trigger, he sprayed the viny leg, then followed it up the torso of the creature. Jalen prayed it would work, but he was not sure if they had some sort of magical immunity to the stuff. If they did, he always had the fire to fall back on. To his great joy, the creature shrieked, grabbed at its leg, and fell back, grasping at trees for support along the way. Jalen yelled a whoop of excitement into his mask. Taking advantage of the moment, he ran toward the creature and kept spraying, making sure to coat the poison all over it. The monster writhed in pain, the glow of its pumpkin head flickering as if it was going out. Satisfied it would die, or at least not be able to interfere, Jalen started to jog again.

Finally arriving at his destination in the backyard of Ms. Patterson, he set down the tank in his left hand, reached behind his back, and grabbed the machete out of a sheath. Then, with his newly muscular leg, he kicked in the door. Killing an old lady didn't get him excited, but it would raise his body count and buy him time. A younger person could fight back or call the cops quicker, so he wanted to start slow, then build his way up. The noise of the door busting in was deafening, but he had watched Ms. Patterson and knew she took her hearing aids out at night—she probably wouldn't flinch. Sure enough, when he reached the bedroom, he saw the sweet old lady lying in bed, her back to the door, sleeping like a log. Raising up the machete, he took a deep breath and brought it down for a good . . . slice.

Cuthump. The blade hit her, but it wasn't soft and doughy like a normal body. Jalen pulled out the blade and waited for the blood to start pooling into the white comforter, but nothing came. Suddenly, he felt sick. *What was going on?* The room, which was already dark, suddenly got darker as the window became covered in vines.

How the hell could they know what house I was going to? Where was Ms. Patterson?

Clare - October 31st - 8:22 p.m.

The detective at that poor woman's house would be one. The house fires, which would spread to nine total houses, destroying almost an entire street, would kill seven. Exactly the eight needed to keep the darkness at bay. The warriors showed her this, but they also showed Jalen killing over fifteen other people that night without ever getting caught; she couldn't let that happen. If more than eight died, then the balance would be off and darkness could get suspicious and slip into the world. So she made her plan. Let the eight happen, then trap Jalen until after midnight. If she could hold him off and get the police to find him with the incendiary devices, then he would be stopped for good and her warriors could be saved.

Faking the body was easy, but encasing the house in vines, that was a bit harder. Her warriors could use vines to stretch and shoot and wrap, but they only went so far and grew so much when they were not attached to the master seeds at her house. In order to encase something,

Clare had to bring the seeds with her. That night around seven, she knocked on the front door of Ms. Patterson's, a woman she had never met but instantly liked as her sweet face was that of a picturesque grandma who reminded her of her nana. Clare was ready for a protest from the old lady, but for some reason, the woman looked at her and simply said, "I understand, dear, let me grab some things."

Clare was shocked, but then the woman gave her a simple wink and she understood that the woman *knew*, just like she herself knew. Within seconds, the woman showed up with two old duffel bags, dropping them at the door and turning to look at the house with her hand on the doorframe. She rubbed it lightly and sighed.

"I'll miss her, this old home. My entire life was lived here, but you do what you have to do to keep them safe," Ms. Patterson said before slipping out the door and walking down the front steps. She got in her own car, gave Clare one last sad smile, and drove off.

Clare understood then that the vines had visited Ms. Patterson. Standing alone in the front yard, Clare took out the seeds and set about planting one on each side of the house by simply digging with one finger, setting the seed in, covering it up, and pouring a bit of bottled water on it. Within seconds, a small sprout came out of each one, making her smile. Then it was time to wait.

When she heard the sirens across town, she understood Jalen was on his way. But then a few minutes later, a pain unlike anything she had ever felt shot through her skull. It was like a tiny bullet entered her right temple, turned left, then right, then shot back out her left eye. The pain dropped her to her knees. Gasping for air, she heard the first screams. Jalen had killed the lookout. Clare stood up with an enraged yell and began to cry.

He was supposed to just watch, to tell them when he was close. Why did he show himself to him? Why?

Molly - October 31st - 8:29 p.m.

Molly sat in the back of the ambulance, a jacket or blanket—she couldn't tell which—draped over her shoulders. A man, or maybe a woman, was attending to the cut on her eye. The cop, she thinks they were a cop, had punched her. Or maybe it was a backhand? She didn't care. It was deserved. The detective was dead. *Dead. Dead.* Just like Chet. Although at least he still had a head, what was left of it. *Dead.* She wanted to be dead. *Dead.* The person touching her face talked, but it sounded like it was all underwater, she couldn't hear their words and she didn't care. She wanted to be dead. Looking around, she saw a pair of shiny, long scissors in the belt of the body in front of her, the body of the person touching her face. *Were they sharp enough?* Looking around, she saw guns on hips everywhere. All over her yard, men and women—some in uniform, others in plainclothes—were crying and screaming, some siting with their hands in their faces. She wasn't strong enough to grab a gun, but even if the scissors didn't work, she could attack this person and then someone would shoot her, shoot her dead.

Looking up to see the if the person attending to her cut was paying attention, she saw her new neighbor—*what was his name?* —staring down from his upstairs window. She didn't care about him, but something he was holding made her stare. It was a small bag, he was pointing to it, then to his own head, over and over. The bag was, dark blue, almost like a bowling bag or an old lady's purse, and it was big enough to fit . . . a head inside. Why would he be pointing at it and then to his . . ..

Molly grabbed the scissors. They were crooked and not sharp, but they were something. The person in front of her protested, but then she pushed them hard and ran towards her neighbor's house, never looking away from the window. Of course, as soon as she started to run, the man pulled the shade.

Five feet, that is all she made before hands came from everywhere to grab her. She swung the scissors, hitting something. There were screams, and then her face was slammed into the road. The tiny rocks hurt a lot, but she screamed and told them it was *him* all along. But they didn't listen, she had already killed one of their own, she had just attacked another, but she needed to tell them. Needed . . . *a needle*. The needle slammed into her arm. It hurt, but not as much as the rocks digging into her face. Everything swirled. Everything blurred. Everything started to fade. He . . . was . . . going . . . *Darker*. To get . . . *Really dark*. Away . . . *Total darkness*.

Jalen/Mr. Slice - October 31st - 9:05pm

After running from room to room and realizing the entire house was covered in vines. Jalen started to have a panic attack. These monsters were not going to take away the perfect night from him. There was no way out, but he could make one—he had fire and poison. Opening the back door, he was met with a wall of writhing vines. The image of them all slithering around made him think of his mother's snake tattoo. He had to live, for *her*, she needed him. Grabbing the nozzle of poison, he started to spray the hive of vines. Instantly, they screamed out in pain and moved, showing small gaps of the night beyond them. In the other hand, he pulled out his machete and started hacking. Piece after piece of vines fell as others pulled back, but just as quickly as they recoiled or dropped, new ones took their place.

Jalen stopped his attack and thought for a moment before rushing to the front door. Opening the door, he sheathed his blade, took out the butane torch, and lit it. Holding the glowing flame against the vines, they retreated and writhed—some even caught fire, but not enough. Moving the torch, he set the doorframe on fire, then reached over and grabbed a chair from the front entry. Using his foot, he pushed the chair into the vines and set it on fire. It went up fast and stayed lit as the vines moved back and forth, trying to not get burned.

Satisfied that the chair would keep burning for a bit, Jalen ran to the back door and set that doorframe on fire as well. Then he grabbed an old Victorian chair with padding on it and pushed it into the vines by the back door before setting it on fire. Racing back and forth, he stoked the fires and added more chairs and items to each. Before long the house was catching a blaze, but that was fine, he was going to make his break in a second. Standing in the middle of the house, he looked to the front door and then to the back door. Each had small gaps in the vines as they fought around the fire, but the back door had just a bit bigger one, and the Victorian chair was also crumbling enough to run through it rather than over it. Readying his blade, he took a deep breath and ran toward the door. In one swift, action movie–type move, Jalen swung the machete, cutting a path through the vines as he turned and slammed his shoulder into the burning door. The vines broke free, and Jalen stumbled outside into the Halloween night.

Clare - October 31st - 9:12 p.m.

Standing in the backyard, her warriors surrounding her, Clare couldn't believe that Jalen broke through and made it out. The visions didn't show this, but then again, her trapping Jalen inside wasn't in the vision either, so she had altered the outcome herself. Out here, they couldn't touch him, they could only intimidate and threaten him. Her five available warriors—the others were escorting the blackness—quickly took up positions, doing their best to lock down the yard. Clare felt sick, she knew they would not all make it out alive.

Jalen looked at them like a trapped cat, part scared and part pissed. She could tell he was assessing his options, a machete in one hand and the torch blazing hot in the other. Standing behind the legs of her tallest warrior, she felt rage bubble up in her as she stared at the sick young man. But then, Jalen saw *her*. A slick, slimy, and sinister smile crossed his face that turned her guts to liquid. Jalen started to shake his head as if he understood her importance. Suddenly, he ran straight at her, the machete raised high.

Clare's faithful warrior shot its fingers down between its legs, making a makeshift curtain of vines, instantly blocking her view of the approaching madman. Instinctively, she backed up, then cried as she saw the blade cut through. She screamed in her head for them to grab Jalen, wrap him in vines, and hang him from a tree, but they couldn't, *he is a chosen one.* But then Clare realized that while *they* couldn't, *she* could. There was nothing stopping *her* from killing Jalen. Except for the fact that if there were more than eight deaths tonight, the balance would be off. Maybe she could just incapacitate him and make sure he didn't die until after midnight. Pulling the pumpkin-carving knife out of her waistband, Clare settled into a fighting stance and prepared for Jalen, who was about to break through the wall of vines and attack. A burst of flames shot through the gaps like angry little hornets. Clare got ready to swing the knife and then, she was in the air.

The vines wouldn't let her get hurt, they wouldn't let her risk anything. She understood it the second they wrapped around her. Fully incased in their embrace, she felt safer than she ever had, but her rage boiled even hotter. There was no ground below her, she could tell she was being carried, but she didn't know if she was upright, lying down, or if she was a foot or ten feet off the ground. She was completely cocooned in their vines. She heard screams inside of her head from her beloved. There were yells outside of her womb as well—they all mixed together in a cacophony of pain and terror that was unbearable. Were the screams Jalen's or were they—they sounded like a woman—no, more than that— there were several people yelling.

Clare demanded to be let go, but the vines ignored her pleas as some sort of battle raged on. When she felt another of her warriors fall, she stopped fighting and screaming and cried. When the third disappeared from her consciousness, she almost fainted. The one encasing her suddenly started to run. She felt the jostling and moving as he fled. Clare held onto the vines and sobbed as a thousand thoughts of panic and frantic communication between them ran through her head in an overwhelming wave.

Mr. Tricks - October 31st - 8:50 p.m.

Holding the bag up and having Molly see it, man, it was a rush of pleasure unlike anything I have ever experienced! But the rush disappeared quicker than it came as I realized how much of the night I was deprived of. Worst off, if she goes to jail, I'll never get to her again. *Fuck!*

Kicking the wall was stupid, but thankfully I didn't break anything, although I am perturbed that I lost my temper—I never do that, and I'll have to analyze why that was later. But that will come later, now I have to get out and get away. They will not believe what she says, but they will still eventually come and ask me questions. Thankfully, I planned for this as well.

Checking the camera on the back fence, I was relieved to see no authorities out there—there shouldn't be, it was just woods back there and they were not looking for a suspect. Grabbing the bag with Chet's head, I slipped it into a backpack, then hit the emergency switch. I never planned on using it, but it was there for this exact reason. This is why you have a backup plan to a backup plan. Heading out the back door, I knew I had exactly fourteen minutes to get to the car that I kept behind the old, abandoned Bradlees department store a mile away. It was a junker and looked abandoned itself, but it worked perfectly, and I checked every other day to make sure it was there and running. All I had to do was walk through the woods for a mile and come out in that back lot, get in that car, and drive off. Then I could lick my wounds and make a new plan when the dust settled, literally.

As I started to walk, I saw brilliant, flickering orange light off in the distance, lighting up the night sky. It looked as if there were several houses on fire. I laughed to myself because Haven was already having one hell of a night, yet they were about to have an even more explosive evening in . . . I looked at my watch . . . five, four, three . . .

BOOM!

Shit. Jesus, that was loud! And I was off by a few seconds. As mad as I was that my timer was off, I couldn't help but laugh. There had to be three dozen emergency personnel on site and that house just went up like an atom bomb. Goodbye, Haven emergency services!

You know what, I can spin this, I can make it look like this was my plan all along. I'll send a letter to the media telling them that this year's trick was . . . explosive! Maybe things aren't going to be that bad after . . . *What the fuck was that?*

At the edge of the woods, there was a large black mass with, I must have been losing it. Were there moving trees walking next to the black mass? Was I having a delusion? It made no sense, all my mental functions were in place, and I was well-adjusted and prepared for the night's events—I couldn't be going into shock. I had no history of delusions or paranoia, so there was no way I could be hallucinating. The things were now blocking my path out. They couldn't be real, could they?

I could leave the path and cut through the woods, but they might hear me fighting through the branches and brush. *Shit.* The best option was to stay back and wait until they moved. No one will be looking for me anyway, most likely they will think the poor old neighbor next to Molly died in the explosion. They won't know it was an initial gas leak for days. I'd just have to wait for this delusion or whatever it was to move on. Thick bushes off to the side of the path hid me pretty well, but I couldn't see them or the path, so I'd have to just wait and look out every few minutes. Closing my eyes, I took a deep breath and tried to assess the situation and figure out if it was a delusion stopping myself from getting away or if there really was something otherworldly going on. But that wasn't possible. I didn't believe in things like that, so it just couldn't be, but at the same time, I didn't want to think that I was.

I can't say that the thing that shot out in front of me was beautiful, it's more like it was . . . a perfect reflection of myself: dark, black, and soulless. It had a shape and could be confused for a creature in the night, but it was more than that, it was . . . I couldn't stop myself, I reached out and tried to touch its effervescence. It was almost like putty, yet cloudlike and colder than dry ice, but it somehow also felt like it was on fire. It made no sense, but I could feel it looking through and inside me. I knew it could see everything I had done and planned to do, and it adamantly approved of my actions. It wanted me to do more. I pulled back my hand

and a small dark chunk floated around my fingers, breaking off from the beast. It was like floating cotton candy around my hands, then just as fast as it appeared, the essence on my fingers was gone, absorbed into my skin. My heart suddenly stopped, and for a solid ten seconds I couldn't breathe. My eyes shut in pain, and I felt like death had arrived, but then my heart beat again and I understood this blackness was now a part of me. When I opened my eyes and sucked in air, the beast and its tree companions were gone. This was not a delusion, it was a gift for my work.

I had been chosen.

Jalen/Mr. Slice - October 31st - 9:33 p.m.

All Jalen could think was, *Well, that wasn't expected.* Standing in the yard, three dead giant vine creatures on the ground, six crispy neighbors and two others bleeding out around him, his brain was having a hard time contemplating what just happened. He was prepared to take on the monsters, but then the "neighborhood watch" showed up like a classic mob with pitchforks. When they saw the monsters, half of them ran away, but the other half got ready for battle as if they had been waiting for this very moment their whole lives. Jalen lifted his mask and told them he had been fighting the monsters all night and needed help, and without hesitation they joined in. As soon as the last beast fell, with the last two creatures running away, Jalen turned the blowtorch on the helpful vigilantes. Six easily went up in flames—it was so much fun watching them scream and try to stop, drop, and roll to no avail, but then his propane ran out. The two who were left tried to help their friends, and while they were distracted, he simply snuck up behind them and *sliced, sliced, sliced.* It wasn't what he planned, it was *better.*

After getting his bearings and feeling like a warrior, Jalen took off his mask and knelt down next to the two non-burning bodies. He had to leave his mark. Pulling out a hunting knife, he cut off the men's shirts and carved "Mr. Slice Was Here!" on both of their torsos. As he made the last exclamation point on the second man, who was so overweight it was hard to carve the words clearly, a black mass grabbed his hand. The second the icy hot stuff touched him, he knew what it was and he knew to not fear it. In a way, after making eye contact with it last year—if you could call it that—he knew it would come back for him, that it would give its approval. With the darkness dancing around in his head, he smiled and started to cry. The tears made him feel embarrassed, but he couldn't help it. It was the first time he ever felt . . . important. When it pulled back its touch, Jalen closed his eyes and nodded, understanding that the darkness would now be with him and that it would expect a whole lot more next year.

Clare - October 31st - 9:41 p.m.

We lost. It's out. It's over. Clare and the remaining vines mourned their lost warriors and embraced, knowing they only had two hours before going back to purgatory, having failed to keep the darkness at bay.

Haven Gazette - Facebook Post - November 1st, 4:07 a.m.

BREAKING NEWS: Reports of multiple house fires and numerous casualties throughout all of Haven have been reported. With the amount of emergencies, town officials have not made a statement. But eyewitnesses say there are numerous houses burnt to the ground from intentional fires and that there are at least two dozen people dead, including first responders at the site of a house explosion that was heard four towns over. Reports of the national guard being called in have been reported but not confirmed. Updates will be posted throughout the day, and we will be live on the scene for our 5:30 a.m. newscast.

Haven Gazette will have updates as things progress.

The Future of All Hallows' Eve

Molly sat by the window in the hospital, the same hospital where she used to work, only now she was a patient and on a different floor, the one she never had security clearance to enter. The meds and constant surveillance made it impossible for her to kill herself like she so desperately wanted to, so she sat like a rotting vegetable, staring out the window, fantasizing about death and killing Mr. Tricks. She had not shown one smile or had even one moment of clarity in the past few months—it was nothing but medicated numbness.

The closest she got to feeling anything was sitting at the large double-paned glass door, the type with the metal mesh built into it, to watch the children on the other side of the ward. She always knew there was a hush-hush psychiatric unit for children, but now she realized how many kids were there. Patients were not allowed to sit there or even go close to it, but since she used to work at this hospital and they pitied her, they would let her wander over and observe the children from time to time. Sitting by the door, she would watch the kids playing and pretend to be watching Chet. He loved to play with his superhero action figures.

After the first week, a small girl with horrific scars running across her face showed up. Molly watched her intently, understanding that the girl had gone through something horrific to get that scar. The poor child would sit in the play area all alone on the bright-colored carpet. The girl was small and frail, but she looked to be almost ten, even if she acted more like a six-year-old. She looked so sad, it made Molly cry even more. When the girl saw Molly crying, she came over and put her hand on the door. Molly placed her own hand against the glass, causing a smile to break out across the poor girl's grotesquely broken face. Molly wanted to take care of the girl and wondered what happened to her and how she ended up here. On the third day of playing games with the little girl through the glass, Molly asked her favorite nurse—a plump, short woman named Julie, who smiled no matter how awful a patient was to her—what the girl's story was. When she found out that the girl killed her quadriplegic father, Molly swallowed hard.

The next day, she saw the girl sitting against the wall, her hand clamped tight over her ears. She was rocking, and while Molly couldn't hear through the glass, it seemed that the girl was humming to herself. She tried in vain to get the girl's attention, but she couldn't. Molly just watched, slowly crying. After being forced to leave for lunch, Molly came back and was relieved to see that the girl seemed better, *normal* almost. After a few minutes, she got the child to come to the window. They played a tapping game where Molly poked a part of the window and the girl had to poke it back. It was like Simon Says, only with glass. As she watched the girl giggle, she knew that the death of the kid's father had to be an accident. As they started the second round, a little boy came up to the girl and held up a Captain Flame action figure. Through the muffled glass, she could hear the boy make fun of the girl, then he told Captain Flame to *kill* the monster. But Molly didn't care about the bullying, all she saw was Captain Flame. *Captain Flame.*

"Mom! Don't call me Chet!"

"Sorry, I mean . . . Captain Flame!"

The memory made Molly scream and scream. The next four days she was restrained and lost the privilege of looking out the door she wasn't really supposed to go by anyway. Time passed—she had no clue how long. But eventually the restraints came off and the snow started to melt, then one day Julie came by, in a chipper mood like always.

"You got a letter! A lovely man just dropped it off. I'm not supposed to give you mail yet, but he was just so nice, and I figured you could use a pick-me-up. So, do me a favor and hide it when you finish reading it, okay sweetheart? He said he wanted to visit, but you can't have any visitors just yet. I told him to check back next month, that the doctor should allow visitors soon. And if he doesn't, don't worry, I'll advocate for you," Julie chirped.

At first, Molly didn't realize Julie was talking to her. She hadn't gotten any mail or visitors who weren't reporters since she had been deemed unfit for human interaction. The nurse placed the letter on her lap and walked away, humming a familiar tune. The tune snapped her out of the daze. She turned around to ask her where she heard that song, but the nurse had already left the room. Instead, she turned her attention to the letter. It simply had her name on it. Flipping it over to open it up, she saw a jack-o'-lantern sticker on the back. She started to tremble.

Pulling out the letter, she knew it was from him. It had to be. Trying not to scream, she took a deep, trembling breath and read it.

Molly,

I'm sorry we didn't get to spend more time together on Halloween. But before I could visit, you were already being taken away. Was that axe meant for me, by the way? Guess you now have blood on your hands too. It's a wonderful feeling, isn't it?

Anyway, just wanted to let you know that I have been taking good care of your son. He makes a great pencil holder. I keep him on my desk. If you ever want his head back, I suggest you become an ideal patient and get yourself out of there.

Though I must tell you, I also have a new . . . passenger, you might call it, that is helping me along my journey. With its help, I will be able to make the entire world feel the pain Chet's death caused in you. Wouldn't that be glorious? I am telling you this because I want you to know that you won't be alone in your pain long, you will have thousands of others to grieve alongside you next Halloween. Yet I promise to not forget about you, you started it all, after all. Get yourself better and I'll make sure to return him next year, as promised.

Your Trick-or-Treat friend,
Mr. Tricks & Chet

Molly folded the letter gently and set it in her lap, silently vowing to get out before next Halloween so she could finally end it all.

The same night Molly got that letter, the Haven City Council was voting on changing the town name to Crestline. Clare, as one of the few remaining residents, ignored the constant requests to attend the town hall meeting and instead sat in her kitchen poring over a stack of ancient books she got on her trip to Europe. The texts cost her life's savings, but she had to learn everything she could about the blackness before next Halloween, not just for herself and the warriors, but for the world. Things had been quiet since the horrific day, but she knew it was out there, growing and thriving, getting its servants ready. As best as she could tell, on the next Halloween, the blackness would use its human counterparts to call back its own master to this world, and if that happened, there would never be Halloween again, let alone another day on Earth.

The weight of being the only person in the world who knew this . . . was crushing. At times, she felt like she were mad and that the past two years were a prolonged mental breakdown. Really, what proof did she have other than a few photos of her yard covered in vines? At one point, she was so worried about her mental state, she scheduled a psychologist appointment, but she quickly canceled when she looked at the jar of seeds she kept in a fireproof safe in her closet. Even if it was all in her head, she'd rather live in this fantasy world where she was a queen battling to save her kingdom over being just a lonely woman with a desk job and three weeks' vacation a year.

Just as she was about to call it a night, she heard a noise. It was muffled, but it sounded like rattling coming from the safe. Running upstairs, she moved aside the empty boxes that hid the four-grand, top-of-the-line vault and quickly spun the dial around and around until it opened with a yawn of stale air. Inside, her mason jar full of exactly thirty-one seeds was shaking and trembling as if it were filled with Mexican jumping beans having seizures. Clare grabbed the jar and held it to her chest like she were calming a colicky baby.

"No, no, no. What is wrong, what is wrong?" She cried as she started to rock herself. Holding up the jar, she looked at them and saw that two of the seeds had turned brown and were drying out rapidly. Spinning the cap off, she poured a quarter of the seeds in her hand and pulled out the two rotting ones. Tears were flowing down her face now. Swallowing hard, she tried to communicate with them like she would when they were grown, but she could only hear the slightest muffled moans and cries, like they were a thousand miles under the Earth screaming at the top of their lungs.

Putting the two dead seeds on top of the safe, she put the good ones back in the jar. They seemed to settle down a bit, as the far-off cries calmed. It was the blackness, it had to be, it was somehow already infecting them, weakening the defense from the inside out. Not sure if it was contagious, Molly put the jar back, locked the safe, and took the two black seeds with her.

Ten minutes later, the dried seeds were floating their way down the Connecticut River, and Clare was heading to the craft store to buy dozens of tiny jars to separate the other seeds in the hopes of stopping any infection. An hour later, they were all lined up, twenty-eight tiny jars with wooden corks. The seeds were all calm, sitting there staring back at her as if she were someone losing her marbles. That night, she took all her pillows and blankets and slept on the floor next to the safe. She had nightmares of the blackness that woke her every thirty minutes with screams. That morning, she knew she needed to find the farmer who sold her the pumpkins two years ago.

Sweet Sydney. Sweet, Sweet Sydney. It was the words she heard in her head all the time on repeat. It was like there were someone standing on a street corner in her mind with one of those megaphone things, just saying it over and over again. But the man wasn't close to her, he was across the street. And the man never stopped saying it. She wished it were her father's voice saying it in her head, but it wasn't, it was a voice she didn't know, muffled through an odd distortion of electric static and distance. *And it never stopped.* At times it screamed at her, at times it said it in a monotone drone. *Sweet Sydney.* Other times it screamed it as if accusing her of something. *SWEET SYDNEY.* But the one she hated the most was when the man sang the name like he was happy and trying to coax her out of a hiding spot, just like her dad used to: *Sweeeeet Sydney. Sweet, Sweet, Syyyyydney.* After a year of it never stopping, not even when she

203

slept, she became able to ignore it, but when the sing-song version started, she had to cover her ears, hunker down, and hum to herself. The worst part, and the one thing she couldn't understand, was that her scar would ache when the singing started. With the gash going across her whole face, it meant everything screamed in pain.

Sydney often wondered if she would still be hearing those words if her father had said anything else to her on that night. Instead of screaming or swearing as he laid there, newly paralyzed, he whispered her name over and over, trying to make sure she was all right. It was the only thing she could remember about what happened. Just lying, stunned and in pain, hearing those two words over and over and over and over. When she unplugged his breathing machine and laid next to him in bed as he slowly slipped away, she eagerly waited for the words to stop. They were his words, his name for her, after all. If he was gone, they would be gone too, but as her father grew cold, the words got louder and louder, making the scar flair up so much she scratched and pawed at it as if it would tear off and reveal a new face. When they found her, covered in blood and chunks of her own flesh, lying on top of her father's dead body, they took her away. *Away, away, away, away, away.*

They told her, but she didn't understand where she was or the full magnitude of her confinement. With no living relatives, she had no one, except for Cathy, an old sad lady who wore fuzzy brown dresses and big glasses and always had her arms full of folders and papers. She was the only one who came and checked on her. Cathy would explain things about money and where she would go when . . . *if* she got out of here. Cathy told her she would have to be placed in a foster family, and that it would be, difficult. The lady didn't say why, but Sydney—*Sweet, Sweet Sydney*—understood it was because of her face. Not only did it look grotesque, but she always had to keep her mouth open to breath, as her nasal passages were too scarred from all the surgeries. She was like a constantly panting abused dog. A dog that no one would want, one that you'd find behind a dumpster and feel bad for, one that you'd pray would just die rather than suffer. Some of the nurses said that one night when they thought she was sleeping: "Poor thing would have been better dying along with her father."

She wasn't in school for a big part of her childhood, as she "bravely fought" the cancer that tried to destroy her. She hated that phrase so much: *bravely fought*. She didn't fight anything. She sat in a bed while nurses poked and prodded her and filled her with swimming pools full of chemicals that made her sicker than she ever felt with the cancer. Yet everyone told her day in and day out how "brave" she was, like she had a choice. People said she was a "fighter" when she did nothing but watch cartoons, read, and sleep. It was all lies and cruel. People would come and pray with her, and when she asked these "servants of God" why God would do this to her, they smiled and said, "He didn't, God is curing you," or, "He works in mysterious ways." When she was six, she told them to stop coming, but they came anyway. When she fought back and told them she didn't think anyone who was all-powerful would make someone suffer, they told her she was too young to understand. But she did understand, the world was cruel and dumb. She knew this at six years old, when her mother died while getting her hot cocoa from the vending machine in the hospital waiting area. The thief meant to slash the strap to her purse, but instead the blade slit her mom's throat across the main veins or arteries, she couldn't recall which was which. She bled out . . . in a hospital waiting room. All while Sweet Sydney waited and waited for her cocoa.

When she heard screaming, she had taken her IV stand and went for a walk, and soon she saw her mother on the floor, blood spreading out like spilled Kool-Aid. There was so much blood on her face, Sydney could only tell it was her mother by the green ring on the hand sticking out from the crowd of doctors working on her; it was the ring she had given her on Mother's Day a month before. There was a small knife— one like her friend Brady showed her once, a pocketknife he called it— on the ground a few feet from her mom's hand. Even farther away there was a man, dirty and stringy thin on the floor—a big muscly, angry man wearing a green baseball hat had his knee on the guy's back. The dirty man was not fighting back—he looked calm, in fact. Sydney took her eyes off the blood around her mother and looked to the man, now knowing what happened. The man looked at her, spread his lips in a grin of broken teeth, and winked. Being polite, because she was always Sweet, Sweet Sydney, she smiled back.

At the funeral, all she could think about was the Kool-Aid spreading and the smile—she wished she could take back the smile and make the puddle of sticky red liquid move from her mom's body to the man's. The red liquid should have come out of him. As she sat staring at her mom's cold, stoic body posed in a position she thought was too uncomfortable for her—her mom always liked her arms above her head, not on her stomach—she thought about that day and pictured herself picking up the pocketknife. She thought about taking the knife to the man and making him stop smiling.

After that, Dad was different—*so, so* different. But he tried and tried for his *Sweet Sydney*. But things were never the same. When she got out of the hospital and finally came home, the house no longer felt like *home*. It felt like a, museum—one where she was scared to touch things and walked around silently to not disturb anything as she tried her best to preserve what was left of her mother. It wasn't until a week after being home, when she went into the kitchen cabinet for a glass and she saw the box of instant hot cocoa, that she realized her mother was dead because of *her*, because *she* wanted cocoa. Because she pouted and squeezed out a fake tear about *needing* cocoa. No matter what anyone told her at the funeral or in countless therapy sessions, in her mind there was no question that she—*Sweet Sydney herself*—killed her own mother.

That is why after the accident, when she heard her dad cry and cry every night about wanting to be with Mom, about not wanting to be alive, she thought she could kill again. Besides, she'd be doing him a favor. She considered it for many nights, but it wasn't until that megaphone man's dang sing-song voice wouldn't go away in her head that she finally unplugged all of those wires.

Suffering, death, then calm, then more suffering. Now there was nothing but surgeries and pills and strangers. Most nights she wished she could just unplug her own wires like she did with Dad, but that wasn't possible here—she was watched constantly, even when she showered.

In fact, one male nurse watched her a bit too closely when she showered, he even offered to help on a few occasions, but she snarled at him each time—a trick she learned to do. If she scrunched up her nose and snarled, it spread her scars wide. The sight made most kids cry and caused adults to back up. It didn't make the man cry, but it did keep him back . . . *so far*. When she realized that the showers he made her take were in the middle of the night (she hadn't been able to tell night from day for the first few months in the facility), she decided he needed to be "shut off" as well, but that would take a lot of planning.

In ten years of life, she understood all she needed about the world. It was cruel, cruel, cruel, and then it killed you. And she was tired of it, so tired, so, so tired. But then *he* arrived.

Cathy, in a rumpled brown outfit like always, showed up one day, which wasn't unusual but certainly not common. What was uncommon was being pulled into one of the "family" rooms that she saw the other kids go when their families visited. She had never gone into one, until today. The room was too bright and filled with bins of toys, a couch, beanbag chairs, a television, and a table in the corner. It still looked like a hospital, but it made her miss her home, the home she would never see again. Cathy sat down, setting down the stacks of paper on the table, then turned the chair to face into the room. Sydney—*Sweet Sydney*—stood in the center, not sure where to sit or what to do.

"You can sit wherever you are comfortable, dear," Cathy said before wiping her brow as if she were sweating, though the room was borderline freezing to Sydney.

"Remember how I said placing you with a family might be a long journey? Well, a young man came to us recently, and he has expressed an interest in . . . looking out for you."

Sydney quickly thought about every person she ever knew and could not think of a single young man who would want to take her.

"It is an unusual situation," Cathy continued. "In all my years I've never seen anyone under twenty-eight take in a child, but the law states that as long as they are eighteen and have a stable income, they can apply to do just that."

Sydney felt prickles of goosebumps start to pop up all over her body like excited little groundhogs, but she couldn't tell if they were ones of fear or excitement.

"This boy . . . or rather, this *young man*, has a very similar issue. I'm sorry, Sydney, that wasn't nice calling it an 'issue.' He has, well, you'll see in a moment. Anyway, we want you to meet him. If you get along, you'll have several supervised visits here for a few months, then outside visits when the doctor allows them. If all goes well, he can foster you. But the earliest that would be is six months to a year down the road. Regardless, it is a unique situation that I am hopeful for."

Sydney still didn't move, the goosebumps started to vibrate as if communicating with her, telling her this was going to be the reason to not unplug her own system. Cathy then looked at the door and nodded. Sydney didn't turn around as she heard the door unlatch and creak open.

"Sydney, I want you to meet Jalen."

Sucking in a deep breath, Sydney, putting on a sweet smile—well, sweet for her—turned around and looked at the man. The tiny, forced smile on her face grew and grew as tears filled her eyes. *The man was just like her.* He had different scars, but he was just like her, damaged and discarded by the world. When her eyes met his, she could see something in them, something dark. In her head, she saw the man with the megaphone get scared, she saw him look up to the sky as black thunderclouds swept in. He dropped the damn megaphone and ran. *The . . . sing-song . . . words . . . stopped.* There was no more "Sweet, Sweet Sydney" on repeat. *It was finally silent.*

Then she heard the most beautiful voice speak. *Hello, Syd, I think we are going to get along just great.* The voice was also in her head, but she knew it came from the darkness inside this man . . . and she loved it, for it stopped the megaphone man. In her head she said *hello* back, then she stuck out her hand and said "hello" out loud. For the first time she could remember, she felt sane and excited to live . . . *and get back at the world, we have a lot to do before Halloween,* the darkness added to her thought. Just as Sydney's not-so-sweet smile spread wider across her scarred face, the darkness came into her mind and set up a board where the megaphone man used to stand. It read:

271 Days Until Next Halloween

About the Author

The enigmatic and reclusive Mr. Gore is the author of three dark and twisted short story collections, *Tales From a Mortician*, *Skeletons in the Attic* and *Do Not Open*. His stories have appeared in numerous anthologies with several being optioned for film rights. A former mortician, Mr. Gore lives alone in New England where he writes in an isolated cabin, shunning the outside world.

Visit AuthorMike.com to read more of his work.

Read

More

Gore…

Books to Kill For
Est. 2010

DarkInkBooks.com